A Novel

Way Downtown

John Patrick Walsh

This book is a work of fiction. The names, characters, places, incidents and dialogue are products of the author's imagination or are used fictitiously and are not to be construed as real. Any resemblance to actual events, locales, organizations, or persons, living or dead, is entirely coincidental.

to NB & Papa

"You're kidding, there isn't a downtown?"

- Confused tourist in Moscow

GOAL

As the ball completed its descent from a high-arced shot, it snapped the net with a distinctive crack. Near mid court, up in the ninth row, the three-point shooter's mother only appeared to be unexcited, almost disinterested. *My God, she thought, that's the sweetest sound I've ever heard.*

Way Downtown

Chapter 1

Ivan Stogov stood by his window. He could see the pine trees becoming the evergreen forest. He'd just finished reading a report out of French Guiana. Some of it seemed strange. The deputy director for operational planning and analysis didn't easily put aside such a feeling.

From within the headquarters of the SVR, the Foreign Intelligence Service, in the Yasenevo district of southwest Moscow, referred to as the Center, he could also see the blue sky and distant dark clouds. He liked to stand by the window to think. To let things settle in his mind.

Stogov's office was large, but not elegantly or even nicely furnished, as one would expect at this top rung of the administrative ladder. Instead, his office was a cavernous room of confounding starkness dominated by its occupant.

The deputy director was by nature austere and rigorous, and he has always shunned trappings of power and influence. He considers them unnecessary and only a cause for distraction from his vital role.

He sees himself as the most steadfast and formidable guardian of the SVR mission. He meets his responsibilities with a penetrating focus, is methodical in quirky ways and meticulous to a fault. He loathes failure and is harshly dismissive of those who would bring it.

Many years ago, Stogov was an Olympic wrestler. With his burly physique, very short haircut, gruff demeanor and unwillingness to suffer fools, it's easy to imagine why wrestling opponents called him the Beast.

In recent decades, this Center boss has been the mastermind behind many of the most challenging and complicated undertakings in Russian intelligence. A succession of directors and presidents have always deferred to his judgment.

He no longer fights or struggles with anyone. He questions, but rarely argues. When he finds it necessary, he never hesitates to quickly ax a plan or career. His decisions are the law.

He's supposed to be told about anything significant that might be happening at the spaceport in Guiana. The more he thought about what he'd just read, the more he suspected that a secret strategic payload was being prepared for launch and his agents were clueless.

It was ten after eight in the morning when his concentration by the window was broken by the sound of a phone. He went to his desk and picked up a handset to answer a call on his restricted direct line.

One of his pet peeves is the reflex action of answering calls on speakerphones, by supposedly smart people, who seem to have zero awareness that we're creatures of habit, and this particular bad habit inevitably results in the exposure of things meant to be confidential.

"Good morning, this is Stogov.

"Yes, yes, I know who you are, Viktor A. Bravchuk, and I know who gave you my number.

"I know they have a major interest, which is why we considered it.

"I'm not disclosing the reasons.

"Viktor A. Bravchuk, have you heard about the Rutgers mug?

"Then I'll tell you about it. Listen closely." Stogov activated a phone interception system. A red light appeared. It would change to green when the target phone was compromised, probably in about thirty seconds. With officious troublemakers like this, he amused himself by asserting some wacky drivel while he kept them on the line just long enough to wiretap their phones.

"So, a young agent in the U.S. was asked to go under the bed of a known source of high-value chatter. The subject was an alluring magnet for conversations filled with remarkable insights. But our electronic devices were useless. It seemed that, in her bedroom, everything got jammed.

"Our guy was fantastic. In college, he made money in street theatre as a living statue. He was so good people would stand and stare at him for long periods of time. Many started to think he really was a statue.

"This intriguing bedroom caper seemed doable. Her daily routines were quite predictable. The agent had amazing intrusion skills and his work was always excellent. Even so, the case officer wisely counseled a practice run.

"From the street, our guy got under the bed incredibly fast. Once in position, he found a wrapped gift, apparently hidden there. He had a little tool kit and couldn't resist seeing what was inside. He'd take a peek without any sign of tampering.

"It was an American university coffee mug. It was a Rutgers mug. Its handle was broken off and in several pieces. Later, we figured it was probably a gift for her boyfriend's birthday, which got smashed under the bed." Stogov saw the green light from the intercept system.

"The case officer canceled the plan. End of story.

"Hello, are you still there?

"Of course, it's ludicrous. Can you decipher the hidden message?

"It's a warning. Don't ever call this number again."

Stogov hung up his restricted direct line and clicked on a desktop screen where he could see the two visitors he was expecting sitting in his waiting room. He buzzed his secretary of thirty-seven years. "Please send them in," he told her, handset to handset.

The first to enter was Regina Baranova from the political intelligence directorate. In her early forties, she was stately in her appearance and manners, smooth and decisive, and rapidly gaining prominence with a reputation for good instincts and being very clever.

She was followed by Anton Malenkov, about ten years her senior, a high-ranking official from the illegals directorate, who managed to always be dressed in a finely-tailored traditional suit from Savile Row, and was always calm, reflective and philosophical.

The meeting was about Kim Jong Un, the ruler of North Korea, and Bo Tenbinakov, a former Russian basketball player. Baranova and Malenkov would like one of the most elusive prizes in the game of espionage -- having ears next to an unguarded freewheeling Kim.

Like most Kim watchers, they know he's fascinated with basketball. They're part of a small cadre of officials and operatives who are keeping a most unusual top secret.

The former basketball star is going to be recruited to develop a close personal relationship with Kim.

As they took their seats at the conference table, Stogov offered tea. With anyone else, it would be considered polite to accept. But these visitors knew Stogov valued efficiency and speed, and preferred to skip such niceties. They thanked him and declined. Then without hesitation or any indication from Stogov, Baranova began.

"Sir, as you requested, we're here to highlight two aspects of this plan, the vulnerability of Kim Jong Un and the suitability of Bo Tenbinakov. I'll talk about Kim. Mr. Malenkov will talk about Bo. Then I'll wrap up."

As she talks, she doesn't take her eyes off of Stogov, except to occasionally glance over at Malenkov.

"Many people are aware that Kim is a basketball enthusiast. What few realize is the extent of it. He's an absolute fanatic. It's an obsession. He idolizes star players and has fantasies about himself.

"He does not appear to have any significant athletic skills. At least he has never demonstrated anything out of the ordinary. Yet he envisions himself as having some natural, untapped, basketball talent. Sometimes, he sneaks away from his official duties to travel incognito to a secluded basketball facility in the city of Anju, which is about fifty miles north of the capital.

"Apparently, he has a tutor for rules and terminology, a trainer, who he seems to have little time for, and a coach for practices. We're told he competes in games against opponents that his aides consider suitable. But all this is very hush-hush.

"The people involved in such games or practices are constantly warned not to divulge anything to anyone. There's no tolerance for any gossip or rumor suggesting that their supreme leader may be lacking in some athletic ability.

"There was an incident when a few players failed to keep their lips sealed. They were dealt with swiftly by his sister Kim Yo Jong, the iron fist in the velvet glove. All the offenders were severely punished. Even the people who listened to them suffered disciplinary measures.

"Kim has fun with basketball, but he also takes it very seriously. Millions do what he does -- watch games, have favorites, follow news, recite statistics, play themselves or wish they could. But he seems to be taking it into another dimension.

"We think he has a burning desire to somehow display a basketball prowess of his own that would leave a lasting impression to validate his general supremacy. So, we drop the hook. Suddenly, here's Bo offering to make that possible, like a genie out of a magic lamp.

"We think Bo will become an adored and trusted strategist, and then a close buddy. We're convinced this is achievable. If you mix that kind of relationship with Kim's propensity to drink and entertain late into the night, this could be very fruitful. We think there's a good chance an intoxicated Kim will treat Bo as a confidant.

"As a side note, and not a significant one, but I should mention it, some years back, a former American basketball player, a very bizarre publicity hound, made several trips to North Korea. He was granted a little time with Kim. It didn't amount to anything." A phone rang.

"Please excuse me," Stogov said, as he picked up a handset in front of him on the conference table.

"Yes, go ahead." While he listened, he watched his visitors, who were both looking down at their folded hands on the table. He trusted these two and thought they complemented each other. *What a relief, not dealing with idiots for a change,* he thought.

"It's too sensitive to be entrusted to digital transfer. Have a TS3 courier take him a copy of the file. Do this immediately. Then have lunch set up in a partitioned area of the Primakov Room. And make sure they offer him his favorite dessert, that flaky apple croustade." He hung up and nodded at Baranova to continue.

"Sir, if the Foreign Ministry knew what we're planning, they'd object most strenuously. 'You propose to dispatch an untrained, untested amateur into the top of the most security-policed state on the planet! Are you nuts?' That's what they'd say.

"And internally, word of a celebrity action can be hard to contain. There must be the strictest adherence to a need to know. Including the three of us, that's currently a dozen people."

"You understand," Stogov said, "as soon as anything comes of this, we'll need to inform GRU, probably Denis Kulick."

"Yes, of course. Sir, as we move forward with this, it'll always be with the realization that Bo is a national figure with legions of admirers. It's not just foreign relations, but also his safety, that will be foremost on our minds. We'll always proceed with the utmost care."

She then looked over at her colleague and motioned for him to take over.

Like her, he didn't have any file or notes.

"Sir, we think the plan to recruit Bo for this rather exotic mission is based on solid assumptions. We're sure he can be trusted. His father was a decorated air force test pilot who died in a crash, and his grandfather was an army officer killed in combat. They're his heroes. He has a profound gratitude for their sacrifices.

"He's a person with strong patriotic beliefs, who has never served. Once introduced to this plan, he'll realize he's the only one who can do it. We have no doubt that he'll answer his country's call to duty.

"Bo grew up in Kazan. The rest of his family still live there. His mother is a respected pediatrician. She eventually remarried after his father's death. Her new husband runs a medical laboratory and is on the board of advisors for a private hospital.

"Bo's only sibling, an older sister, is a track coach and physical education instructor at a local college. She lives with her girlfriend of about ten years, a freelance graphic artist. Bo and his sister have since made peace, but there was a period when she treated him with extreme animosity.

"We learned from the Kazan police that eight years ago his sister faced criminal charges for threatening him with an illegal offensive weapon, an Italian-made stiletto switchblade, in a jealous altercation over the girlfriend. Fearing for his life, a neighbor called the police.

"Eventually, the most serious charge was dropped and she only paid a small fine and court costs. She even got to keep the switchblade on the condition it be kept at home. She claimed it was a treasured family heirloom and necessary for protection.

"Twice previously, she'd been a crime victim. One was a stalking case. The other was an attempted assault. In the latter case, she turned the tables on the assailant and push him down a flight of stairs.

"At this point, it seems that Bo is on speaking terms with all of his family. But as the years have passed, their contact has lessened. They rarely see each other anymore, not even on holidays and birthdays, even though Bo epitomizes the most frequent traveler. It's safe to say, they're no longer particularly close.

"Bo studied economics at Saint Petersburg State University, and during his time there developed an impressive athletic training program. Soon after graduation, at the age of twenty-one, he began playing professional basketball. His ascendancy in the sport was meteoric. For nine years, he was spectacular in the EuroLeague.

"Then his career was suddenly interrupted when he broke his left ankle, near the end of a three-year contract with Khimki. Over a period of eleven months, he went through two surgeries and extensive rehabilitation, before gaining full recovery.

"But while he was disabled, something quite surprising happened. Rather than planning a return to the basketball courts to continue his stellar playing career, he almost immediately transitioned into what he has become today.

"But before I get into that, a little more about his playing days, which we know Kim would be very familiar with. Since he attended school in Switzerland, Kim has closely followed the EuroLeague.

"Bo was fast. In a flash, he could attack anywhere on the court. He had an athleticism and basketball IQ that frequently stunned his opponents. His ball handling and passing were dazzling. His shooting percentages were always up near the top in the league.

"He was fantastic on defense. Frequently, he would anticipate what opponents were going to do. His ability to steal the ball was amazing.

"He was always a fierce competitor. Regardless of the opponent, he was usually able to dominate the game.

"His most impressive skill of all was his ability to fake people out, to trick them. His ability to get people looking the wrong way was astonishing. He almost always led the league in assists.

"It's been five years since his playing days ended. For a long time, people will be asking, what if he had returned? And his legend grows. He probably figured that would happen.

"He's now a prosperous entrepreneur. His rise to prominence in the business world has been as rapid as his rise to stardom as a player.

"He's a consultant and strategist. He connects players and coaches with agents, endorsements and investors. He develops partnerships and all sorts of marketing networks. He provides ticketing, lighting, backboards, scoreboards, uniforms, jackets, caps. You name it, he sells it.

"One of his strong suits is media production. Whether it's vivid coverage of a real game, or bringing fantasy basketball to life, his company's made-for-television work is brilliant.

"Simply put, he's the provider of the total basketball experience and all the value it can generate. And he's become an ambassador of sorts for the universal appeal of the game.

"His success is based on his fame, his ability to foster dreams and goals, and his personal warmth. He is always thoughtful and gracious with everyone. In a word, he's a charmer.

"And one more important thing, which is key to our plan. He has an exceptionally good memory.

"Our globetrotting sensation has a girlfriend in Romania by the name of Zella Rosetti. By all accounts, they're very much in love. She's twenty-six, a language teacher, and devoted to the care of her ailing mother. That's all we know about Zella. We have some work to do there. We're currently getting set up in her area.

"Sir, there's one thing about Bo that's a little puzzling. We've had some sharp people posing as freelance sports reporters, supposedly digging for a human-interest story. They've learned a lot from his friends, acquaintances, teammates, business associates and so on.

"Obviously, many women are very attracted to Bo. And it appears he has an insatiable sexual appetite. We've heard so many stories about countless dalliances with allusions to mysterious beautiful women, who always seem to remain in the background out of view.

"Regina noticed this first. It's odd. There must be a lot of them, but except for the Romanian, it's like none of these women exist. We keep asking ourselves, how does such a famous guy have so many affairs and yet none of the women can be identified?"

Malenkov then nodded to Baranova to continue.

Without pause, she did so. "We're going to help Bo expand his operations into the Far East. Then, when he makes his first contact with Kim as a business proposition, it will seem like a logical move.

"Kim will definitely want what Bo has to offer, and we're confident that he'll be willing to pay for it.

"Of course, Bo will certainly appear to be motivated by the money, lots of it. His fees will be hefty.

"They both speak English, so they'll be able to converse directly with each other in private. Kim has a laid-back, easygoing, cool type of personality. Bo is very adaptable and charmingly engaging. Odds are, this is a bromance in the making.

"Sir, may we answer any questions?"

"I don't have any questions, but I'm going to state the obvious. If they ever find out what Bo was really up to, he's dead, and you and I will end up with nice jobs in a shoe factory."

No one said anything for a moment, as they all dutifully recognized that possibility.

"Unless either of you have anything further, that'll be it. Thank you both. Please continue to give me advance briefings. I want to be in front on this one."

Everyone got up from the table. Malenkov was out the door first. His colleague started to follow. Stogov knew she was the initiator of the plan.

"Regina Baranova..." She stopped and looked back to catch his final words. "...good move."

Her face showed a slight smile, barely detectable, and then she continued out.

Chapter 2

The city of Cluj-Napoca is surrounded by grasslands, forests and medieval castles, in a lush river valley in northwest Romania. It is the unofficial capital of the historical province of Transylvania.

The novel *Dracula* has guaranteed that Transylvania is forever associated with vampires. Bram Stoker, its Irish author, never set foot in Transylvania, or anywhere in Eastern Europe for that matter.

Russian frequent traveler Oleg Pankova has been to Transylvania dozens of times. Ostensibly, for leisure and study. He tells people that he has fallen in love with this part of Romania.

As his wife keeps reminding him, Oleg was supposed to become a pensioner a long time ago. She never stops explaining what they're missing by his inexplicable failure to retire.

But Oleg knows that the Center's right. If older people aren't part of the Service, too much would be lost. Besides, he doesn't want to stop. It's part of his nature. It's a parallel life he doesn't want to end.

His latest assignment is probably one of the easiest he's ever had. It almost seems like a vacation. He must learn everything he can about an alluring girlfriend of a Russian sports celebrity. As always, he's well prepared. As of late, he's become an aficionado of European professional basketball.

Some institutions in Cluj, such as the country's largest university, the national museum of art, and the largest Romanian-owned commercial bank, are very well known. Unlike Oleg, most visitors and many residents are not aware that Cluj also has a professional basketball team with championship banners.

Romania is like a fairy-tale land, filled with stunning vistas across its verdant hills, plains and mountains. It's one of the most scenic countries in the world. Oleg has often marveled at its sheer beauty.

There have also been a few occasions when he has recoiled at what he has sensed and felt. Experiences he finds hard to describe. For in the recesses of this vast, unspoiled, natural beauty there is also the mysterious, the unearthly, the unexplainable.

*

The central district of Cluj spreads out in all directions from the towering Gothic-style Saint Michael's Church in Union Square. This Roman Catholic edifice, which dates from the fourteenth century, is named after Archangel Michael, the city's patron saint.

A few blocks away from St. Michael's, on an upper floor of a bustling, prosperous side street, is the local branch of the very prestigious Zürich-based International Academy for Language and Culture. Zella Rosetti is the youngest member of its professional staff. She is also its top-rated and most talented instructor.

It's a twenty-minute walk from her work to the three-bedroom terraced house she shares with her mother. Their place is part of a quartet of buildings surrounding a small square with a neighborhood flower garden. There are twelve residences, three in each building.

These are spacious homes built in the 1920s with much attention to fine architectural detail. They join harmoniously as one in this quiet enchanting enclave, originally named and still called Home Court.

Zella's mother Maria, a long-time resident, has always said that if she could live anywhere, it would be here. It is also where she wants to die. Maria was a heavy smoker most of her life. She now has lung cancer, which has spread to her liver. She has less than three months to live.

Before she had to quit her job because of the illness, Maria was a very accomplished civil engineer whose work had included bridges, tunnels, roadways and other vital infrastructure.

When she left, her management told her, if she ever wanted to return, her job would be waiting for her. They told her that she was irreplaceable.

Near the end of her last day at work, everyone who had any connection with Maria gathered around her office. They all wished her well as she departed. A few wished her a speedy recovery.

Maria could see tears in some of their eyes. She knew they couldn't say it directly. She knew what they meant. This was their way of saying goodbye. They knew she was never coming back.

Maria was determined to accept her fate with a certain dignity and peaceful resignation. She told the doctors that she didn't want any therapy. She told her daughter she didn't want to suffer through treatments to fight a losing battle, and she didn't want Zella to watch her trying to tolerate them.

Maria's care is now completely focused on providing as much comfort as possible during the time that remains. She takes pain medication. She keeps getting weaker.

When Zella is at the Academy, her mother is attended to by Sabrina, whose mother and father are good friends of Maria. It was Sabrina's parents who started the talks that led to this arrangement.

Sabrina recently graduated from high school. She has decided that she wants to be a hospital nurse. She knew from the beginning that, sadly, her job of taking care of Maria wouldn't last long. When it's finished, she's applying to nursing school.

Sabrina is good-natured, compassionate, smart and disciplined. Someday a hospital and its patients will be very lucky to have her.

Sabrina has a boyfriend, Stelian, a nineteen-year-old university student. He has no idea what he wants to do, except smoke weed, have lots of wild sex, and somehow get through his classes.

Zella is a bit leery of Stelian, but she sees Sabrina as responsible and strong-willed.

Maria no longer wants to see visitors. Some of her close friends persist. But, through Zella or Sabrina, she now always declines with expressions of regret.

She does make one exception, for "my Zella's Bo." She welcomes him to her bedside. She is comforted by his presence. As she rapidly approaches the end of her life, it gives her a sense of solace and gratitude to think that her daughter will be happy.

Zella's parents divorced when she was just an infant. Zella was their only child. Soon after the divorce, her father remarried, moved to Germany and at last count had eight more children. Over the years, Zella has had little contact with him.

After Zella's father left, Maria stayed single. She flourished in her engineering career and has always enjoyed a close relationship with her daughter.

Maria feels that she's had a share of good fortune, but she has hoped her daughter will have something she did not. She has hoped Zella will have a good partner with whom she can share her life.

Zella knows that she will always have Bo, but she doesn't want to explain why to her mother, so she's glad her mom assumes this.

*

It has become somewhat of a routine that Sabrina will prepare dinner and have it with Zella before she leaves. They're now, in a way, co-workers who have become friends. They both enjoy their talks at the dinner table.

This day was typical. After stopping to grab a few groceries, Zella arrived home on her bicycle at about half past six, knowing that Sabrina was making their evening meal. After spending some time with her mother, Zella joined Sabrina in the kitchen and dining room and then the two of them sat down for dinner.

Zella usually didn't talk about her individual students, but on this evening, it was different.

"I had a wonderful client today. An old man, retired, probably in his mid-seventies. He's Russian, he worked for their space agency. Now he likes to travel a lot. A very nice, kindhearted gentleman.

"I don't know how we got on the subject, but when he found out that I'm close to Bo, he got so excited. As it turns out, he's quite a basketball fan and thinks that Bo was the greatest."

After carefully pouring a little wine into Sabrina's glass, she continued, "I'm telling you, I don't think that nice Russian gentleman got much out of his lesson because he was just so thrilled to hear things about his basketball hero. The more I told him, the more delighted he was. It felt like I was giving special chocolate candy treats to a child. I must say, it felt good to make him so happy.

"I shouldn't feel guilty, like he got cheated out of a proper lesson. I noticed he has twelve more scheduled in the next four weeks, so I can easily help him make up for it.

"Sabrina, you know how sometimes when you first meet someone you almost immediately feel relaxed and comfortable around them. He's like that, the kind of person you'd want to get to know as a friend."

After they finished the meal and started clearing the table, Zella said, "Sabrina, you're a jewel. My mom doesn't say much anymore, but she always manages to tell me how much she likes you, how good you are to her, what a blessing you are. I know we're very lucky. Thank you for being with us."

Sabrina put some things back down that she'd just picked up and came over and hugged Zella.

"I'm so very sorry about your mom. She's such a wonderful lady and..."

She released the hug and stepped back. "I must not cry. I must learn not to cry. People will need me to be strong.

Maria needs me to be strong." And then she hurried into the kitchen to the sink and cried.

*

Later that night, when Zella was finally alone, she started thinking about the great distances between Bo and herself. This is something she has started thinking about a lot.

For her, in what is otherwise a strong bond, it's the only negative thing between them. It bothers her now. She knows that after her mom passes away, it's going to be even harder to accept.

It's not that she will expect him to stay home all the time, wherever that may be. She understands the nature of his business enough to know that's not feasible. She just wants to lessen the separation.

Her dream is that they will build a nest and he won't fly away so often and for so long.

She knows he loves her. But she's disappointed that he hasn't talked about plans that would allow them to be together more of the time. To her, it's a matter of balance and priorities.

She wants him to realize this, and to act accordingly, of his own volition. Ultimately, if he doesn't, she will have to use the power she possesses.

She put on a light jacket, walked out of the house, across the cobblestone street and onto the path into the flower garden.

As was typical for this time of night, there was no one else about. A soft, pleasant, orange glow emanated from inside of several houses. Everything was still. It was completely quiet. The air was cool, crisp and refreshing.

She stopped and stood near the center of the garden, and relished a slow, deep breath of the delicious air.

Soon the only light in the square would be the street lamps and a few porch lights. As she looked around, instead of the usual enjoyment of this setting, she felt a lonely darkness closing in. And then, strangely, a shiver.

Her heart began to feel heavy as she thought about how much she's going to miss the one person who's always been close to her.

She folded her arms together tightly against her chest and looked up at the starry sky, just in time to catch a meteor streak by. It was incredibly brilliant, and then it was gone, all in a flash.

She told herself that she was fortunate to see it, especially at this moment. It instantly took her into a positive state of mind.

She looked over at an almost full moon, probably only a day away. She fondly remembered how her mother would always point out the full moons. Since she was a small child, it has been her favorite light.

The bright lunar presence brought back another fond memory, a dreamy Rolling Stones ballad her mom had played so many times. Zella smiled as gentle waves of the music floated through her head, *But I'm just about a moonlight mile on down the road.* It reminded Zella that her mom would always be there.

She also started remembering her mother showing her the Jovian System, through a little telescope on a tripod. Zella was astonished to actually see, with her own eyes, four moons orbiting around that giant planet Jupiter.

As she continued to gaze into the clear sparkling sky, with even more wonder and awe than she experienced as a child, she suddenly felt like she had abandoned her post.

She was getting lost in the cosmos while her mother might be calling for help.

As Zella walked back to the house, she thought about how sad it was that some people never bother to look up.

*

After her final check on her mom for the night, just before crawling into bed, she again read the latest exchange of text messages with Bo, from and to New Zealand, nine time zones away.

> Zella
> I'm still in Auckland
> Things are going well
> I dream of you to
> know
> True beauty and true
> love
>
> Bo
> Miss you beyond
> description
> Pray you're safe
> Always

*

The next day, as she does every now and then, Zella went home for lunch. As soon as she walked into the kitchen, she could smell the marijuana. Sabrina was leaning against the sink with her arms folded, looking at Zella and looking ashamed.

"Sabrina, what's going on?"

"It was Stelian, while I was in with Maria. When I came out and realized what he was doing, I showed him an anger he hasn't seen in me before.

"I told him that I could get fired, and that would certainly be a very big problem for me. I told him that I have to be sober and alert while I'm on duty here. I can't have Zella thinking I might be smoking weed while I'm taking care of her mother. I made him leave immediately. I think it scared him. I'm sure he's not going to do that again. He left about twenty minutes ago."

"Good," Zella said. She believed Sabrina. She didn't see any need to discuss it further. But to not trivialize the matter, she looked concerned and waited for a few moments before she went on to the next subject.

"How's Maria?"

"She's sleeping right now. She was awake most of the morning."

As Zella went to the fridge to start putting together her lunch, she said, "Did you see that big van out in front with all that strange-looking equipment on top? I wonder what that's about."

"Oh, I can sort of tell you. They were parking when Stelian arrived and he stopped and asked them. He's like that. I can hear him now, 'Hi, how's it going? What's happening? What are you guys going to be doing?'

"He said they were very friendly. They told him they're working on a communications industry survey for some private consultant. I didn't exactly get it all. He mentioned things like radio waves, satellites, mobile devices. I think Stelian said it was about the strength of signals. I guess they're measuring the quality of different services.

"If you're looking for the olives, they're on the table."

"Oh good, thanks," Zella replied.

"But here's the part Stelian and I thought was funny. He said when he heard it, his jaw dropped and he must have looked dumbfounded. He asked the guy to repeat what he said. So, the guy did, and the second time he heard it, Stelian tried to memorized it, but wasn't quite able to. So, Stelian tells the guy it's so cool and he's really got style, and just about begs him to say it one more time. Which the guy then happily does. The third time, Stelian got it memorized.

"When he got in here, he repeated it to me three times.

"So, three times, apparently with a straight face, speaking slowly, and clearly enunciating every word, this comedian says to Stelian, 'We aspire to be inconspicuous, failing that, hope to be unobtrusive, disappointed still, surely, attaining without harm or consequence.' Stelian said this guy acted like he was at a poetry or prose recital.

"I thought it sounded pretty comical."

Obviously, Zella wasn't amused or interested. "What was Maria like when she was awake earlier?"

"She seemed to be lost in her thoughts. I tried a couple of times to read to her, she usually likes that, but this morning she waived it off both times. She held my hand for a moment, patted my arm and thanked me."

"I'll go look in on her after I eat," Zella said, as she finished putting together a sandwich and salad. "Even if she's asleep, it would be nice to just sit next to her for a while before I go back. It'll help me get my rhythm back after a difficult morning with a group of malcontents.

"You wouldn't believe how these people acted. From the minute we started, for no reason whatsoever, it was as if their sole purpose was to irritate me."

Zella sat down and took several bites of her sandwich. Sabrina got a glass of water and sat down across from her at the table to listen sympathetically.

"They were so exasperating. There was no attempt at trying to learn anything. They were totally preoccupied with telling me how I should teach.

"What I'd really like to do is give them an honest assessment of their self-defeating attitude, but I won't. If I did that, if I said what I really think, I'm sure they'd go all out bad-mouthing me on some review sites. A couple of these people are downright mean. I'm sure they'd get a kick out of trashing me.

"And then I'd have to respond. And that wouldn't be the end of it. It would just go on. It would be a ridiculous waste of time and energy to get more engaged with these troublemakers. I'll just ride it out. Apparently, they only have two sessions scheduled.

"But it's really hard to fathom. It seems like their only purpose in taking these expensive classes was to test the patience of the teacher. It doesn't make any sense. Why would they do that?"

Chapter 3

Bo Tenbinakov had a vague theory, which he never dwelt on, about why there were, disproportionately, so many very attractive women in airports. As he entered an international departures concourse in Singapore Changi, his visual acuity was expansive with a continuous sweeping awareness. If there was an especially good-looking woman anywhere, he'd spot her.

When he was alone, he was usually on the hunt in airports. This proclivity was intensified at Changi, where the airport code is SIN. That moniker added to the titillation. He was definitely ready for his next irresistible temptation. Many of his airport encounters have brought sweet results. The occasional failure only added to the thrill of it all.

Then his phone showed that his office was calling. He moved over against a wall away from the flow of people to answer. An important client needed some guidance and needed it quickly.

After he put the phone back in his pocket, Bo closed his eyes for a moment, to transition, to refocus. He was disappointed. He realized he couldn't begin any amorous adventure before his next flight.

He picked out a secluded corner in his airline's first-class lounge. He had just finished setting up his laptop and collecting the files he would need when he was politely interrupted by a soft-spoken, white-haired gentleman impeccably dressed in a three-piece suit and holding a carry-on bag and a copy of the *Financial Times.*

"Excuse me, Mr. Tenbinakov, may I bother you for just a very brief moment to tell you something?"

"Sure, of course. Please, have a seat."

"Thank you."

As he sat, the man put down his bag, held his newspaper with both hands and leaned over towards Bo.

"Sir, I'm with Russian Foreign Intelligence. I have been asked to convey a message to you. Please understand that I am only a messenger. So, what I am about to tell you, is all I can tell you. I'm unable to elaborate or answer any questions.

"Sir, the message is this: Your country is in need of your service. When you get back to your office, you will learn that you had a phone call from someone identified as Coach Gold, who was trying to reach you. There will be a callback number.

"Sir, we know we can trust you not to talk about any of this with anyone. Coach Gold will explain everything. Now I must excuse myself. Thank you for your courtesy, Mr. Tenbinakov."

The old gentleman stood up, picked up his bag, smiled at Bo and walked away.

Bo smiled in return, and for a moment watched the man as he left. But after only a couple of seconds, he went back to looking at his computer screen, expressionless and seemingly unfazed. Instinctively, he figured that this is how he should act under the circumstances.

This was a jolt out of nowhere. Maybe he was being recruited by the SVR to be a spy. He felt a burst of excitement in his chest. It also felt like the force of gravity had suddenly increased.

*

On the last leg of his journey, as soon as his plane came to its final stop, Bo sent two texts. The first was to Max, his personal assistant.

> Just arrived
> See you regular spot
>
> Zella
> Just landed back
> home
> I'll call tonight

It was about six thirty in the evening when Bo and his personal assistant connected outside of baggage claim at Sochi International Airport.

Along the shores of the Black Sea near the Caucasus Mountains, Sochi is Russia's largest resort city. It is one of the few places in the country with a subtropical climate of warm to hot summers and mild winters. Nearby is an excellent ski resort. Sochi has hosted Olympic Games and the World Cup. When Bo was starting his basketball business, he decided this was the ideal place to establish it, and make his home.

"It's so nice to be back," Bo said, as they got into a company-leased late-model luxury sedan.

"I can imagine," Max said. "It's been a long trip for you. You've done a lot of traveling, a lot more than usual."

"Max, when we get to the office, please, I'd like to go over the phone messages with you before you leave."

"Sure. Looking for anything in particular?"

"No, it would just be better if you helped me with it."

"Of course. No problem."

For the rest of the ride, neither one of them said anything. Bo seemed to have a lot on his mind, and Max knew when it was good to be quiet and leave the boss alone.

Back at the office, at Bo's desk, as they went through messages, Max said, "There was a call from a Coach Gold, from his office. They wouldn't say what it was about, except that they knew you wanted to be in contact. Would you like me to find out what it's about?"

"No, thanks, just give me the number, I'll take care of that one."

When they were done conferring, Bo asked Max to shut the door on his way out.

As soon as he was alone, Bo took a deep breath. He didn't know what to think. He made the call.

It rang only once. "Yes, is this Mr. Tenbinakov?"

"It is."

"Sir, thank you for returning the call. Coach Gold can meet you at the Cathedral of Saint Michael the Archangel tomorrow at ten o'clock in the morning. Would that be convenient?"

"Yes, I can do that."

"Very good. When you get there, please take a seat in the back of the church. Thank you, sir, and good evening to you."

Immediately, the line went dead.

Bo put down the phone and sat motionless. He had always prided himself in his ability to move forward and concentrate on what needed to be done, regardless of any adversity or distraction. But this was different. Although there were many things that needed his careful attention, it was going to be impossible to really concentrate on anything else until he found out what this was about.

He left the office after only a cursory look at several matters described as requiring urgent attention. Then he stopped at a quiet neighborhood café and had a quick, unusually light dinner. When he got home, he didn't unpack. He put some ice and Beluga vodka in a small crystal glass, put some water into a tumbler, and sat down to call Zella.

"Oh Bo, I'm so glad you called! How are you?"

"Zella, it's so wonderful to hear your voice. Before I say anything else, please, just talk some more, about anything, just let me hear your beautiful voice. Please, I crave it."

"I love you, Bo. I miss you every minute you're gone. And you've been gone a long time. Bo, it's been too long.

"Now what I want to know is how soon can you get to Cluj? I want to touch you. I want you standing in front of me so I can touch you.

"Sabrina can watch my mom for a couple of days. You need to rent one of those sport cars. We need to go hide in the woods somewhere.

"Bo, do you hear me?"

"Yes, I hear you, and you make me melt."

"Bo, I crave you."

"Oh Zella, I'm just letting it soak in."

He knew, at the moment, he was unable to focus on a Cluj visit and getaway plan.

After a moment of silence, he continued, "Oh Zella, I'm exhausted right now, and I need to get some idea about the situation in the office. Of course, things have really piled up. It'll take a little time to figure out the schedule for my next trip."

"Okay, hopefully you can figure it out tomorrow. How about we FaceTime tomorrow evening?"

"Yes, that sounds good, let's do that. And tomorrow evening I'll look fresh for my girl.

"How's Maria doing?"

"She's about the same, except she seems to be getting weaker. She's been wanting to know when she'll see you. I told her soon."

"Yes, I'll see her soon.

"Oh Zella, I better get off the phone. I am very tired. I'm about to collapse."

"Okay, Bo, good night. I love you."

"I love you too."

*

As Bo sat down in the back of St. Michael's, he noticed something going on with a small group of people up near the front of the church. He wondered if maybe it was a wedding practice.

He imagined Zella in a white wedding gown. He knew it would be breathtaking.

He didn't see her coming. He didn't notice her until she was standing right next to him. She was heavyset, probably in her fifties, probably Chinese. "Hello Bo, I'm Coach Gold. Please, let's see if we can find a place to sit and talk outside."

This woman he followed out of the church was a seasoned Russian intelligence officer. She was ethnic Chinese. For generations her family has lived in the Russian Far East. She's from Vladivostok, the Russian city closest to North Korea.

She exudes a warm motherly wisdom. She can also play rough and be very intimidating. In her younger days, she loved to play basketball. Sometimes, she found it most exhilarating to knock bodies around and spike games with war cries and taunts.

Outside, they found an empty bench and sat down. "Bo, the first thing I want to do is apologize for how the first contact with you was handled, that drama at Changi airport. That's how the Center wanted it. The Center being Moscow headquarters. I don't think it had to be done like that, and it wasn't very nice leaving you hanging in suspense.

"I've tried to figure out their reasoning." She shook her head with a look of disgust. "Well, you're hard to catch alone. They wanted to show how important this is. They think it gives people confidence to know we can be anywhere. They want to get moving on this. Security outweighed mental vexation."

Again, she shook her head with a look of disgust. "Whatever. I would have done it differently. But it wasn't my call. All I can do is say I'm sorry it happened like that.

"Now, without any more unnecessary suspense, I'll get right to why we need you.

"We want to find out anything we can about what North Korean leader Kim Jong Un is thinking these days. As you may know, he's nuts about basketball. That's where you come in.

"Like the rest of us, Kim sees famous basketball players become TV commentators or product advertisers. Things like that. He can idolize them. But he can't use them.

"He'll quickly realize that you're different and unique. He'll realize that you can do a lot for him, I mean a lot; you can be transformative.

"He's an ideal prospect for what you sell. He will be most receptive and then very excited. In his psyche, he may even see a parallel to the Soviet help given to his grandfather.

"He'll view what you offer as a fabulous opportunity to make his dream come true. You're really the sole source for what he wants. All you need to do is make contact and explain what you offer. Then it's inevitable that a deal will be made. A very positive relationship will be established. It's a sure thing.

"You can fulfill his dream and be his prized advisor. You're Russian and you're charming. You'd be able to gain his trust. You could be a buddy at his lavish late-night parties. You could become a confidant.

"Now before I go on, I'd like to say a few things about you and me. Coach Gold is the name I use for contacting you. Please call me Lucy; that's my real name. I was given this assignment because I know a lot about North Korea, I'm a native of Vladivostok, where this mission would be launched, and I'm a basketball junkie.

"Bo, whether you do this or not, I know we can trust you. If you do it, you're going to have to trust me. I'll be the only person you can talk with about your secret. I'll be your only link to the Center.

"You're going to ask yourself, how do I know the guy at the airport and Lucy are really who they say they are, and not foreign agents or part of some elaborate hoax?

The answer is, right now, you don't. But if you decide to do this, rest assured, before you embark on your mission, you will quite literally have ironclad proof. There will be no possible doubt in your mind.

"Bo, you're the only one who can do this. If you pull it off, and you can, it will be an extraordinary achievement for your country."

As several people approached and walked by, Lucy paused, and Bo hid his face by bending down and putting his forehead against his clasped hands between his knees, in what appeared to be a prayerful or contemplative pose.

After Bo sat back up, Lucy looked over at him and then forward. She frowned as she continued.

"To be honest, I have several misgivings about what the Center wants you to do. First, you don't have the proper training. Second, it's a lot to ask. Any foreigner inside North Korea is at risk, and anyone who is going to be close to Kim for an extended period of time is going to be constantly scrutinized by his security apparatus.

"But my biggest concern is the third one. We don't ever embark on highly-sensitive missions without first trying to obtain all relevant information. We have to find out about vulnerabilities. We have to figure out suitability. We have to do our type of due diligence.

"I'm talking now about your sweetheart in Romania. This could be very tough on your relationship. The fact that you will have to keep her completely in the dark is a big concern. It could have some very bad consequences. That's what I would worry about.

"You can't ever tell her. You can't ever tell anyone. Not now, not while it's happening, not when it's over, not when it's been over for many years, not ever.

"This is a volunteer mission. If you decide to take it on, you must do so with a clear understanding of what *secret* will mean for you. I want to be certain you realize what you'd be getting into." She paused for a moment.

"Now let me tell you about some particulars we have in mind. Your solicitation of Kim would be part of an overall expansion of your operations in the Pacific region. You'd open up a branch office in Vladivostok with funds we'd provide.

"Kim would be charged the same rates you'd charge any other wealthy client. To those who may criticize you for doing business with him, you'd reply with comments about basketball building bridges and spreading goodwill.

"This would be very financially rewarding, but I know for you that's only going to be a secondary matter. What's going to matter the most is keeping this secret from the love of your life while you have to be away from her for long stretches.

"Bo, please take some time to really think about this. When you want to talk again, you can reach me at the same number.

"Is there anything you'd like to ask me now?"

"How could I become his pal, I don't speak Korean?"

"He'll always speak Korean in public and even in small private groups. In North Korea it's almost a crime to speak anything other than Korean. But you both speak English. When he wants to talk with you alone, that will be your lingua franca."

"You've got this all figured out, how I'd do this, don't you?"

"Yes, from beginning to end."

"What's the time frame estimate?"

"Two or three years."

"Okay, I'll think about it. I certainly appreciate what you've told me."

Lucy stood up first, and then Bo.

For a moment, they maintained a penetrating eye contact, as if each was trying to explore the other's soul. Finally, Lucy extended her hand and they shook firmly. Nothing else was said, and they walked away in different directions.

Chapter 4

It all made sense to Bo, including the part about a branch office in Vladivostok. He imagined how the plan would unfold, just like the SVR expected.

Sure, there could be danger. A slipup by someone involved in this scheme, or loose lips by someone with knowledge of it, and he could die in a staged accident.

In any event, a fear of what Kim's security people may have discovered might creep into his life. He entertained the thought that he might end up nervous every time he got in a taxi, walked into a public restroom, ran around a park or answered his doorbell.

But he had no doubt that he could pull this off. He'd probably just cruise through it with his natural instincts.

And he felt the pull of a powerful calling, the march onward of his family in the Russian history of honor and sacrifice. Something he'd not been a part of before. Now, here it was beckoning.

Even though he had worked hard to earn his fame, wealth and place of privilege, it was all for his personal gain. This, he thought, was his chance to be a part of something much bigger than himself. This was his chance to be a patriot. He felt grateful that this day had suddenly, unexpectedly, arrived.

He thought about his father and grandfather. As much as anything in his being, he felt profound gratitude and love for them. Now it was his turn to do his duty. Now it was his turn to answer the call.

He became anxious to tell Lucy that he was in. But he forced himself to wait. He decided to sleep on it for a couple of days.

He began to think that maybe his sacrifice would be no more than making lots of money and going to strange parties. He was amazed at how the Center's plan for a Vladivostok branch office could have been lifted right out of his own business plan for expansion in the Pacific.

He got off his high horse of patriotism and reflected on how this wouldn't be any sort of heroism like that shown by his father and grandfather. This would be nothing compared with what they did.

But Lucy was right, one thing was for sure, the big fear factor was Zella. Long stretches of being far away could be devastating. And she wouldn't be able to understand. While he'd secretly be doing his duty for his country, he'd look insensitive, mercenary and greedy.

What if this caused him to lose her?

*

Tonight, they'd FaceTime.

Sure, there was something that no one else would ever know about him. There was something he'd never share with anyone, not even Zella: How he saw the world. What he really focused on. What really occupied his thoughts.

His preoccupation with lust. That just on the other side of his outward appearance, there lurked a hawk-eyed hunter of sexy women, willing to be discreet. He was by nature a powerful sexual prowler, whose seductions and exploits were kept a secret to protect everyone involved.

But to him, not sharing that secret was different. It was different because sex wasn't a choice, not any more than food. It was a predisposition, something you're born with. Therefore, not disclosing it could never breach a trust.

But tonight, he would make a real choice in his life, and he knew a real duplicity was about to begin. With anyone else, that wouldn't be a problem. But with Zella, it seemed wicked. He dreaded changing their relationship like this. He had told her that tonight he'd be fresh for his girl. Instead, he would be wearing a mask of deceit.

Even though he was preparing to accept the assignment, he was having a hard time getting rid of this one lingering and most important doubt. He wasn't sure he could, or should, do this to her. It felt like it would be demeaning to his better half. And, he could lose her.

He realized he had to come to terms with what was suddenly the biggest conflict in his life.

*

It was nine o'clock at night in Cluj, when Zella answered his call.

Their images were a dramatic contrast.

Her black hair in a shoulder-length bob with bangs, which vividly framed striking blue-grey eyes. Her soft, melodious, seductive voice. She sat motionless with an aura of certitude.

He was a picture of contemporary hip, with blonde hair in a trendy fashionable cut. His sparkling brown eyes. His more uniform and assertive speech. His almost constant fluid body movements.

She looked to be from another, more romantic era. The camera seemed to be coming to her. He seemed to be coming to the camera.

"Oh Bo, it's so nice to see you."

"Zella, you are gorgeous. I don't want to talk. I just want to sit here and look at you."

"My darling Bo, I could do the same, but I do very much want to hear how things are going."

"Well, I'm so lucky to have Youri running things. He's amazing. And he's the master of concise briefings. Without him, my catch-up would take weeks. With him, it'll probably take a couple of days.

"My sweet Zella, please, let's talk about our next escapade out in the woods. Right now, that's all I can think about. How about the weekend after next, including Friday? Can you see if Sabrina can do that and how early you could leave? If that's not good, how about trying for the following weekend?"

"Sure, I should be able to find out about that and let you know tomorrow night."

At first, Bo thought about facetiously approaching the serious topic, but quickly discarded that bad idea. It would add insult to injury. He kept trying to think of some way to ease into it. He could think of none. Finally, he decided to try to generate some sympathy for the position he was in. It wouldn't work, but it was the best he could do.

"Zella, I'm a little bit anxious about how you might react to the next subject, but honestly, it's really a business necessity, and it won't be as bad as you'll think.

"I'm planning to expand in the Far East and western Pacific by opening a branch office in Vladivostok."

For a few seconds there was silence. Then she broke it with one monosyllabic word, which she stretched out in a way that conveyed both disbelief and disgust.

"Whaaat!?"

At first, he was not able to respond. He was jolted by the degree of hostility in her reaction, the look on her face and the tone of her voice.

She looked up, as if seeking guidance from above, and then back at Bo.

"Why?"

"We're starting to get more and more action in that part of the world and Vladivostok is the closest Russian city and logical spot to more closely manage those operations. It would give us an opportunity to step up our activities in that region, which has lots of potential for us. It may not be as glamorous as Sochi, but the logistics there would be terrific."

"It sounds like you'd be far away even more. I can't pretend that sounds good. I'm going to get some water. I'll be right back."

As she went off screen, Bo knew it wasn't really to get water. It was her way to contain her anger and maintain her composure.

She returned to her seat a few minutes later. "Bo, this is very disappointing."

"Zella, I know this isn't something you wanted to hear. But please, consider the big picture. This business is based on a unique, elaborate, global enterprise. That's what will ensure its long-term growth. That's what I envisioned when I started it. I've told you that all along.

"I have to expand, especially into those markets. It's not optional, it's essential. Eventually, a lot of this will be delegated and become almost self-sustaining. In the meantime, you and I could take this as an opportunity to visit places like Japan and Hawaii. You'd like that.

"It would be wonderful to go skiing in Japan. They have some of the best powder skiing in the world. And maybe we could learn how to surf in Hawaii. That could be a lot of fun."

"Bo, what I'd like is for us to spend more time together, not less. Some occasional vacation trips aren't going to make up for that."

"Look, I'll just need to get this new office set up, and then I can turn it over to a branch manager. The key thing is hiring the right people. It'll probably take about nine months, and then I'll mainly be back in Sochi."

For a long moment they just looked at each other.

Then Zella broke the silence. "This isn't the kind of news I wanted to hear about our lives, about you and me. This will not be a good development. This may be good for business, but it's not good for us. Did you expect me to be okay with this?"

"I was hoping you'd understand and be patient. This is temporary."

"What, your expanding global empire is temporary?

"Bo, you're wealthy. Your business is huge, and very successful. You don't need to do this."

Once again, for a moment, they just looked at each other. Her eyes seemed to change from inviting to cold and piercing. He felt an eerie sensation. He thought he may have seen her upper lip quiver over a repressed snarl. He told himself that it was the picture transmission or his imagination was getting the best of him.

As they continued to just look at each other, their connection seemed to become surreal. He fantasized that if she were to bite him now, he'd really get hurt.

"In the future, I'll find ways to make it up to you, Zella, I promise. And you know that after dear Maria passes, we're going to be able to spend more time together."

She just stared at him.

He looked down, and then back up at her. "Now please, can I look forward to hearing from you tomorrow about our getaway plans?"

She just continued to stare at him.

"Yes," she finally said, "I'll let you know tomorrow. Good night."

She abruptly ended the call.

Bo continued to sit there. He told himself that it's going to be rough, very rough, but her love would probably be strong enough to ride it out.

What he was surprised about was how easy the deception was. It was so easy to do. He told himself, why shouldn't it be? He was doing what had to be done.

He continued to be convinced that he had to take on the assignment. He knew he could do it, and do it well. He also knew no one else could.

He got up, looked out a window for a few minutes and then decided there was no longer any doubt. He was going to have faith that, in the long run, Zella's love would endure.

His whole life, every step of the way, he has been confident, decisive and swift. This would be no different. He called the number for Coach Gold.

After two rings, he heard, "Sir, would tomorrow, the same place and the same time, be okay for you?"

"Yes, that would be fine."

When Bo walked into St. Michael's, he saw Lucy kneeling in the last pew. As he got closer, he could see she was holding a rosary, an unusual thing to see in an Orthodox church. He sat down on the other end of the same pew. He also noticed there was a laptop by her purse. She looked over at him, then forward again, bowed slightly, made the sign of the cross, and got up.

They walked outside without saying anything. Conveniently, there were no other people on the way back to the same bench.

"Bo, I'm all ears."

"I have one condition, that regardless of whatever happens, this can't be for more than two years."

"That's acceptable to us. Believe me, I understand."

"The Center knew for sure that I was going to do this, didn't they?"

"Yes, they knew."

"And, of course, you know the two-year limit is because of Zella."

"Yes."

"I understand why," he said, "and I don't fault you at all for doing it, but it's kind of creepy, how much you people know about me."

"As I told you before," she replied, "this mission demanded our due diligence. It was for your protection, as well as ours. I'm sorry about the intrusions. Thank you for understanding.

"Now Bo, let's talk about the branch office, and some other financial matters.

"We'll cover the costs of rent, staffing, equipment, utilities and so on. I'm sure we'll agree on a suitable location. I realize your operation must look successful.

"When you go to see Kim, we pay you at the hazardous duty rate and reimburse travel expenses.

"Our funding will stop sixty days after your substantial engagement with Kim ends.

"Any questions about the branch office?"

"No."

"I'm giving you this laptop with a Service orientation program. It's thirty-six hours. The passcode is...into deep water...with no caps and no spaces. Don't write the passcode down. Again, that's *into deep water* with no caps or spaces. If it's tampered with, it'll self-destruct.

"You can do this in as many installments as you want. The sooner you finish the better. Please return it to me as soon as possible. It can't be taken on air travel. I need it back before you head east."

She handed him the laptop.

"So, when would you like me to start in Vladivostok?" he asked.

"Would four weeks work for you?" she replied.

"I think so," he answered. After a pause, and with more certainty in his voice, he said, "Yes, I can do that."

"Good," she said.

He looked away and asked a question that wasn't for Lucy, and really wasn't even a question. It was more of a musing. "I wonder how much time I'll need to spend in North Korea?"

She knew that he didn't expect her to answer that one, but responded anyway. "Yeah, at this point it's hard to tell how much time you'll need to spend in North Korea.

"How much time you spend in other west Pacific countries will be up to you. But please keep in mind that it must be enough that your business reason for the branch office is obviously legit and North Korea doesn't suspiciously stand out."

Suddenly, a squirrel raced up to within a few feet, sat down and looked at them sideways. Bo looked at the intruder with a blank stare, lost in thought.

Lucy looked sympathetically at Bo, and then off into the distance.

Bo continued to look at the squirrel with a blank stare. "Where will you be?"

"When you're ready to head east, I'm going back to my home in Vladivostok. Please know that for as long as you're on this mission, I'll always be available for you any time you need me."

He looked over at her with a smile. "Lucy, tell me, are you really a basketball junkie?"

"Yes, definitely. I'm not an avid fan. I'm what would generally be considered a fanatic. I follow the Russian leagues, the EuroLeague, colleges, the Chinese Basketball Association, even the NBA. Can you believe it?

"Bo, unless you have more questions, I'm going to say good-bye for now. I know you'll do the best job that can be done. I wish you success, not only on your mission, but also in your personal life."

"Thank you, Lucy."

They got up and walked away from each other, Bo to his car and Lucy back into the church.

*

Based on what he had seen in that church pew, Bo assumed that Lucy was a devout Roman Catholic. It never occurred to him that she might be faking it. His assumption was correct.

She's a descendant of Russian nationals who were ethnic Chinese and Roman Catholic. In Russia, this was a very small minority, included in *Other* on demographic pie charts.

For a long time, this made life very difficult for her family. After the Communists took over, during the long hellish nightmare of militant atheism, all the churches were confiscated, and people like her family were considered to be subversive outsiders. Up until the end of the Soviet era, they continued to be treated with suspicion.

Things have certainly changed. Roman Catholicism is now vibrant and growing in the far southeast part of Russia, where there are now eleven thriving parishes. In Vladivostok, the Gothic-styled and beautifully restored Most Holy Mother of God Church is a symbol of this revival. Lucy Wong is one of its parishioners.

As a natural inclination to compensate for their outsider status in Russian society, her family has always demonstrated a strong sense of national loyalty and patriotism.

Lucy had two older brothers. They were both always supportive and protective of her. And they always seemed to know how best to navigate through life's trials and tribulations. They brought stability, security and strong family bonds to her childhood.

They both became proud members of the Armed Forces. They were both casualties of the Afghan War.

One was blown to bits by a land mine, the other suffered from an acute hepatitis infection and died in a field hospital.

It's amazing her parents are still alive. Their grief is all-consuming. It never subsides. They never find any peace. They appear to be in a state of permanent shock: two bodies occupying space in a nursing home in Nakhodka, fifty-three miles east of Vladivostok.

After Lucy graduated from the Far Eastern Federal University, her parents had hoped she would have a career, if not in service to her country, at least in a profession dedicated to the betterment of society.

Instead, she had to tell them that she was working as a headhunter for multinational corporations. They privately thought, disparagingly, that she would use her abundant talent to enrich the profiteers, with cleverness, cunning and hard-fisted business dealings.

When Lucy sees her parents, neither one outwardly expresses any disappointment about her career choice. They're both incapable of showing such feelings anyway. They're alive, but deadened. Their expressions are always blank. They rarely talk, except they always ask Lucy to pray for her brothers. Lucy always promises that she will.

Lucy is a widow. She and her husband loved each other and were the best of friends. They delighted in each other's company. They were great companions.

He was a concert pianist. His music was exquisite. On reflection, she can't remember which she fell in love with first, him or his music. She suspects it was his music.

Their professions often took them on separate travels. It was always a great cause for celebration when they were reunited. They were always so happy together.

He was a hiking enthusiast. As he traveled around the globe to concert venues, he would often add noteworthy trails to his itinerary. It was three years ago when he died of a heat stroke while hiking in California.

Somehow, through all of the tragedy and loss in her life, Lucy has managed to find an inner peace, not to just carry on, but to thrive in life's challenges and adventures.

She is perfectly content to live by herself in a cozy little apartment in central Vladivostok. She is friendly with, but not really close to any of the people in her neighborhood or with any of her fellow parishioners.

By all appearances, she is an independent soul and a hardworking, freelance recruitment specialist, whose business is focused primarily on the shipping industry and international trade.

In secret, she's a skilled, dedicated, highly-respected Russian foreign intelligence officer.

She finds satisfaction in doing a good job for her country. She is constantly intrigued by her casework. She is fascinated by her Korean studies. She finds comfort and strength in the practice of her faith. And she very much enjoys the world of basketball.

Chapter 5

Bo could handle it, but his plate was now overflowing.

The SVR orientation program included practices, guidelines, and complicated technical procedures, which needed to be memorized. It would have to be done in many increments, whether he wanted to or not.

He was already working on the staff additions and other changes that would be necessary for the Far East and western Pacific expansion. For his business, the hiring and promotion actions would be the most time-consuming and critical part of the plan.

He was behind on the attention he needed to give to many existing client contracts. Requests for consultation were coming in from all directions, and related orders, quality control, deliveries, installations, and all the rest, were being stalled.

Zella had responded that the weekend after next would be okay and that she could leave the Academy by three o'clock on Friday. He confirmed, and the bookings were made for the country inn, the private jet trips and the rental car.

He would get to Zella's place early, so that, hopefully, he could visit with Maria before she got home. That would speed up their departure into the woods, into privacy, into sex.

He suspended work on all of the upcoming marketing strategies, and redirected those personnel resources into existing contract obligations.

Every evening, after all the others were gone, he stayed in his office and worked on the orientation program into the late hours.

*

Applications were pouring in for the Vladivostok job openings, which was not surprising. One of the many advantages of celebrity was having your help wanted listing stand out from all the others.

Youri was given the new title of director of global operations, and a handsome increase in salary. Although Bo believed that he was very loyal, this was meant to ensure that he would not at all be tempted to consider some other opportunity. At this juncture, his loss would be a serious blow. And besides, Bo was very grateful to Youri; he greatly valued his work.

The single most challenging human resources task would be to find the right person to be what Bo had tentatively decided to call the Pacific operations manager.

Nine days later, as he approached his long-awaited romantic weekend in Romania, it felt like things were starting to get under control.

He discovered that, fortuitously, Zella's employer, the International Academy for Language and Culture, had a branch in Vladivostok.

He decided that he would ask her to make inquiries about their Korean capabilities, especially tutoring to help someone better understand English spoken with a thick Korean accent, in a Pyongyang dialect.

Such a conversation would broach the subject of his plan to make an unsolicited proposal to Kim Jong Un, which hopefully would eventually result in multiple trips into North Korea, and a very lucrative business deal.

He didn't know what her reaction would be. Whatever it would be, he figured it would be better to observe it in person. That way he'd get a better reading of her true feelings, and if they were extremely negative, he'd be in a better position to deal with it.

He still contemplated the nature of what he'd been asked to do. He kept trying to gauge its significance. Even though he knew he'd be a fool to compare himself with them, he couldn't help thinking again and again about his father and grandfather. They'd gone into the face of danger, for their country. If he's taken in and trusted by Kim, and becomes a confidant and learns any state secrets, and then they find out what he'd been up to, he'd most likely be killed too.

*

As he began his journey in a small jet on a chartered flight to Cluj, Bo's thoughts turned to the love of his life.

It has always seemed somewhat providential the way they met. It was three months after he opened his office in Sochi...

...while he was showing some prospective clients from Greece the Archangel Column, a landmark with a statue of Sochi's patron saint, Michael the Archangel, on the top.

As he finished telling his guests about what they were looking at, he heard a beautiful voice right behind him. "He's also the patron saint of Cluj-Napoca, my hometown in Romania."

Strangely, he felt her voice more than he heard it. When he turned around, it was like being in a schoolboy's dream. She was drop-dead gorgeous, and giving him a seductive smile. It seemed like she was sent by angels, or maybe even was one.

Whatever was happening, he wasn't going to lose her. In sharp contrast to his trademark politeness, he didn't care about his guests or what they might think. The love train had pulled into the station and he wasn't going to miss it.

"Well greetings, I'm Bo, and I'd be delighted if I could have the opportunity to show you some wonderful hidden secrets here in Sochi, if..." Before he could go any further, she interrupted. "I'm Zella, and I'd like that. But please, I don't want to interrupt your tour anymore." She pulled a card out of her purse and handed it to him. "It was nice to meet you, Bo." She then bowed slightly at his visitors, and walked away.

He stood there for a moment, stunned, before he again became aware of his guests. As it turned out, they'd been closely watching, like an audience in a romantic play, and expressed hearty approval.

After he got off the plane, Bo picked up the reserved rental car near the airport. He knew Zella would approve.

It was a bright yellow Ferrari capable of doing zero to sixty miles per hour in less than three seconds.

He arrived at her residence an hour early, and was enthusiastically greeted by Sabrina. He told her how nice it was to see her again, that he knew Maria and Zella were very grateful for her help, and how much he appreciated her staying through the weekend. She told him that she didn't mind at all doing around-the-clock weekends, every now and then.

He asked her to say that she'd already been paid when Zella goes to pay her after the trip. He gave her what amounted to more than triple time. She thanked him, and said that Maria was awake, and would be happy to see him. Then he excused himself, used the bathroom, and went in to visit Maria.

When Zella arrived home, Bo was back in the kitchen talking with Sabrina. He told Zella he had a lovely visit with Maria. That after about thirty minutes she said she needed to rest. Zella finished packing quickly, went in and looked at the now sleeping Maria, was reassured by Sabrina that everything would be fine, and they were off.

They were staying at the same country inn they'd been to before several times. It was in lush green surroundings, setback from the road, carved into the edge of a forest. The staff was friendly and helpful. The rooms were comfortable. The food was good.

And surprisingly it had two tennis courts, which were in excellent condition and even had night lighting. Bo and Zella figured there were probably avid tennis players in the family that owned the place, which would explain such an unusual feature in this location.

They considered it their good fortune to discover such an idyllic place. It was charming, quiet, relaxing, and secluded. When they weren't in bed, they had a lot of fun playing tennis, hiking in the woods, lounging on the balcony, and eating in the cutest little bar and dining room they'd ever seen. It was wonderful.

Friday evening was going to be unusually warm. They had decided it would be perfect for tennis. That would be the first thing they'd do after having a light meal in that cute dining room.

After they finished eating and returned to their room, Zella put on her tennis outfit: a t-shirt, very-short cutoff blue jeans and her favorite shoes, *Bo Brand* high-top black tennies. Suddenly, all Bo could see was her legs, his vision uncontrollably locked on, his breath taken away.

He realized his body was rapidly changing. He tried to snap out of it for the sake of tennis, to have a game first. Then he looked at her face and melted. There was no stopping it. They'd play tennis some other time.

For hours, they handled each other and submitted to each other with total abandon. The desire, pent up for so long, a combustible now finally ignited, flared into a wild indulgence of mutual cravings.

When they finally burnt out, and laid still, they could hear, through an open window, the distant howling of wolves.

For these wilderness animals, it's a trait that strengthens the bond between packmates. Bo and Zella each felt like this nocturnal chorus affirmed and strengthened their bond, which seemed to be endowed with not only physical, but also supernatural powers. A fitting end to their first night in the woods.

*

On Saturday, in between slower sex, they enjoyed a tennis match, a long hike, nice meals, and many conversations. Bo didn't want to risk ruining the weekend, or at least most of it, so he decided not to bring up North Korea until the last day.

It was while they were finishing a nice leisurely Sunday brunch out on the veranda, that he brought it up.

"I see that your school has a branch in Vladivostok. Could you make some inquiries for me? I'd like to find out about their Korean capabilities, both language and customs. I also have an interest in a particular listening skill. I'd like to find out if they can tutor me to better understand English spoken by someone who has a thick accent in the dialect of Pyongyang, the North Korean capital and largest city.

"I'd like to spread our business into that market. Kim Jong Un, the North Korean leader, is a huge basketball fan. Actually, he's obsessed with basketball. I'm very optimistic about the possibility of landing a very lucrative contract with him. It may take a couple of trips, but I really think I can make that happen."

Her head dropped down a few inches, and she looked over the top of her sunglasses, not at Bo, but off into the distance. Nothing was said for a moment, then she took off her sunglasses and looked straight into his eyes. It was a piercing gaze. "Are you really...actually... telling me that you're going into North Korea?"

"Yes," he answered.

"Bo, how would you feel about me going there?"

"Well, you're not, so what's it matter?" he said.

"I'll tell you why it matters! You know damn well you wouldn't want me going into North Korea. And why?

Because it's dangerous! Only a fool would go there if they didn't have to. And you don't have to!"

Her voice had risen to an unprecedented level.

"I'm supposed to live with the fear that you might make some slight miscue or unintentionally commit a serious offense and then end up suffering in unimaginable ways. Bo Tenbinakov, you've got about a zillion places you can grow your business between Europe and the Far East; you don't need to go into North Korea!"

There was a long silence. Bo decided it would be smart to pause this. He wouldn't say anything further at the moment.

"I'm going to take walk," she said. "I won't be gone long. I just need to walk for a while. I'm sorry I yelled, but I stand by everything I said." She got up and left.

Bo knew he needed to talk about this some more with her when she returned. This needed to be done in person. Hopefully, in the next round he could lessen her fears. Hopefully.

About thirty minutes later she returned and joined Bo sitting by a window in their room. "Zella, please let me say a few more things about North Korea."

"Of course, go ahead."

"If I was from a lot of other countries in the world, sure, there could be some real danger, and I might be a fool to go there. But the facts are I'm a well-known Russian sports figure with many adoring fans. Kim's not stupid. He's not going to intentionally do something awful to a Russian sports celebrity. That's not going to happen.

"Besides, trust me, he's going to like me. He idolizes basketball stars, and I'd be there to give him what he wants. And believe me, he's going to want what I have to offer. I should be able to make a lot of money.

"I imagine some people will be critical of me having anything to do with that regime, but I'm certainly not going to apologize for promoting basketball. It's becoming a universal game, a way to build bridges and spread goodwill. It could be an antidote for the insular condition of that country. It could reduce the isolation. It could open up doors of opportunity for more engagement with the outside world.

"Please, Zella, don't worry about it. I'll be safe."

"Bo, considering your flight time, we should probably start getting ready to head back."

And that was the end of it, at least for now. There was no more talk about Bo going into North Korea for the remainder of the weekend. The weather was now turning cooler. And between them, a chill had set in. There was very little talk about anything at all during their last few hours together.

As they were saying goodbye to each other outside of Zella's place, Bo went back to the car and got an envelope, which he gave her and said, "I've made arrangements with a private-duty nurses service. They will provide an around-the-clock hospice care in your home. Oncological care is their specialty. They're state of the art. They are experts in the administration of morphine. This is the best care your mom could possibly have. We know this for certain.

"My close staff and I did a lot of research, and made many inquiries. Youri's involvement was phenomenal. He's brilliant when it comes to somehow getting to the right people, and then getting them to talk candidly. And we even had a private investigator look into it.

"Zella, I'm a person who's blessed with considerable wealth; please allow me to help your mother.

"These nurses are the absolute best. All you have to do is call, tell whomever you're talking with that I've made prior arrangements, which both the director and deputy director are familiar with, and then say when you would like them to start. It's all in the envelope."

They looked at each other.

Both of their faces turned to slight, poignant smiles.

Then she looked away and then down and started to cry, which soon became a convulsive sobbing. After a few moments she stopped, took a deep breath, let out a sigh, looked again at him, and resumed the slight, poignant smile.

They kissed, not passionately, but longingly, and then they hugged tightly, for a long time. "Thanks," she said.

*

Later, as Bo sat in his charter flight passenger seat before takeoff, his thoughts did not turn to all the work he had ahead of him.

Instead, his thoughts stayed with Zella, and he felt terribly conflicted. He felt sad. He felt empty. He wanted to tell her that he would do anything for her. But he couldn't. And he missed her already. He pulled out his phone and sent a text.

> Zella
> You are the light of
> my life
> You make my heart
> dance
> You bring love into
> my soul
> Now and forever

About ten seconds later, she responded.

> I am with you
> Always

Chapter 6

Back in Sochi, Bo was determined to stay on schedule with Lucy.

There were over a hundred applications for the two management jobs in Vladivostok. Video teleconferencing was going to play a big part in the selection process.

The online search for commercial office space had so far resulted in half a dozen possibilities.

The increased emphasis on the servicing of existing clients seemed to be going well.

Bo was almost done with his orientation program. He would finish it in a day or two.

Things were moving along. He was satisfied with the progress.

Lucy had indicated that she preferred they head east in four weeks. He had told her that was doable. Now he was certain that was going to happen.

The travel reservations were made. Bo would arrive in Vladivostok twenty-eight days after the last St. Michael's meeting. He'd be accompanied by Max and by Garry, a sophisticated acquisitions negotiator, who would remain there until the office space was leased, any significant modifications were taken care of, and both of the new managers were in place.

Four days before departure, Bo called for Coach Gold. They'd meet in two days, this time at the Arboretum. He was reminded to return the orientation program.

*

The meeting was brief. Lucy grumbled a little about his fame creating a visibility problem. She was appreciative that he was on schedule. She said that twice.

"This will be our last loosey-goosey meeting," she said. "After we get to Vlad, and especially after contact with North Korea, we're going to need to take extraordinary measures to avoid surveillance.

"The place is crawling with spies. You wouldn't believe how much is out there -- Chinese, North Korean, South Korean, American, Japanese, British, Australian. I'm telling you, it's pretty wild. Which is to be expected; it is an international port after all.

"We'll even have to avoid Russian surveillance. Your mission is highly restricted, on a need-to-know basis, among a small number of people within the SVR. The Federal Security Service, for example, will not and should not ever know about this operation. It seems crazy to use countersurveillance on your own people, but that will happen."

She handed him a piece of paper.

"That's the new Coach Gold phone number for use in the Far East. I'll be there before you are. I'm leaving early tomorrow morning."

"Lucy, please don't worry about my ability to maintain secrecy. I've been obsessed with being able to do it since my childhood. I'm a master at it. Eventually, I think you'll appreciate what I mean."

"Bo, listen to me. When it comes to maintaining secrecy, you need to do what you've been instructed in that program you just finished, and what I tell you. No shortcuts, abbreviated versions, or substitutes. Our country's vital interests and your personal safety depend on it.

"Bo, do you read me?"

"Yes, I got it."

"Okay," she said, "I'll see you in Vlad."

*

On the evening of his last full day in Sochi, Bo called Zella. He knew they would be texting, but because of all the work that would be going on while they were seven time zones apart, he assumed it might be quite a while before they got a chance to talk again.

During their phone conversation, they shared fond memories of the country inn. Zella pointed out what was now obvious, that they wouldn't have any more weekends away together until after Maria passes on.

She asked him when he thought he might return from the Far East. She realized there would be a lot involved in setting up that branch office. She only half-jokingly said that she hoped he'd be back in time for Christmas.

There was no mention of North Korea. Bo figured she had made her passionate objection and was going to stand by it. He figured she wouldn't talk about it anymore, as that might diminish or compromise her plea. Instead, she would continue to register her strong objection with a wall of complete silence.

But he realized that he was mistaken about that near the end of their conversation. She told him that she wasn't going to make any insider inquiries like he had asked of her. She said that she wouldn't do anything that might in any way help him go into North Korea.

She said that Maria wanted him to know that she was grateful for his last visit, that she cherished it.

Then she said that she had to go and hung up. Her closing was rapid and tense. He didn't get a chance to respond. He sensed that she was starting to cry. And he knew, he was letting her down.

Chapter 7

Bo, Garry and Max had set up shop in a large business-friendly hotel near the center of Vladivostok. Bo liked Garry, and was glad to have him on the team. Garry was a smooth operator. He was amiable, easy to get along with, easy to deal with, and a skilled negotiator who never missed any details.

The office space possibilities had grown to fifteen. Garry had started scheduling tours he would take with commercial real estate brokers, property managers or owners themselves. Bo's interviews with the nine finalists for the two key positions were being scheduled in a hotel conference room. There were four remaining candidates for the position of Pacific operations manager, and five still in the running for branch manager. Bo and Youri agreed, they all looked like good possibilities.

Lucy drove by and picked up Bo as he was walking down the street a half block from where he was staying. She avoided the cameras at the hotel. The driver and front passenger side windows were lightly tinted. In a look he hadn't seen before, she was wearing a hat with a large brim and big sunglasses.

She drove to a spot near the beautiful historic railway station, in an area busy with buses and taxis. They stayed in the car. She gave him another secure laptop with an instructional program. She explained how the SVR funds would be moved through other entities before being transferred into his company bank account.

She told him that he would soon be receiving an invitation to the Pacific Fleet's annual officers and veterans basketball game where he was going to be the honored guest.

Before the game, he would be taken onboard a ship to view a personal greeting from the Center. Then, during the pre-game festivities, he would be introduced by the commanding officer, say a few words himself and then toss up the jump ball to start the game.

Bo asked her about a Korean language translator and a tutor for North Korean customs.

He told her Zella had declined to help and why.

She said that she already had someone identified for the help he'd need. She just needed to doublecheck on it.

Then she drove him back to the vicinity of his hotel. She dropped him off near a coffeehouse a few blocks away. He went in and bought a latte.

*

Two days later, a Russian Navy junior lieutenant found Bo walking out of a hotel conference room. The young officer introduced himself and then presented Bo with a black and gold embossed invitation to *The Seventeenth Annual Russian Pacific Fleet Officers and Veterans*

Basketball Game, which was from the event's official host, Capt. Alexei Yenotov.

Bo looked at the invitation, and then smiled at the messenger. "Lt. Petrenko, could you give a message to Capt. Yenotov for me?"

"Yes, sir, of course."

"Please, tell him that I proudly accept this invitation, and consider it to be a great honor. And thank you for delivering it, Lt. Petrenko."

"Yes, sir. A pleasure, sir!"

*

Each year, after this event's honored guest has accepted the invitation, black and gold embossed copies of the invitation and an open letter from the official host to the officers and veterans informing them of the invitee's acceptance are posted on the fleet's website and inside of locked glass display cases throughout the base and at several facilities that provide benefits to veterans.

*

Bo's transparent visit to the captain's quarters would be the perfect way for the Center to provide, as Lucy had promised, ironclad proof, both figuratively and literally, of his mission's authenticity.

And this celebrity event exposure of Bo's presence in the Far East would appear to be advantageous to his growing business interests, an impressive promotion of his expansion into the Pacific.

Chapter 8

On the day of the Pacific Fleet basketball event, a Navy driver arrived at the hotel to take the honored guest to the ship of the official host. On the trip to the base, the driver explained how, over the years, this annual game has become a much-anticipated event.

"And the brass has done a great job of hyping this thing up with celebrities. Now, every year, people are expecting someone famous. Last year, we had singer Vera Fradkov. Talk about being radiant; she was something else! Nobody wanted to miss that."

Bo was projecting a calm poised image, but underneath that appearance, he was very excited to be doing this. He wanted to relish every minute.

As they approached the base's main gate, he noted that it was a slightly overcast, pleasant afternoon. The driver had mentioned that the cool comfortable weather was rather typical for an early October. The driver wished it was like this all the time.

The Pacific Fleet was composed of fifty-three warships and an estimated twenty-three submarines. Its principal port was Vladivostok. Bo had expected the base would be large. As he rode across it, he found it was even larger than he had imagined.

He was driven to an edge of the harbor, to Capt. Yenotov's ship, which he was told was a guided-missile destroyer. When the car came to a stop, he was immediately greeted by a lieutenant who expressed pleasure at being able to escort him to the captain's quarters.

For such a high-ranking military officer, Capt. Yenotov was fairly young. He was handsome and athletic-looking. He had played on the officers' team at this event the last two years.

He was very pleased that Bo could be their guest this year. He told Bo that there is no mandatory attendance for this event, which means these will be mostly people who really like basketball.

"Which means, Mr. Tenbinakov, you're going to have a lot of fans out there."

"Captain, please sir, call me Bo."

The captain insisted that they have a liquid refreshment before leaving for the game. He offered a variety of beverages, including Russian vodka. Bo chose chilled apple cider.

The captain ordered two of those, and then went over and unlocked and opened the door for what had appeared to be a closet, until you could see what was inside. He motioned for Bo to enter.

"Bo, please take the seat in there in front of the screen. I'm going to activate a recording, which is for you personally and confidentially, and then I'm going to shut the door. When it's over, please, just come back out."

After looking at the seal of the SVR for about half a minute, the picture changed and Bo saw a woman sitting in a dark green, high-backed, plush chair against a dark-wood-paneled wall. Next to her was a small table. On it was a lamp with a white shade and a yellow vase with yellow roses.

"Bo, greetings from Moscow. I'm Regina Baranova at the headquarters of the Foreign Intelligence Service of the Russian Federation.

"On behalf of your government, I want to welcome you to the service of our country. As part of our foreign intelligence, you are now part of an amazing global team, which is seldom publicly recognized and sometimes not appreciated enough, but whose work ensures the security of our country.

"In order to protect you and your mission, except through your case officer Lucy Wong, we will never be contacting you and we will never be recognizing you. But please know, Bo, we will always be aware of your courage and dedication. You are part of that invisible corps that our nation is indebted to.

"Bo, we'll always be cheering for you. I hope you enjoy the game today. I know the Navy's very proud to have you there."

She stood up.

"Mr. Bo Tenbinakov, on behalf of your grateful government and the Russian people, I salute you, thank you for your service, and wish you the very best."

The screen returned to the seal of the SVR for a few seconds and then went dark. Bo got up. As he walked back into the room, their beverages were being brought in. The captain toasted to "a great day for basketball" and they clinked glasses.

Before they had a chance to finish their drinks, the lieutenant was knocking on the door and advising the captain it was time to go.

"Bo, excuse me for a moment, I need to erase your message and lock up the equipment."

After the captain secured his communications closet, they headed off for the game.

The gymnasium was huge. It was made to also accommodate base assemblies. The place was packed and very noisy.

It was explained to Bo that in order to help level the playing field, starting this year, only officers who have been on active duty for more than ten years were allowed to play.

During his address to the crowd, the captain said that he was proud to introduce the honored guest as, "...the incomparable Bo Tenbinakov...one of the greatest to ever play the game...a transcendent figure in the world of sports...someone who exemplified team spirit, good sportsmanship, humility, dedication and excellence."

Bo said very little. "Captain, thanks for inviting me and thanks for your kind words. It is my honor to be here, one I will always treasure. And thanks to all of you veterans, officers and sailors. Thank you for your service to our country."

To no one's surprise, when Bo tossed up the jump ball to start the game, it went very high, perfectly straight and right where it was supposed to be.

As he sat with the captain, in the middle of an enthusiastic crowd, watching a spirited contest, Bo realized that both teams were really pumped up. This wasn't just some go-through-the-motions exhibition game. This was going to be a hard-fought battle. The captain confided in him that even though it was officially frowned upon, there was a lot of betting. Bo wondered how much of the enthusiasm was due to such monetary interests. Regardless, he found it to be quite entertaining, and by halftime, he had a favorite, which he kept to himself.

Chapter 9

With adeptness, speed and some amazing luck, Bo and his team had the Vladivostok branch up and running in two weeks. There were some office space modifications that needed to be finished, and the furniture was still temporary and makeshift, but the new place was perfectly suitable.

The new hires -- Nick, the Pacific operations manager, and Valeria, the branch manager -- were enthusiastically onboard. The computers were working flawlessly. Updates to the company website were done. There were nice views of the harbor, which gave it an international feel. The immediate neighborhood was quite appealing. There were popular cafés nearby.

Bo received a message he knew was from Lucy that told him to contact a tutor and translator by the name of Svetlana Baranovichi at the International Academy for Language and Culture. Max was able to get him an appointment to see her later the same day.

When he arrived, a receptionist took him into a conference room. A few minutes later, Svetlana walked in

-- a tall, leggy blonde with an engaging smile, who looked to be about thirty. He was first drawn to her lips. Without saying a word, she went up close to him and shook hands. Then it was the look in her eyes. Right off, he could feel himself getting hooked.

After she introduced herself, she told him that she didn't follow basketball, but she knew enough to know that he had been a famous player. By the time she asked if she could call him by his first name, he was addicted, and he knew what he wanted to do with her.

She spent about fifteen minutes giving him an overview of the services she could provide. And then for probably another forty-five minutes, they exchanged questions and answers.

He found her to be personable, and a good listener. She made it clear that she would be able to satisfy all of his needs, including verbal and written translations, and tutoring about customs and nuances of dialect and body language.

It didn't take him long to realize he wanted her to work for him. He was convinced she was an expert on Korea and a talented linguist. Fortuitously, she had this seductive aura, which felt really good. Almost too good, as it could be distracting. But he'd be happy to deal with that kind of a problem.

After meeting for over an hour, she asked to be excused for a few minutes. She left, and a very courteous receptionist came in and offered him something to drink, which made him think that it was probably going to be more than a few minutes.

About fifteen minutes later, Svetlana returned with a gentleman she introduced as her manager. They both proceeded to tell Bo, if he wanted to make a major push into either Korea, he should hire her as a contractor employee working in his offices and accompanying him on trips. They both urged him to consider that contract option as essential for his objectives.

When they were done with their sales pitch and answering Bo's questions, the manager exchanged pleasantries and left. Svetlana told Bo that she was going to go get some things she wanted to give him. She quickly returned with more background information, glowing references, contract terms and their fee schedule.

He promised to get in touch with her again the next morning. As he left, he really had no doubt about doing it. Because of Zella, he already knew this organization could be trusted. And then, of course, there was Lucy's prompt.

On the way back to his office, he thought to himself that she was more than capable and, he agreed, as a contractor employee, essential for his mission. He considered himself lucky that she was available.

He wondered about the disarming and almost flirtatious way she looked at him. He wanted to interpret *her* body language. It seemed like the sexual attraction was mutual. But then again, maybe he was reading too much into it. Maybe what he had observed was her usual professional demeanor. Maybe she puts everyone under her spell.

That night, he flipped through the material she had given him. Early the next morning, Max made an appointment to execute the contract, and obtained an advance copy. Bo had ordered that it only needed to be reviewed by Garry, who, although now in Manila, would be ready to look at it.

Bo and Svetlana's manager signed it at noontime. Afterwards, Svetlana told Bo that, since she was now going to be working for him to sell basketball, she looked forward to becoming an avid student of the game. She was sure she could help him achieve much success, and that it should be lots of fun.

Chapter 10

A couple of hours after hiring Svetlana, Bo received a signal to contact Coach Gold. For her calls, he now used burners -- pre-paid-in-cash disposable phones -- which were then methodically destroyed. He was now keenly aware of eavesdropping on mobiles, why texts weren't secure, and location tracking. They'd meet the next morning by the ice-skating rink in Minny Gorodok Park.

*

That evening he reflected on all the admonitions he had received from the Service instructional programs and Lucy. How imperative it was to always apply appropriate protection measures.

He had this recurring thought that maybe he didn't worry enough about the inherent danger in his mission.

Out in the everyday world of her hometown, people wouldn't know what Lucy did. But the RGB, the North Korean intelligence service? They might. Or some other foreign spies might. And sometimes, information was traded, even among adversaries.

It might take only one detection of some connection between Bo and Lucy for a fatal result. It was a sobering thing to consider. When safeguards were appropriate, he began to routinely repeat the warning to himself. *Just one detection of any connection.*

For his mission, he now understood how compelling it was to adopt SVR methods over his own instincts. He'd spent about a hundred and thirty hours intensely studying, imagining, absorbing...

Wearing bland clothes, not easily spotted from discreet distances... Taking long, circuitous, surveillance-detection routes...Focusing on the middle distance...Changing pace through traffic...Spotting repeat pedestrians or vehicles, or other anomalies...Using disguises...

Making the actual meeting time three hours earlier than the one in a message...Using times that were fifteen or forty-five past the hour, not the top of or half past the hour...Giving places code names...

He'd been introduced to the tradecraft, but it was only in his mind. He'd never done any of it. He knew that he was a master of deception, but his tricks were of a different kind. He was surprised that Lucy considered Zella a bigger concern than his inexperience at this game.

Of course, there were some things that only Lucy could do. She could provide cutting-edge countersurveillance. She could create diversions. She could have an operative impersonate a hotel manager, supply a fake taxi or a phony cop. She could create an elaborate hoax.

But they both had to always know when to wave off a rendezvous, without waving.

The next morning, as he approached the closed ice-skating rink, he found her sitting on a bench. They had done an appearance reversal. She looked like her normal self. He was barely recognizable, and she was impressed. He was wearing a hooded jacket, with the hood up and over his head, covering all of his hair, with the cords pulled tight and tied under his chin. And he had on sunglasses.

He sat down next to her, and put the second instructional laptop next to her purse.

"Are you trying to hide your identity or something?" she asked.

"Yeah, I'm tired of signing autographs."

They chuckled together, for the first time.

"Well, I just finished a damn two-hour surveillance detection route," she said. "This'll be the last time you get off so easy.

"Now, please, tell me, did you enjoy the Navy's annual game and your personal message from the Center?"

"Oh, I had a great time, and I appreciated the Center's message."

But then he shook his head. "With all due respect to the captain who introduced me to the crowd, I think he went overboard the way he described me, all that stuff about virtues, especially the part about humility. I didn't recognize the person he described."

"Bo, I was a huge fan of yours. You were, and still are, my favorite player ever. The fact that a basketball fanatic like me never said anything about your playing days, and you never asked me about that omission, is a testament to your humility. I wasn't there, but I saw a video of what the captain said. I recognized the person he described."

"Oh Lucy, you're so kind, and too diplomatic to say anything else." And then he told her about hiring Svetlana. How he thought she was probably perfect for the mission. Lucy listened, and said she agreed; it sounded like a good decision.

Then they talked about Bo's unsolicited proposal to Kim, and his anticipated trips into North Korea.

Lucy said that he should not initiate any sort of contact with the Russian embassy or any of its personnel in Pyongyang. The contacts should be exclusively between Bo's business and Kim's government.

She handed him a note about how to submit his proposal to Kim. He would use a DPRK-authorized dedicated courier service for multiple hand-deliveries, with routing to obtain a security inspection certificate, and an annotation by the sports liaison officer, Ro Chung Ju, who was in the office of the DPRK-Russia business and trade council.

The note included contact information for two such authorized couriers in Vladivostok.

Then she touched on the heart of his mission.

"We have the tiniest audio recording devices. They're amazing. It's incredible how tiny they are. They capture everything, and they're never discovered. But for you in North Korea, even that's too risky. We have to rely solely on your memory."

Bo nodded. "Of course, since the Service knows so much about me, you know I have an exceptionally good memory, don't you?"

"Yes, we're well aware of that," she answered. "It's a critical part of this mission." As she pulled a paperback book out of her purse and pretended to be reading, she said, "It's about to get crowded here." In his peripheral vision, Bo could now see four people and two dogs approaching in the distance. They were quite a way off, and coming from a point slightly behind them. And he had not seen Lucy look that way. He was impressed with her perception. He got up and left in the opposite direction.

*

When Svetlana arrived in Bo's office to begin working the following Monday, he already had a draft proposal ready for her translation and comments.

It didn't show any humility under the headings of Gifted Player, Magical Coach, Inspirational Consultant and Brilliant Strategist. It explained how he was a single source for everything in the world of basketball. It said that whatever you needed -- a one-on-one trainer, state-of-the-art scoreboard, team jackets -- whatever it was, he could provide it. For those who could afford the best, he would take their game to a higher level.

The proposal package was marked *Confidential* and started with a personal letter to Kim expressing how honored and happy Bo would be to share his secrets of basketball success with such an important leader and devotee of the game.

He suggested that, if he visited Kim, the benefits of media attention would be short-lived, whereas a confidential relationship could serve to bring amazing long-term benefits.

He explained that he had recently opened a branch office in Vladivostok to expand his operations in the

Pacific region. If Kim was interested and summoned him, subject to visa processing, he would be delighted to catch a flight and make the short trip into Pyongyang.

Before she started translating, Svetlana reviewed it and gave Bo her comments. Youri, back in Sochi, also gave him comments. Within two days, all the changes and corrections were made, the translation was finished, and the package was taken to a courier.

After the package was on its way, Bo had a talk with everyone who was involved in the project, about protecting their business position. He issued a stern warning. He told them, if it has anything to do with North Korea, be careful when you use any form of communication. He told them, before you talk or write, ask yourself this question: Would you want their intelligence people to hear or read what you were going to say? He added that such snooping was unlikely, but since it was a possibility, we have to be cautious.

*

Seven days later, Bo was contacted by Mr. Pak Hak Su, "on behalf of the Supreme Leader of the Democratic People's Republic of Korea." Kim was inviting Bo to meet with him, "out of the glare of the media limelight," and wished to know if Bo could spend a weekend in Pyongyang.

The trip was scheduled for the weekend after next, nine days hence. Bo would take Svetlana with him. By next Wednesday, they'd receive their visas, "expedited by the Escort Bureau." They booked flights with Air Koryo. They made reservations at the Yanggakdo International Hotel, which was "highly recommended" by Pak.

After it was all set, Bo sat down alone at his desk and reflected on how impressive it was that this was actually happening, and so quickly.

About nine hours later, seven time zones behind, Zella would also be sitting alone at her desk, but she would be in a very different state of mind. She had decided to check the client database in the Academy's information system. She saw that Bo had hired a staff member named Svetlana Baranovichi as a contractor employee, for the purpose she feared.

Chapter 11

Lana Vasiliev had survived some very wild, risk-taking, teenage years when, at the age of sixteen, she married a professional footballer, the father of her eleven-month-old daughter.

Lana grew up in Novosibirsk, in southwestern Siberia, a large city on the banks of the Ob River. The young Yegor Baranovichi was the most talented player on FC Sibir Novosibirsk. Lana met Yegor at a private team party. An older friend had been invited and asked Lana to come along.

Just before their wedding, Yegor bought a very large house, more aptly called a mansion, in the city's wealthiest neighborhood. He was twenty-one. To some, it seemed absurd. But he was a bankable asset with injury insurance. And that's what stardom-bound footballers do. At least, Yegor thought so.

Ten months later, he signed a four-year contract with a team in the English Premier League for a staggering amount of money. Yegor wanted Lana to remain with their young child in the Novosibirsk mansion. Their marriage lasted two and a half years.

As she moved on with her life, Lana kept her ex-husband's last name, so that it would be the same as her daughter's. In the divorce settlement, Lana was granted full custody of four-year-old Natasha, the mansion was sold, and Lana was given the financial wherewithal to raise her daughter in a life of privilege and to build a prosperous future for herself.

They moved into a more suitable residence, a three-bedroom house near a desirable private school. Lana was a devoted mother, who did a great job raising her daughter.

Lana also worked on her own personal goal -- a gradual, but steady pursuit of higher education. Eventually, she would be a part-time university student. And then when Natasha was old enough to take care of herself, she would go full bore on becoming a credentialed, sophisticated professional.

Lana was determined to be a scholar in East Asia studies. She was fascinated by the history and culture of China and Japan. She didn't know exactly where this would lead, but she was sure there would be rewarding opportunities involving such a vital part of the world.

During Natasha's child-rearing years, Lana managed to do quite a bit of dating, but no one ever really entered the nest and world she had created for herself and her daughter. She wanted to find the right guy, she longed for a thrilling romance and true love, but instead it was only an endless procession of boy toys.

Occasionally, Lana felt bored, disappointed, alone and isolated. But most of the time, she was buoyed by her dreams of academia and a career. Both she and her daughter continuously received the highest grades and scholastic honors. They shared the joys of stellar achievements and dreams about the future.

After Natasha graduated from high school and turned eighteen, Lana decided it was time to cut loose. Her daughter agreed. They were close, the best of friends, but they knew it was time. They were excited for each other, about their ambitions, and the adventures that would lie ahead. Of course, they'd always be close, but now they'd be independent of each other.

It seemed ironic, almost comical, that they'd be going their separate ways, but that would be to the same destination, over three thousand five hundred miles away, to the Far Eastern Federal University in Vladivostok.

Natasha was going to be an oceanography major.

Lana was going to continue her East Asia studies, which had veered into the Korean peninsula. That was where she was going to focus and establish her specialty. Her aspirations were to become more than an expert, more than a professional; she had her mind set on becoming a widely-respected and highly-valued authority.

She put the house up for sale. In Vladivostok, these two university students would each find their own cozy one-bedroom apartment.

Before they left Novosibirsk, she told Natasha that, in her new life, she was going to revert to her birth first name, Svetlana, and that her full name henceforth would be Svetlana Vasiliev Baranovichi.

*

By the time Bo first met Svetlana in the conference room at the International Academy of Language and Culture,

85

she had two university degrees and two years of experience working as a specialist in Korean language and customs. She was well on the way to reaching her goals.

She was now thirty-nine. He would have guessed she was about ten years younger. Paradoxically, in her teens she looked old for her age, and now as she approached her forties she looked much younger than her years.

Chapter 12

It was now the week of the trip to Pyongyang. Bo didn't know what to do about Zella. She wasn't responding to his messages. Twice, he sent flowers, which Max confirmed were delivered. She was probably glad to put them in Maria's room.

It had now been a month since she hung up on him during his last call from Sochi. He didn't know what to think. Emotionally, this was probably a very difficult time for her. She would be feeling the pain of losing her dear mother. And maybe Maria's care had gotten more complicated and difficult. And he was only making things worse. Although he thought that her fears were exaggerated, obviously the North Korea thing scared her.

*

Pak had given instruction on how to access a special Escort Bureau website, where Bo and Svetlana could fill out their visa applications, which they did right away.

On Monday, Svetlana received a call from a consular officer, who wanted to ask some further questions. It was about her ex-husband. Svetlana was not surprised. She said that she would be more than happy to tell them whatever they wanted to know.

The caller was very courteous, even apologetic. He told her that he hoped she'd understand their need to ask some further questions, "due to Mr. Yegor Baranovichi's residence in Great Britain."

At the end of the call, he repeatedly thanked her for her indulgence and assured her that this further inquiry in no way was meant to cast any aspersions on her character, which they viewed with respect.

Bo and Svetlana received their visas the next day.

Not yet fully grasping the extent and effects of Kim's basketball worship, she was amazed by the attitude of the consular officer who called and questioned her, the speed of receiving their documents and the duration of stay permitted.

She knew that the processing of visas for North Korea usually took at least four weeks. They had theirs in five days. And normally, they last two months. Both of theirs were for six.

*

On Tuesday, the same day the visas arrived, Bo finally received a text from Zella.

> Nurses a godsend
> We're grateful

That's all she said. He was disappointed there wasn't more. But he figured, at least it was something. At least she contacted him.

*

The regular Air Koryo direct flight from Vladivostok to Pyongyang was scheduled to depart at twelve forty-five on Friday. They were booked in business class. There was no first class.

The flight time was ninety minutes. Because Pyongyang is only one time zone behind Vladivostok, most first-time travelers would expect to arrive at one fifteen. But the scheduled arrival in Pyongyang was twelve forty-five.

Svetlana noted and explained the discrepancy to Bo and Max. Four years into his reign, Kim ordered a permanent time change. All clocks in North Korean were moved back thirty minutes. He declared that this was done to assert his country's sovereignty, and to purge a remnant of the past, a leftover theft of time from the period of Japanese colonial rule.

Max noted that, surprisingly, there weren't any Air Koryo charges appearing on the company credit card account.

*

On Thursday, their last day in the office, as Bo and Svetlana discussed some details about the trip, Svetlana reflected on the two months she stayed in Pyongyang as part of her graduate studies.

89

"One of the things that stands out in my mind, is what that city is like at night. A city of about three million three hundred thousand.

"Honestly, it gave me the creeps, in a way I can't imagine I'd experience anywhere else in the world.

"As soon as it gets dark, the whole city loses its sound. It becomes absolutely silent. And it's a silence that's eerie.

"You can walk outside for a long time to try to hear something. Anything. But there's nothing. Not ever. How can that be in such a big city?

"I don't mean to sound negative; I think this will be a very positive trip. But I think it's good to know in advance that Pyongyang is very strange at night."

*

On Thursday evening, Bo and Lucy met briefly at a fast-food place called Bell Burger.

When Bo walked inside, the only customers he saw were seven teenagers siting at adjoining tables against a side wall. He stood back from the counter and started looking at a displayed menu. The side door from the parking lot opened. He glanced over, and then did a double take. It was a woman in an outrageous, heavy metal outfit. This generated some whistling and hooting from the teenagers.

She had long pink hair. Her face was painted white, with black around the eyes and on the lips. She wore tight leather pants with studs and straps. Her vest had a human skull on one side and a Metallica patch on the other. She had very high heels. And she was holding a half-unfolded map.

As she approached Bo, he assumed she was going to a concert, club or party, and was lost. She certainly looked lost. He probably wouldn't be able to, but he would try to help her.

"Sir, I'm trying to figure out where I'm at. Could you show me on this map?" She was hoping Bo would recognize her voice. He did.

"Sure," he said. "Let's put your map down on a table over here." And he led her to a table away from the teenagers.

They stood at the table and she spread out her map.

"The trip's on for this weekend," he said.

She already knew the flight schedules for Pyongyang.

"Let's meet at twelve noon on Tuesday, the day after you get back," she said. "I'll bring lunch."

Then she pointed to a spot on the map. "Burdenko Lane, number twenty. As you enter the street, it's the second apartment building on the right. Around on the right side of the property is apartment F. It's accessible from the street, the alley behind or the apartment building next door. Again, twenty Burdenko Lane, unit F, a garden apartment around on the right side.

"Memorize this, don't write it down," she continued. "Now point to it and repeat what I said."

He put an index finger on the spot and said, "Tuesday twelve noon, twenty Burdenko Lane, second building on the right, apartment F, around on the right side."

"Okay, I'll see you there," she said. "And remember, from now on, level-three surveillance-evasion measures must always be used."

She raised a fist, pulled her map off the table, and stepped back. "Thank you, sir!" she said in a gleeful voice, then dashed out, holding up the unfolded fluttering map like a kite being launched.

*

On Friday morning, Max drove Bo and Svetlana to the airport.

First, he picked up Bo.

Then at Svetlana's, he went to the door, and took her bag as she locked up. Max was trying to hide his attraction to her. Bo could see that he was trying, but it was still obvious; he was hooked too.

As Bo watched them walk down the path, he scolded himself for an unkind thought about his loyal assistant. *That's one of the differences between us. I've got the ability to conceal. That's one of the reasons why I'm the tycoon and you're the chauffeur.*

As the two approached the car, Bo studied what he now realized was her signature attire: a dress or skirt about an inch above the knee and mid-calf low-heel boots.

He wouldn't tell her how good she looked. He wouldn't talk about her appearance at all. He was going to rigidly submit to his company's policy on appropriate professional behavior. At least for now.

As they continued on to the airport, Bo felt very confident about the trip. With Svetlana as his travel companion, he knew he'd be able to successfully navigate a delicate journey into an unfamiliar land.

Chapter 13

Bo had two special things with him on the trip to Pyongyang.

He had a new phone, which had a new number, and was unused, except that the three numbers for the Sochi and Vladivostok offices and Svetlana had been put in its contacts. It didn't have any history of incoming or outgoing calls or messages. He didn't bring his regular phone or laptop.

And he had a gift for Kim. In his carry-on bag, he had ten of the finest Montecristo cigars from Cuba, which were on a silk cushion in an extra-thick, specially-engraved, wooden box. He was sure this would be appreciated.

Their plane left the gate a few minutes early. As it taxied to the runway, Svetlana thought about how fortunate and how advantageous this trip, and possibly more to come, would be for her career. There were many Korean specialists, she thought, but how many are able to say they know the leader of North Korea, that they have actually spent time with him?

During the flight, Bo overheard some other Russian passenger talking about the waiting line at Pyongyang airport border inspection. How the inspections were very rigorous. How the inspecting officers did things like look at videos on a traveler's tablet. How sometimes it seemed to take forever to get through that line.

Bo had a hunch that wouldn't be happening to them.

They arrived at Pyongyang Sunan International Airport at twelve thirty-five, ten minutes early.

Sure enough, as they approached the border inspection line, they were intercepted by a man and a woman, differing only by gender. Each of them was young, tall, slender, athletic-looking, in a snug black business suit and wearing sunglasses.

The woman told Svetlana that she and her partner had the honor of being the official escorts for their entire visit. She asked Svetlana to please tell Bo that it was a pleasure to welcome them.

Svetlana translated for Bo, thanked them and told them that it was exciting to be here.

Bo and Svetlana both figured that these two escorts were probably an elite security detail.

They were taken to a nearby office, where they were greeted by three uniformed customs officers, all smiling young women, who said it was a pleasure to quickly conduct the required inspections.

They both emptied their pockets, Bo took off his belt, and each of them slowly walked through a scanner. Their carry-on bags and Svetlana's purse disappeared into an adjoining room.

Bo asked Svetlana to tell them the cigars were for Chairman Kim.

She told their female escort, who replied, "Don't worry, they won't disturb anything without talking to us first."

A few minutes later, their belongings were handed back, their documents were stamped, and they were told, "Welcome to the Democratic People's Republic of Korea. Please, enjoy your visit."

Then they were led outside to a late-model, large, black, Mercedes Benz sedan with tinted windows, illegally parked curbside near an arrivals exit. They were told their luggage would follow. The woman drove.

They went into the city, a trip of about twenty miles, onto a small island in what Svetlana recognized as the Taedong River, about a mile from the center of the capital. They parked by the main entrance to the enormous Yanggakdo International Hotel.

Before they got out of the car, the driver explained the evening schedule to Svetlana.

First, there was a six o'clock dinner reservation for Bo and her in the fabulous hotel restaurant on the forty-seventh floor.

Second, they had been invited by the Supreme Leader to the Ryongsong Residence, a presidential palace in northern Pyongyang. This was for an after-dinner party and to see an advanced screening of a Moranbong Band concert in the palace cinema.

At eight o'clock, their escorts would be back at the hotel to take them to the palace.

"Any questions?"

"May I ask, what are your names?"

"Our boss gave us nicknames, so we use them, because it's fun and they're easy to remember. I'm Tiger, and he's Lucky."

Then Bo and Svetlana were led into the hotel.

Inside its gigantic lobby, the four of them were met by another couple, in hotel uniforms. Tiger told Svetlana that they would now be assisted by hotel staff. Svetlana thanked the departing escorts. Tiger said that it was their pleasure, and then she nodded to the hotel staff, which seemed to signify an official transfer of responsibility.

Bo and Svetlana were then led to the elevators by the hotel staff. The front desk was bypassed. They were taken to the thirty-second floor, where the woman took Svetlana in one direction to her room, and the man took Bo in a different direction to his.

In her room, Svetlana was shown the phone extensions for Bo, herself and the front desk, and a directory of all the hotel amenities. The guide flipped to the section showing all the entertainment options in the basement and pointed out a casino with a bar, a billiards room with a bar, a bowling alley with a bar, and a karaoke bar.

Svetlana was told, if they wanted a snack before dinner, there were several options downstairs, or they could have anything they wanted brought to their room.

She was told that five minutes before their dinner reservation, someone from hotel engineering would be out in the hallway by the elevators, to provide them with quick elevator service.

And she was asked to please tell Bo about the phone extensions and the dinner elevator arrangement.

Then the woman excused herself and left.

Obviously, everyone knew it was only Svetlana who spoke Korean.

*

The views from their rooms were spectacular, looking out over much of the city. The bedding was luxurious. Everything was immaculate. The towels and toiletries were high-end. The televisions had large, high-definition, flat screens. The channel lineup included two popular Russian sports channels. Mini refrigerators and tabletop bowls were filled with a delectable assortment of food and beverages.

They both assumed that these particular provisions were far from standard.

About twenty minutes later, their luggage arrived.

After they unpacked, they got together and spent a couple of hours downstairs strolling around, checking out some of the hotel offerings. They browsed in the bookstore and the souvenir shop. In the billiards room, they had nuts and sodas at the bar, and played a game of pool.

Bo was getting ready to put his last ball in a side pocket. He paused, not to contemplate the shot, but to decide whether or not he was going to wink at Svetlana when it went in.

Suddenly, a very inebriated Russian man stumbled into the room, came to an abrupt halt close to them, and stared at Bo.

"Holy shit, you're Bo Tenbinakov. I don't believe it."

As he looked over a Svetlana for a few seconds, his eyes got much bigger, he leaned forward, almost fell, caught himself, slapped himself on the chest, and then refocused on Bo.

"I love this place. I mean they've got good cheap beer and all these freebies. But this is too much. Damn! I can't believe it. Bo's here."

He took a couple of short steps to get even closer.

"Uh, could I take a picture? You know, with me in it with you."

"Sure, why not?" Bo replied.

"Wow. That's so wonderful. I can't believe it."

He reached in his pocket, then another pocket, then another, and then he started patting all over his clothes.

"Oh no! Where's my phone?"

His jaw dropped. He eyes rolled around. He patted his clothes again.

"I'll be back. I've got to find my phone. Everything's on it. I've got to find it."

Then he staggered to the exit, turned around to take one last look at Bo and Svetlana, and disappeared.

Bo put his last ball in the pocket. He didn't wink, instead he just thanked her for the game.

It was four thirty. They decided to head back to their rooms. They figured, it was probably going to be a long night, and probably a good idea to take it easy before dinner.

Instead of waiting for an elevator, they went to the stairs to go up to the main floor.

"I think they've tried to create a miniature Macau down here in this basement," Bo said.

"It's probably only Chinese nationals who don't speak Korean working down here, and it's probably off-limits to North Koreans," Svetlana said.

Suddenly, they had to move to the side and squeeze up against the wall, as three police officers rushed past, going downstairs.

"They try to hire foreigners who don't speak Korean to prevent contact with locals," she added. "And for workers down here, contact would already be very limited because they probably wouldn't be allowed to leave the island."

"I wonder if those cops are for that drunk?" he said.

"Probably," she replied.

*

At exactly five fifty-four, Bo and Svetlana left their rooms and walked to the elevator bay, where they met a man wearing denim overalls with a hotel insignia patch, standing by an open elevator and holding a tool bag. He said that he was from hotel engineering. He told them he was a systems electrician.

He assured them that all the elevators were top-notch. But not all of them went to the forty-seventh floor, and sometimes there were a lot of people waiting to go to that restaurant. He thanked them for allowing him to provide this special assistance.

Then he opened his tool bag, took out a long protective case, opened that up, and took out a selfie stick. After he unfolded it and carefully attached his phone, he asked if the "illustrious guests" would be so kind as to let him take a picture of the three of them. He said that his wife and children would be very proud.

As she posed with Bo and the systems electrician, Svetlana smiled, and thought about this elevator situation. She wondered how long this guy has held the restaurant elevator here, and how long people may be waiting on other floors.

She was beginning to fully realize the extent of Kim's basketball fanaticism. She would no longer be surprised by its effects.

*

It was about a half hour after sunset as Bo and Svetlana were warmly greeted in the restaurant and taken to their table, which was next to a window and beautifully decorated with flowers. After they sat down and the receptionist left, what appeared to be the head waitress, with two assistants in tow, came over and stood next to Svetlana.

"The restaurant will now be revolving, because of you, our honored guests," she said. Then she gave them food and beverage menus, and asked if they would like to begin with something to drink. They both asked for tea.

As the restaurant slowly moved three hundred sixty degrees, what they could see outside was so much darkness for such a large city. Bo couldn't tell if this was due to the view being blocked by interior lights reflected off the window glass, or if this vast cityscape was actually all dark.

"The illumination of monuments and headlights of an occasional car or truck are probably the only lights out there," Svetlana said.

Earlier, they talked about how there would probably be a hidden microphone somewhere on their dinner table. With this in mind, as they studied the table, they both looked at the flower arrangements with suspicion, and knew they had to be careful not to offend.

"It's admirable how they use lighting to show proper respect for their leaders and ideals, and also do a great job with conservation," she added, with a wink.

*

As they progressed through the several courses of dinner, they talked about the food. Bo was glad to be with someone who knew so much about it and could clearly describe everything. But for the most part, they didn't talk.

During one stretch of silence, Svetlana had a flashback, from twenty-four years ago.

It was after she first met Yegor at the football club party. It was during a championship match two weeks later, in which he had arranged for her to be in a special row of seats closest to the field.

He had just done an incredibly amazing thing, moving the ball through heavy traffic, and in to score. It was a dramatic, stunning goal. Many fans later said it was the highlight of the season.

The stadium had erupted into prolonged thunderous applause. As Yegor completed his victory glidepath, he trotted by Svetlana's seat. As he passed by, he gracefully looked over at her and winked. She immediately fell in love.

Then she thought about something that happened last month.

She was in the weight room at the gym she frequents. She was moving from one machine to another when she crossed paths with an older woman, a regular she'd seen a number of times, but had never talked with. As they passed each other, this woman winked at her.

For as long as she could remember, Svetlana has felt incapable of winking as an act of flirtation. She didn't understand why. With many people, it was so easy and happened so naturally. With Svetlana, there seemed to be some mental block.

She most certainly didn't lack the capacity to flirt. She just couldn't flirt by winking. She figured it was similar to what some people experience with public speaking, when they freeze up. There was a disconnect between desire and performance.

Sometimes, she marveled at the winking phenomenon. How this slight, delicate, split-second body movement can have an effect on the relationship between two people. And in many public situations, it can be done secretly.

There was no physical attraction to that woman in the weight room. She had no interest in her whatsoever. Yet, she was affected by that wink. It caused a pleasant sensation to wash across her body. Again, it made her realize how much potential a wink has -- to communicate, to influence, to touch, to impact.

The wink she had given Bo at the beginning of the meal was a signal that tagged her remark as a joke. It was a professional gesture. It was an appropriate way to make certain that the actual meaning was understood.

It was not at all flirtatious.

Yes, she thought Bo was very attractive, but she had no intention of any romantic involvement. It was against Academy policy and there was that employment contract she had signed with them. Under these circumstances, it would offend her personal sense of professionalism. And, thanks to Max, she knew about Zella.

No, this was strictly business. Nevertheless, for wink-challenged Svetlana, it was sort of a bold thing to do.

She was satisfied that she had done it perfectly. The eye contact was there. The timing was spot-on. It was artfully done. For her, it was an accomplishment.

*

Bo analyzed a lot of things from a basketball perspective. He did that now, as he again, pointlessly, peered out the restaurant window.

He was disappointed in himself.

He couldn't believe he got beat to the wink.

She didn't hesitate, like he did down in the basement. He had to admit, it was a nice move.

And she delivered it with impunity. Under the circumstances, it was the proper thing to do. It was professionally appropriate. The situation -- that supposed mic in the flowers -- had given her an assist. His pool shot scene would have been nothing but grandstanding.

It was such a little thing. But in the game of love, he knew it was often the little things that mattered the most.

The wink was one of his most valued moves in the beginning stages of seduction. And she took it away.

If losing the wink wasn't bad enough, she stole it in a context that prevented any insight into whether or not she was sexually attracted to him.

She's so fucking smooth, he thought. He couldn't stand it anymore. He had to take over this game.

Chapter 14

After dinner, Bo and Svetlana found the same systems electrician standing next to open elevator doors. He took them down, with a stop to go to their rooms for a few minutes. As they stepped into the main lobby at about ten before eight, they found their escorts waiting.

As they walked out of the hotel and drove off the island, Tiger seemed to have shed her stiffness and constant seriousness.

"As I told you earlier, we're going to the Ryongsong Residence," she said. "That's its official name. It's a presidential palace. Many of the locals call it the central luxury mansion. My partner and I have our own nomenclature. We call it number fifty-five. Don't ask why, because that's a big secret. Isn't that right, Lucky?"

Lucky smiled, but he didn't say anything.

Tiger now seemed to be acting like some jocular guide.

"It's about eight miles north of the city," she continued. "It won't take us long to get there, to the palace compound that is, but then as we enter and move through the grounds, it'll take quite a while.

"We'll be driving very slowly, just creeping along, through a dark forest on a narrow road. And the place is crawling with what I like to call *exuberant* guards, who only care about one thing -- ensuring the safety of Marshal Kim.

"Lucky and I have been on the grounds before, several times, but neither of us has ever seen the inside of the palace past the entry hall. We hear it's an impressive place."

Svetlana wondered if Lucky ever talked.

"You can't see it right now because it's too dark," Tiger said, "but we're passing by the Koryo Hotel."

Svetlana strained to see what she was talking about, but she couldn't discern any hotel in the direction Tiger was pointing.

"But in daylight, it's obvious from far off. It's very distinctive. Tall twin towers with a bridge near the top. A lot of foreign visitors stay there. It's an interesting and fun place. If you have time before you leave and want to check it out, let us know, we'll take you over there.

"When you were here before, did you ride the Metro?"

"Yes, I did."

"So, you know what it's like down there. If he has a chance before you leave, we should take your boss down there."

"Oh, I definitely agree, but he may not have time on this trip."

"One more thing, before I stop acting like a tourist guide. Did you visit the Taedonggang Beer Brewery?"

"No. I've heard of it, but I've never been there."

"It's on the eastern outskirts of the city. I'm telling you, it's well worth the trip. You'd really enjoy it. Again, if you can fit it into your schedule, let us know, we'd be happy to take you out there."

"If we did want to take you up on your offer to go to any of those places, how would we get a hold of you?"

"Just ring the front desk. They know how to reach us, any time, day or night."

It only took about fifteen minutes to get to the palace compound. As they approached the entrance, Tiger looked over at her partner.

"Okay Lucky, look alive. It's time to let them do their thing."

They were stopped and inspected at three different checkpoints, each with many heavily-armed guards, who all watched every move with cold stares and looked like they were trained to kill instantly and ask questions later.

Through these rings of high security, there were no exchanges of pleasantries or jokes or casual remarks. Nothing like that.

These gatekeepers were aggressively circumspect and suspicious. They pointed powerful flashlights everywhere, including in people's faces, intensely eyeballed everyone and their possessions, glared while they interrogated, and ignored distractions while deploying detection devices.

At each checkpoint, when the crossbar was finally being raised, the lead gatekeeper bent down close to the open driver's window, with his left hand on top of the car, and looked again at all the occupants.

"Thank you for your patience and cooperation. Please proceed."

Throughout all of these inspections, Lucky just looked ahead with a bored-looking poker face.

Tiger responded to the guards with all the correct answers, but in a surprisingly offhanded manner and with an almost flippant attitude.

Under the circumstances, Svetlana couldn't tell if Tiger and Lucky's petulant ways were caused by some sort of a service rivalry or whether it was a show intended to demonstrate their professional and personal superiority. Either way, it again made her think that these escorts were probably an elite pair in the security apparatus.

As they drove out of the other side of the wooded grounds and the narrow one-way road became the circular palace driveway, they were met by palace valets who directed Tiger to a parking spot near the entrance.

After they walked inside the front door, Bo and Svetlana were turned over to smiling, very attentive palace staff.

They were then ushered down long, enormous, marble-floored hallways. There were high ceilings everywhere. The doors were open to many of the rooms they passed by, which mostly displayed glittering ornate chandeliers, French Baroque furnishings and deep plush carpets.

They ended up in a large reception hall with a gathering of about seventy people, including half a dozen high-ranking military officers. Some of the guests were sitting, but most were standing. Bo and Svetlana were told that everyone was waiting for Kim's arrival.

Everyone else was North Korean. Svetlana knew that a gathering like this would be composed of nothing but very influential people.

Although they were trying to be inconspicuous about it, the other guests were obviously curious about the presence of two Russians. Svetlana figured it was probably highly unusual for any foreigners to be at something like this.

The reception hall was an opulent setting. Exquisite tapestries hung from its rich-wood-paneled walls. Around much of the perimeter there were high-back velvet chairs and side tables with floral bouquets.

After about five minutes, Svetlana saw Kim's sister Kim Yo Jong enter through a door on the other side of the room and slide into a conversation with a nearby group of people.

Svetlana told herself that she wouldn't be surprised if it was Kim Yo Jong who selected Tiger and Lucky as their escorts. She knew that Kim's sister managed his bodyguards, and anyone who would be having close contact with Kim would get extra attention.

The thought also crossed her mind that after the first escorting from the airport, maybe she counseled Tiger to lighten up in the handling of her Russian charges. After all, Bo was one of her brother's basketball idols.

About ten minutes later, a woman with a hand-held microphone stood up on a riser at the front of the room, and in a loud voice made an announcement.

"Please, may I have quiet and everyone's attention.

"I am sorry that I have to announce that a beloved member of the palace staff has suddenly taken very ill. It may be a ruptured appendix.

"It's a serious situation and our Great Host wants to do everything he can to help. He's very distressed about it. Understandably, as a result, he will not be joining us, and unfortunately the cocktail party and concert movie must be postponed or canceled. Of course, we are all disappointed.

"*However*, there is some good news. We are fortunate in that we have been able to replace the scheduled events with another program. And I must say, under these particular circumstances, it is indeed a most appropriate substitution.

"Now, please be patient as we bring in a larger riser and a podium, and folding chairs for everyone, so you can all sit close.

"Then, we will have the privilege of hearing an enlightening address on preventive healthcare, specifically, the prevention of osteoporosis, to be given by a representative from the Ministry of Public health.

"As it turns out, the distinguished professor of nursing, An Yong Myong, was already here at the palace and has generously offered to do this on such short notice.

"And, as an added benefit, she said that after her lecture she will be delighted to answer questions, address particular concerns you may have, and lead you in discussions about this important topic.

"Again, give us a few minutes to set up her podium and your lecture seats, and then we can welcome the professor.

"Finally, and most importantly, you should know that Our Great and Benevolent Host, as anxious and worried as he may be at the moment, was pleased to learn that this cancellation has been turned into an advantageous event for the greater glory of public health.

"Thank you for your patience."

The announcer then scurried away very quickly.

Nobody moved. No one said anything. Everyone looked stunned and bewildered. Slowly, the guests began looking at each other with blank expressions. The minister of finance was suffering from emphysema. Those near him could now hear his wheezing. But otherwise, not a sound could be heard in the reception hall.

And then all the lights went out. It was completely dark for a few seconds, and then several moveable spotlights came on and pointed to a side door, which swung open, and out marched the Great Host. "Just kidding!" he shouted into the microphone he was holding.

He stepped aside, and out flew a group of shapely young women wearing basketball uniforms with Bo's name and number. Some were waiving pom-poms, some were playing tambourines, three were doing cartwheels, all to the famous sports anthem *Rock and Roll, Part Two*, which was now blasting out of the hall speakers.

In three minutes, it was over. The music known as "The 'Hey' Song" ended, the cheerleaders dashed back out the door, the spotlights went off, and the regular ambient lighting returned.

Everybody was laughing, some hysterically.

A large crew of servers was now hurriedly entering the room and setting up bars for drinks and mini desserts. Other palace staff were hooking up large video monitors, which began showing highlights of Bo's playing days in the EuroLeague.

Kim went over and stood on the riser at the front of the hall.

"Nothing like a little comedy to set the right tone," he said, and then paused to slowly survey the crowd.

"A hearty good evening, welcome to you all, welcome to everyone.

"I want to especially recognize the presence of General Han and the other heroic officers from our glorious People's Army, and also our special guest from the Russian Federation, who is a revered figure in the world of basketball, the great Bo Tenbinakov, and also from Russia, his learned assistant, the lovely Svetlana Vasiliev Baranovichi.

"Fortunately, no one has taken ill and I'm told that the osteoporosis lecture will be given at another more suitable time. So, let's party!"

Then he stepped down, handed the microphone to an aide, and started mingling with the guests.

He first tried to talk with General Han, the ranking military officer, the one with the most medals. But Han was still laughing too hard, so they just shook hands. He moved on and chatted briefly with several other officers. Then he came over to meet Bo. He was accompanied by an aide and a bodyguard, but no interpreter.

Svetlana was surprised and flattered that he had chosen to converse with Bo through her.

He welcomed them to his country and said that he hoped their accommodations were fine and that everyone has been treating them as most-favored guests, as he had ordered.

Bo said that it was an honor to meet him, he was very happy to be here, and, yes, they have been treated very well, with many courtesies. Then he presented the gift of Montecristo Cuban cigars, which Kim carefully opened, and then broke into a broad smile. He said that he was a cigar connoisseur and that this was a very thoughtful gift and a delightful treat.

He then handed the box of cigars to his aide with an instruction to keep them handy. He told Bo that he looked forward to enjoying the first one with him later in the weekend in a more private setting.

He told Bo and Svetlana that Han loves his gags. He asked if they saw how hard the general was laughing. He lowered his voice and leaned closer when he said that someday the old man was probably going to die laughing.

He was very gracious with Svetlana. He seemed very interested in her academic background and her professional work. He said that he was very pleased that she had decided to grace his country once again with her presence.

He introduced Bo and Svetlana to about twenty of the attendees, including military officers, Workers' Party officials, cabinet members, and his sister.

Like a lot of the guests, he and Bo were drinking some fine cognac. So was Svetlana, but at a much slower pace, just a couple of tiny sips. He smoked one cigarette. Bo recognized the French brand.

He wanted to know if either Bo or Svetlana had ever seen a performance by his all-female band. Neither had, and they both thanked him for the invitation to see them tonight.

He told them that he selected every band member. He alluded to his musical aptitude and mentioned that he was a composer. He said that his mother was an opera singer.

He told Bo that he looked forward to talking all about basketball and Bo's intriguing proposal, which they would do tomorrow. But right now, he did have to ask Bo just a few questions about some of the EuroLeague teams and their prospects for the future.

After about an hour with Bo and Svetlana, he told them that he needed to talk with some of the other guests. And then he started making his way around the room.

After Kim walked away, Svetlana asked Bo, "You know that catchy, rousing, stomping music we heard earlier; are you aware of the artist's dark history?"

"Yeah, I know what you're talking about," he answered. "I forget the guy's name."

"Gary Glitter," she said. "I think he sold all rights to that song many years ago, but I'm not sure." She chuckled. "I don't imagine anybody will be receiving royalties from North Korea."

As this very exclusive party wore on, Kim returned several times to introduce more people to Bo and Svetlana.

And a few of the guests came up to Bo and Svetlana and introduced themselves.

After about two and a half hours, Kim asked a group of ushers to start helping everyone move to the palace cinema. He went ahead with his aides and bodyguards.

The screening was of a documentary titled *Dancing into the Future*, based on a concert by the Moranbong Band last winter in Chongjin, a large city in the northeast part of the country. It was a co-production of DPRK state television and several French partners. This was its first release.

As Bo and Svetlana approached the palace cinema in another enormous hallway, the first thing they noticed were large posters of the band, which were displayed on three-legged stands next to the doorways that led into the theatre.

On the poster, there was a captivating face in the center of a photo of six of the band members, wearing military overcoats and fur hats, walking closely together as a group, in a purposeful movement, seemingly towards the viewer.

The face was of a young woman. She was the only one looking into the camera. It was a haunting image. She was looking right at you. With classic features, she was the face of pure, timeless beauty.

Bo stared at the poster for a long time.

Svetlana was sure that he was fixated on that face. What seemed like crazy thoughts raced through her head. Was he infatuated? Would he use his pull to try and meet her? Could she blame him if he did? At this point, she told herself, nothing would surprise her.

After everyone was seated, Kim walked over and stood in front of the large red-curtained screen. He gave the briefest of introductions.

"This is a movie that speaks for itself. Please, enjoy the show."

After he sat down, the lights dimmed, and the red curtains parted.

As soon as the band came out on stage, Svetlana spotted that young woman on the poster. She was a violin player.

During the movie, the gasps and shrieks made it clear that it was genuinely well-received by the audience. When it ended, everyone cheered and clapped loudly.

The audience had learned more about Kim's involvement in the life of the band, and they had experienced a high-energy, dazzling, symphonic journey through pop, rock and militaristic music.

As soon as the last credits disappeared and the lights came back on, Kim got up and thanked everyone for coming, wished everyone a good night, walked over and shook hands with General Han and another officer standing next to him, and then left with his bodyguards and aides.

The guests waited quietly in place until he was gone, and then exchanged praises of his genius and started leaving.

Two members of the palace staff led Bo and Svetlana back to the palace front entry hall where their escorts were waiting.

As they followed a snaking line of red taillights slowly moving back through the dark woods, Bo thought about the personal chemistry in his initial interaction with Kim. His assessment was that it was all positive.

As they drove back into the city, Tiger said that tomorrow morning they would be picked up in the main lobby at nine thirty.

"The two of you are going to be the first foreign visitors to ever join the Supreme Leader at his special basketball facility in an undisclosed location. Isn't that right, Lucky, *an undisclosed location?*"

Lucky just smiled.

And once again, Svetlana reflected on how beneficial all this would be for her career.

It was a little after one o'clock in the morning when they arrived back at the hotel.

As they quietly headed to their rooms, Bo and Svetlana both knew there was a lot at stake tomorrow. It was likely to be the most critical part of the trip. They both wanted to get as much sleep as possible.

They both said that in the morning they were going to have the hotel buffet breakfast, but didn't see any need to meet at a fixed time for that. They agreed to meet in the main lobby at nine twenty, which would be ten minutes before their escorts were due to arrive.

They said "good night" to each other as they stepped off the elevator on the thirty-second floor.

Chapter 15

In years past, Moon Chang Ho had often found it quite difficult and frustrating to do his job. There were so many unnecessary obstacles -- aggravating idiotic bureaucracies creating ridiculous problems, which were compounded by generous portions of dysfunctional troublemakers, slackers, buffoons and dimwits.

He had tried many times to change things, to improve things, to make it all work better. Undoubtedly, his most significant efforts had been directed at the difficulties and dangers which were inherent in compartmentalization. He understood the reasons for this type of operational structuring, but he knew the disadvantages far outweighed the advantages.

He considered intelligence to be the beating heart of security work, and compartmentalization weakened the heart; it weakened his body of security work. He tried to convince the higher-ups that officers like himself would be more capable of doing their jobs if they did not work in isolation. He tried in vain. And he had not pressed the matter too hard; he knew that could be a career-ending mistake.

He also knew that, for conscientious people like himself, many of these kinds of workplace problems were a fact of life, and this was so in just about every line of professional work the world over. And so, he gradually, eventually, just got over it, and mellowed out.

Moon was now at a stage in his life when he had resigned himself to just go with the flow, even if it was often senselessly diverted, blocked and muddied. He had nobly fought his crusade for more information sharing, and lost. He had thrown in the towel on other reforms as well. He was now content to just try his best to do the job within existing parameters, and enjoy it as much as possible.

He had, after all, much to be grateful for. And he was. Early on, his aptitude for security work had been widely recognized, even admired. And then developed, advanced, and rewarded.

Early in his career, after a series of fortuitous events, he seemed to be forever marked, irrefutably, as a master of security.

On one occasion, in a major training course, during an important evaluation, an imaginary child disappeared in the center of an activity. Immediately, the parents were struck by the fear of kidnapping and were in a panic. In this exercise, each of the trainees quickly, carefully, efficiently, moved outward from the last known location of the child, all that is, except Moon. Instead, he instantly raced as fast as possible to the farthest outside perimeter of egress, and then slowly, carefully, thoroughly, moved inward, ready to stop anything. He was not going to let the perpetrator or perpetrators leave the premises with the child while the others were foolishly on the wrong end of the search area.

That test and others given during the course were about instincts. As the designers of the course knew, there is only so much that can be done with training.

In another session, trainees were faced with a series of inspections to find weak links. An example was a secured storage facility. Under the pressure of having only twenty seconds, the trainees had to rush around the building without the ability to pause and look more closely at anything. When they subsequently wrote down their observations, all but one questioned the sufficiency of the padlock on the door. Moon, alone, viewed the padlock as meaningless. Instead, his focus was on the metal clasp it was attached to. By the looks of it, he noted, it was held to the wood doors by small narrow screws, which would be no more than about five eights of an inch long. A very strong person could use the padlock as a handle and rip the metal clasp right off the doors. With a screwdriver, anyone would be able to easily pry it off.

Again, and again, over the course's six weeks, with its many tests, Moon demonstrated an amazing ability to see and understand what others could not. When this course was over, his image had been sketched out, and the trajectory of his career had been determined. In their scoring, the evaluators gave him the highest possible marks ever recorded.

On another occasion, in the performance of his official duties, he was following a car that was carrying a vice chairman of the state affairs commission. As they were crossing an intersection and approaching a bridge, a truck driver with defective brakes lost control of his vehicle and smashed into the vice chairman's car, propelling it off the road and landing it partly hanging over the edge of a river embankment. The two right side wheels and about half the car were over the side.

In the smoking wreckage, on top of an obliterated guard rail, the car driver was unconscious and his backseat passenger was dazed and semi-conscious. The car was in a precarious position; its right half dangling over the edge. It appeared that the slightest thing might tip it a little and cause it to go crashing down the steep drop into the river.

Moon acted with lightning speed. The buckled-in vice chairman's weight was on the river side of the car. The driver was a very large, very heavy man. At the moment, he was also a critical counterweight, preventing the car from going over the side.

Moon opened the left rear door all the way and told his partner to exert as much constant downward pressure on this door as possible. Then Moon began crawling in the back towards the passenger, sliding horizontally only far enough to be able to reach out and release his seat belt. Suddenly, Moon realized that some unknown person had opened the front left door and was reaching in, apparently to try to remove the driver. "Stop! Don't move him yet!" Moon yelled. After he saw the person step back from the car, he asked his partner if the driver was buckled in. When assured that he was, and thankful that he hadn't just fallen out, Moon went back to work on the passenger.

Once he had the vice chairman out, then he and his partner worked together to pull the driver out. As soon as they had managed to get the huge man out and onto the ground, the car tipped over and went crashing down into the river.

Moon found out later that it was the truck driver who was going to rashly remove the counterweight and send the vice chairman and himself tumbling down to their probable deaths below.

After he recovered from his injuries, the vice chairman arranged for Moon to receive an award for heroism from Marshal Kim, who on presenting it said, "In a grave situation, you unselfishly put your own life at risk for the safety of others. You demonstrated a remarkable presence of mind and incredible courage. You have mightily earned the admiration of a grateful nation. You have our deepest thanks."

Moon appreciated the Supreme Leader's sentiments, but he knew that there would hardly be anyone in the nation who would know about him and what he did. It wouldn't be on television. His picture and name wouldn't be in the newspapers. Maybe it would be reported many years later after he retired.

There had actually been some discussion about the possibility of transferring this act of heroism to some other real or fictitious person, so that full advantage could be taken of all of the publicity angles. It seemed too valuable to keep hidden. Such a scheme started to gain some traction. It increasingly was becoming a golden opportunity to propagate an inspirational story, not only for domestic consumption, but also abroad. When the vice chairman got wind of this, he quickly put an end to it. He called in its promoters and told them, "I do not intend to discourage creative thinking, and I certainly encourage the clever exploitation of events for the greater good. However, in this particular situation, I thank you for your worthwhile efforts, but have ordered that the person, who actually did this, must be recognized and honored."

There was a very nice little ceremony, complete with flags, banners, flowers, champagne and petits fours. The vice chairman brought his wife and children. The counterweight had also recovered, and he was there. The truck driver was not. His physical injuries had been slight; the subsequent humiliation was not.

Anyone perusing Moon's personnel file would also see some very fascinating entries about his marksmanship.

The People's Army Ground Force sponsors an annual series of shooting matches at a base near Kaesong. It is a much-heralded event; all branches of the armed forces, intelligence and security services, and certain police organizations are invited to participate.

In his tenth and fourteenth years in the security service, Moon's bosses entered him in the competition for small arms, in the category for use of a pistol on moving targets. Both times, to the astonishment of the usual military winners and other keen observers, he finished in first place.

After both competitions, during festive closing ceremonies, as he walked to center stage to receive the coveted Jo Myong Rok Trophy, there was quite a bit of whispering about "this remarkable guy," among the powerful and influential people in attendance. Some had heard of him before. Generally, at these events, military and police participants were talked about freely and openly; contestants from the intelligence and security services were not. Thus, the whispering.

Anyone who reviewed his complete record, saw that these were just a few of the many impressive highlights. By the time he was in the middle of his career, Moon Chang Ho was part of a small select group of go-to guys for the ruling family's most critical security assignments.

As Kim's sister searched through the ranks of an elite unit of plainclothes officers in the Escort Bureau to find a good fit for Bo, she saw Moon's listing. She was aware of his distinguished record and likeability. When she discovered how fluent he was in Russian, that cinched it.

During his school days in secondary and higher education, Moon excelled in the Russian language courses he took for five years. In his work, he has often been given assignments involving both written and spoken Russian. This has provided him with the opportunity to keep improving his command of that language. For many years now, he has been completely comfortable carrying on any sort of conversation in Russian.

When Kim's sister talked with him about handling Bo, Moon said that he was sorry that he was not more informed about the sport of basketball. She said it didn't matter. She said that his high level of professional competence and his easy-going manner were the only things they needed.

After he walked out of her office, she thought, *He's so unassuming, he seems so ordinary...that's the beauty of it.*

Chapter 16

At half past seven, Bo was woken from a dream by the alarm on his nightstand clock radio and then a few seconds later by the alarm on his smartphone.

After he turned off the alarms, the first thing he thought of was what Svetlana had said about the Pyongyang morning mist. He got out of bed and went over to the window.

There it was, a mist blanketing the city. Near ground level, visibility was poor or zero, but out of this shroud rose the taller buildings and monuments, which could still be seen sticking up all over the city.

He stood there for a while gazing at this intriguing foreign capital. Then he started thinking about food. After all of the brandy and sweets the night before, he was famished.

Within an hour, with a large plate on a tray, he was perusing the breakfast buffet. He didn't need Svetlana's help to figure it out. There was nothing at all strange about this. He quickly rounded up an orange juice, three fried eggs, a lot of potatoes, a pile of mixed fruit, a cinnamon roll and a coffee.

He sat at one of the many large round tables, which were almost all empty. He was in a huge banquet hall, which was used as a dining room for lunches and dinners and seating area for breakfast buffets. It could probably accommodate a thousand people. At the moment, including himself, he counted eight.

After he finished his breakfast, and was getting up from the table, he saw a man obviously coming to see him. It was perfect timing for his first encounter of the day. As the man got closer, he wondered if it was another security guy. Usually he could tell, but this time he wasn't sure. Compared to Tiger and Lucky, he was older, not very tall, heavier, weathered, more rugged looking. He was wearing an ordinary brown business suit. No badge was displayed. Maybe yes, maybe no. He'd find out in a moment.

"Good news, Mr. Bo Tenbinakov, I speak Russian fluently, and I have the privilege of being your escort today. My name is Moon. Please, just Moon, no mister. May I call you Bo?"

"Yes, of course, please do."

"I don't see your assistant."

"Right, she's probably in her room. She must have had breakfast earlier, before I got here."

"Bo, it looks like you've finished your meal. We can take off any time now, as soon as it's convenient for you."

"Okay, I need to call Svetlana, my assistant, and also go back to my room for a few minutes. I'll call her out in front here, before I go upstairs."

"Excellent, I'll be waiting in the main lobby."

A few minutes later, when Bo called from a house phone, there was no answer.

When he got up to his room, he called her again. No answer.

When he got back down downstairs, he looked around and could see that she wasn't in the main lobby. He tried a house phone again. No answer.

He walked over to Moon, who was standing near the front doors.

"I haven't been able to reach her by phone. I've tried three times. She should have been here by now. We agreed to meet in the main lobby at nine twenty."

"I've seen her picture, I know what she looks like," Moon said. "She hasn't been in the lobby since I've been here."

"Damn it," Bo said. "She knows how important this is. I can't believe she's not here."

"Give her a few minutes," Moon said. "Maybe she had to use the ladies' room. Maybe she's on an elevator that's taking a long time. Sometimes they're crowded and have to make a lot of stops."

"Okay, thank you, I'll try to have some patience. Say, I'm curious, what happened to Tiger and Lucky?"

"Oh nothing, they're still around. You'll be seeing them again soon. It's just that I'm the one who's familiar with your destination today."

Bo moved around and stood next to Moon so he could also watch people coming and going in the hotel's enormous main lobby. They stood there and observed for about five minutes.

"Maybe I should check her room," Bo finally said. "But I don't even know what her room number is and I don't have a key."

"Bo, let me get someone from the hotel staff with a key to take you up there."

"Good. Thanks."

Bo watched Moon go over to the reception counter, show some sort of badge or identification, and talk with several staff members, one of whom then picked up a phone and made a brief call. A few minutes later, a woman from housekeeping showed up, listened to her instructions and then accompanied Moon back over to Bo.

"Bo, this lady is going to accompany you up to Svetlana's room. I'll wait here and keep an eye out for her."

When Bo got to Svetlana's door, he knocked several times and then listened for any response. There was none. He then nodded to the maid, who unlocked the door and stepped aside.

Bo went in and looked everywhere, including the bathroom, the closet, even under the bed.

Then he walked out, checked to make sure the door was locked, and headed back downstairs to Moon.

"She's not there, but I saw her purse and coat sitting on a chair and her room key on the table. Her bed looks slept in. This is puzzling, and disturbing."

"When was the last time you saw her or talked with her?"

"We got back here about one o'clock last night, and we both went directly to our rooms. The last time I had contact with her was when we got off the elevator on our floor."

"Bo, I think it might be a good idea if I talked with the police about this, don't you?"

"Yes, I guess so."

"Okay, give me a few minutes, I'm going to call them now."

Moon walked away as he started to place the call. He was on the phone for at least ten minutes. He paced back and forth across the lobby until the call ended.

"Okay, they're going to assemble a search team, which should be here within thirty minutes. They'll figure out what's happened."

Moon now looked pensive. He blankly looked up, then off to the side away from Bo, then down. He seemed to be lost in thought.

"It's probably one of those crazy things that you'll all laugh about years later," Moon finally said. "She's here somewhere, either in the hotel or somewhere else on the island. Believe me, they'll find her.

"Now, if you don't mind, the police commander wanted me to ask a few questions."

"Sure, go ahead."

"Now please, don't take offense. These are routine questions that are always asked in situations like this, when someone appears to have disappeared."

"Of course, I understand, please, ask away."

"Do you know if she's taking any psychotropic drugs, or if she's on any other medication?"

"Not to my knowledge, but I wouldn't necessarily know that."

"Do you think she might have an alcohol or drug problem?"

"Again, not to my knowledge."

"Have you ever noticed any erratic behavior? Anything that might indicate psychological or emotional problems?"

"No."

"How long have you known her? Are you aware of anything in her past that may have triggered some episode?"

"She's been working for me for only a short period of time, and on a personal level, I don't know anything about her past. But she has impressive professional credentials and she's from a very prestigious organization, which does rigorous vetting in the hiring of its staff."

Moon's phone rang. He answered and then walked away again and started pacing back and forth across the lobby as he carried on a conversation. He ended the call about five minutes later.

"Bo, I'm sorry this happened to you. But now we're going to need to get going. The police will keep me posted, and as soon as there's any news, I'll let you know."

They went outside. When Bo saw the car parked right in front of the entrance, he thought it looked like the same one Tiger drove. Moon opened a back door for Bo. Once he got in, Bo was sure it was the same car. There was a smiley face button that he had noticed before. It was still in the same spot in a cup holder.

Moon didn't say where they were headed, and Bo didn't ask.

"I can't believe this is happening, her disappearance I mean. She's so responsible and conscientious. And she certainly understood the importance of today's trip. It doesn't make any sense that she would just disappear at such an important time. I'm really worried."

"I certainly mean no disrespect to your assistant. And I appreciate your concern for her. But I urge you to please keep in mind that you are about to be joining Marshal Kim. For your benefit, on this auspicious occasion, please allow yourself to concentrate solely on your interaction with the Great Leader. I assure you, the police will take care of the situation with your assistant."

Nothing more was said, until they arrived at their first stop, about thirty minutes later, in an industrial area on the northern outskirts of the city. It was a heliport surrounded by a high concrete wall with a solid steel gate, which started opening as soon as they pulled up.

Moon drove in past three heavily-armed soldiers standing at attention, and then parked off to the side against a wall. One military helicopter of medium size was sitting in the center of the yard.

"We'll just wait here in the car until the pilot's ready to go," Moon said. "It won't be long." Then, with an expression of empathy, he looked at Bo in the rearview mirror.

"Bo, again, please understand I mean no disrespect towards her, but she's a very good-looking woman. When you're desperate for some explanation, you start thinking about all sorts of possibilities. Like imagine, after you last saw her, she decided to go have a nightcap at one of the hotel bars, and she met someone..."

Moon stopped talking as they both saw what Bo assumed was the pilot hurrying out of the small, narrow, three-story heliport building and waiving at them as he rushed toward the chopper.

"Okay, let's go get in before we have to go through a cloud of dust," Moon said.

As they got close to the chopper, the pilot, who was now in his seat with his headset on, looked over at them, but he didn't say anything or even acknowledge them once they were onboard. Moon pointed Bo to his seat, and then once Bo was buckled in, handed him some large, thick, eye shades.

"Bo, my job is to protect you. Please put these on. And then I'm going to give you some earmuffs. I don't want you to know where we're going or our route of travel. This is for your own protection. There are some things you really don't want to know, and this is one of them."

After Bo had both the eye shades and ear muffs on, he could feel Moon touching them to check the fit. And he could feel the engine start up and the rotor blades begin to move, slowly at first, and then at full tilt. He could feel liftoff a few minutes later.

With the earmuffs, the tremendous noise of the chopper was only somewhat reduced, but if there was any conversation between the pilot and Moon or any talking on the radio, he couldn't hear it. And the vibration was overwhelming.

Bo had expected to be able to make mental notes about directions, distances, terrain, land use, landmarks, anything and everything. He wanted to impress Lucy with his extraordinary recall powers. But until he could see and hear again, he could do none of that. He could only sense the vertical and horizontal movements of the aircraft.

About an hour later, Bo could feel the helicopter's descent, the bump of touching down, and the powering down of the rotor blades. Then he felt his earmuffs being removed.

"Bo, you can take off your eye shades now, we've landed."

They were out in the country. As he looked around, the only distinctive thing he saw was what looked like the top of a smoke stack on the other side of some hills.

They were in an open field. There were two soldiers waiting by a vehicle under some nearby trees. As the seemingly impatient pilot started to power up again, they quickly got out and jogged away from the airship's impending dusty windstorm.

As they took their seats behind the two soldiers in the back of a light utility four-door, Moon seemed delighted in telling Bo about it. "This four-wheel drive, off-road machine was made in your country, in Ulyanovsk. It's sturdy, rugged, durable, and very *un*comfortable." Moon chuckled. "It's affectionally known as the Goat."

They drove on dirt roads for about six miles, several times pulling off to stop under canopies of large thick trees. At each of these stops, they would just sit for about ten minutes. It was an elusive maneuver to deal with spy satellites and reconnaissance aircraft, and reminiscent of a shell game.

Their destination turned out to be in another grove of large thick trees, providing cover from above, similar to the intervening stops, except this was near the foot of a mountain. Inside the tree perimeter was a tall chain-link fence topped with barbed wire, all of which was in a matte black. Again, with aerial reconnaissance and spy satellites in mind, all the shiny silvery metal had been darkened.

A couple of heavily-armed soldiers opened a gate. Nearby, there were more heavily-armed soldiers pulling back leashes on half a dozen German shepherds, which were growling or lurching forward with ferocious barking.

Among the trees, there was an assortment of military vehicles and several small bunker-like structures, which couldn't be any more than entryways to elevators or stairs. The driver pulled up to and stopped by one of these structures. There were three soldiers standing next to it. They only had sidearms, and one was holding papers on a clipboard. That one walked over to the Goat and talked with Moon.

Then Moon and Bo went with the other two, one in front of them and one behind them, into the little structure. Once inside, they climbed down through an open hatch with a very thick steel door. At the bottom of the ladder, they walked over to a stairwell and went down five flights to the bottom, which was next to the end of a tunnel, which they walked through and emerged into a network of corridors, in which they walked past occupied offices, conference rooms, toilets, storage rooms and utility closets.

Finally, they went down a very-wide set of stairs and then through an open set of double doors into a small basketball arena, a full court with beautiful hardwood floors, nice-looking backboards, nets and scoreboards, and seating for about fifty. There was also an enclosed area with video recording equipment. Moon told Bo that Kim had already arrived at this location and would be joining them shortly.

Bo figured that, in this deep underground facility, the basketball court was probably a Kim-ordered luxury, an appendage to a strategic military installation. This was a place from which orders might be given to launch missiles, dispatch artillery and tanks, deploy troops in armored personnel carriers, and shoot some hoops.

A few minutes later, they heard an approaching clamor of voices and laughter outside the open double doors on the other side of the court. As he led his laughing entourage into the little arena, Kim shouted in English, "Bo, welcome to the basketball underground!"

Even if it was only one sentence, Bo was surprised that Kim openly used a non-Korean language in front of a fairly large group, including army officers.

Kim motioned for Bo to join him out on the court, and asked everyone else to go take a seat in the stands. He led Bo to center court and stopped. He clapped his hands as he turned his body around and then stopped again and shook hands.

"Bo, I've been told that you are fluent in English. Is this true?"

"Yes, as a matter of fact, I am."

"Well then, this is most fortunate," Kim said. "This will allow us to speak with each other privately, directly and more clearly.

"I chose this spot to start our basketball relationship because of its symbolism," Kim continued. "It is here, at center court, that something begins. And for us, it will be a lot more than a game. The fact that this court is even here, shows how much I value basketball. And the fact that we are underground is also symbolic. The purpose of our relationship must remain deeply hidden. I must have your promise of absolute confidentiality."

Kim paused.

"I understand," Bo replied. "I will take you to your basketball goal in a way that will be, and will always remain, confidential. You have my word."

"Excellent," said Kim. "Now let's go have lunch and talk about life and our favorite sport."

Kim's entourage had just gotten settled in their seats in the stands, and now he waived for them to get up, and led everyone to the officers' canteen.

Once inside, he told the others that he was going to briefly sit privately with Bo to discuss some tentative business arrangements. He then took Bo to a table on the other side of the very large room, where no one else would be able to hear them.

As soon as they sat down, a server came to the table and ask Kim if he would like his favorite lunch.

"Would today's special be okay?" Kim asked Bo. "It's a plate of grilled chicken breast, mixed vegetables and rice."

"That sounds good to me," Bo replied.

Kim nodded to the server, and she hurried off.

"Bo, I took a careful look at your proposal. I'm very familiar with your basketball career. I'm as familiar as any outsider can be with your business activities. I know of your reputation for being discreet, and as someone who can be trusted to keep a secret. You don't need to sell yourself to me. I know what you offer. We can skip that. So, I'm going to get right to the point about what I need."

Kim stopped and smiled at both Bo and the server as she sat down a tea tray and poured two cups. Then he continued.

"My destiny is inextricably bound with the destiny of my country. It is essential that I be an inspirational figure for my people. It is my solemn duty to continue the preternatural leadership of my father and grandfather. My leadership must embolden my people to move with pride and confidence into a glorious future.

"Of course, basketball is not intrinsically a way to do this. But it's something I'm passionate about, so for me, it's a great way to do it. Your job will be to get my basketball to a higher, preternatural level."

Kim reached over and opened up a tablet computer that one of his aides had handed him as they walked into the canteen. He pulled up a video of a game in which he was playing point guard, turned it around and pushed it toward Bo to look at.

Several minutes later, as two servers began to set down some colorful appetizers, Kim pulled the tablet back and shut it down. As the servers started to walk away, he handed the tablet to one of them, said something and pointed toward the aide who had given it to him.

"Bo, I love basketball. I love playing it, watching it, and everything about it. But more importantly, in a profound sense, I know that I must use it to project an image of talent and skill that will be viewed with amazement and awe. It must be a source of pride and confidence for my people.

"This is the goal I need you to help me achieve."

Bo waited for a brief moment before he responded.

"I understood very well your goal as the leader of your people, and how an awesome display of basketball prowess could play a powerful role in achieving that goal.

"The first thing we would do," Bo continued, "is one-on-one coaching and training, particularly for ball handling and shooting. Then we would have properly conducted actual games. Then we would have staged game scenes. We would also capture large crowds of fans cheering. And we would have staged fan scenes. We would end up with an enormous collection of images, which would be edited down to a tiny fraction of the total.

"I have a special team of videographers, which I call on when it's time to produce a masterpiece. They are gifted artists. When it comes to this type of project, there is no other crew in the world that comes even close to their abilities.

"Now I want you to know upfront that these guys are based in London. I know that might seem unacceptable for a project like this. But I assure you, it is precisely a project like this that calls for these guys. I know them very well. They've done a lot of work for me. They're good friends of mine. I know they can be trusted to protect a client's confidentiality. They'll keep their promises. Sure, like me, they'll sign nondisclosure agreements. More importantly, their word is gold.

"They're not generally well known because they don't work in the entertainment industry. They specialize in image making for private clients. They're behind the scenes guys. They're the best behind the scenes guys in the business.

"If you trust me to know what I'm doing, I'll secretly take you to your goal. You can count on it."

"I believe you," Kim said.

"Does that mean you're accepting my proposal?" Bo asked.

"It does," Kim replied. "So, let's have a toast with our tea cups."

"To your basketball success," Bo said, as they very gently clinked the delicate floral-designed porcelain.

"This too is symbolic," Kim added. "For this job must be handled very carefully."

"Indeed, and it shall." Bo said.

Kim pulled a card out of his pocket and slid it across the table. "That's my assistant Pak Hak Su. He'll be your contact for schedule, logistics, financial arrangements, and so on. He knows a lot about basketball and has all the authority he needs to get things done.

"Now tell me, what's the name of those video guys?"

"Video All Stars, or VAS, and they will tell you emphatically that 'All Stars' is not a reference to them, it's what they help turn their clients into."

Kim smiled broadly, and then nodded approvingly.

"Now, we should go over and join the others," Kim said. "Besides the Army brass, this group includes my favorite coaches and trainers, and some of my key staff, and they're all very excited to meet you.

"I'll tell them about some of the highlights of your legendary career and that you're going to be helping us here in the DPRK to promote the health and recreational benefits of basketball. And then I'll ask them to welcome you with applause. At that point, it would be fantastic if you could go around and shake all their hands. They would love that."

Then Kim motioned to the servers and asked them to move their places settings and dishes over by the others.

After everyone was done eating and Bo had been introduced and greeted, Kim waived good-bye and departed with his close aides and bodyguards. And Bo, Moon and their two soldier escorts left in the other direction, returning up top the same way they came down.

The Goat wasn't there, just the same soldier with paperwork on a clipboard.

"We'll have to wait a little while," Moon said. "As you've seen, the drivers out in these parts have to follow peculiar security routing and time-allocation procedures."

Bo looked around again, more carefully than when they arrived. This time he did some counting: three small bunker-like structures, two troop-carrying trucks, two small all-terrain vehicles, and one tank, which he couldn't believe he didn't notice before. Everything was under the cover of large thick trees and also very well camouflaged.

The thought crossed his mind that what he was looking at and what he had seen below might just be a little piece of a vast underground military installation, perhaps even going under the nearby mountain.

While they waited, Moon talked with the clipboard soldier, and the two escort soldiers stood at attention nearby.

About fifteen minutes later, the Goat arrived, with the same soldiers, who had now switched seats. As they departed through the opened gate past two heavily-armed guards, there were no concerned German shepherds watching them go out.

The new Goat driver did the same thing. Three times, he pulled off the road and parked under the cover of large thick trees and just sat there for about ten minutes. When they arrived back at the same clearing, the chopper was waiting.

It was the same pilot. And once again, he said nothing. Bo donned his eye shades and ear muffs, and away they went, back to Pyongyang.

When they arrived at the heliport, Bo was surprised to see Tiger and Lucky sitting in the front seats of the car. He and Moon got in the back, and they took off for the Yanggakdo Hotel.

As they drove in towards central Pyongyang from the northern outskirts of the city, Moon initiated several exchanges with Tiger and Lucky. Although he didn't say anything, with his looks and nods, Lucky appeared fully engaged. Moon seemed to be asking a lot of questions. Bo had no idea what they were talking about, but he thought it was obvious that Moon was not only of a higher rank, but also highly respected by the two up in front.

At one point, Moon seemed to be getting a little heated up at how they were responding or failing to respond. Then the conversation was interrupted when Moon's phone rang. He answered, apparently identified himself, and then just listened, for quite a long time.

As soon as the call ended, his phone immediately rang a second time, and again, he just listened, for quite a while. When he was finished with the back-to-back calls, he looked over at his charge. "Bo, your assistant has been found. I'm told that when two members of the police search team went back to her room for further investigation, they discovered her asleep in bed."

At first, Bo didn't say anything. He looked at Moon with a blank expression, then turned his head in the opposite direction, as if he was looking out his side window, then turned back ninety degrees to look straight ahead.

"How very strange," Bo finally said, without looking at Moon.

"And I have some other news," Moon said. "Marshal Kim has invited you to his *spectacular* Sunday buffet. Tiger and Lucky will pick you up tomorrow morning at ten o'clock. I am told that your assistant is most welcome, and it is hoped that she will be there.

"But whether or not she joins you, is of course your decision solely. If you choose not to bring her, an interpreter will be provided."

Then Moon started talking to Tiger and Lucky. Bo assumed he was filling them in on the latest. When he finished, Lucky turned around and looked at Moon and then over at Tiger as he said something. It was the first time Bo heard Lucky talk. All three of them started laughing at whatever Lucky said, and they kept it up until Moon's phone rang yet again, a few moments later.

After Moon finished the third call and didn't say anything right away, Bo asked him, "When we get back to the hotel, would you mind talking with the front desk and asking them to give me a key to Svetlana's room?"

"Of course not, in fact, I'll take care of that right now." Moon then made a call and talked briefly. "Done," he said afterward. "When you get back, just go up to the front desk. You'll be handed a key."

When the car stopped in front of the hotel entrance, Bo thanked Moon, and after he got out, waived at Lucky and Tiger.

As soon as he approached the reception counter, a staff member standing in the back moved forward with a big smile and handed him a key.

Bo went to his room and called Svetlana. No answer. After a minute, he tried again. This time she answered. She sounded very groggy. "Svetlana, it's Bo. I'm coming to see you. I'll be there in a few minutes. I just got a key; I can let myself in." He didn't wait for a response, he just hung up.

He scribbled a note in a pad of paper, ripped it out and took off for her room. He knocked, waited just a few seconds, then used the key and went in. She was sitting on the edge of the bed with a blanket around her. He showed her the note.

> *Don't say anything*
> *we can't talk here*
> *if you can do it*
> *get dressed and*
> *we'll take a walk*
> *outside*

She nodded yes. As she got up to do it, he went and sat down on the other side of the bed and looked away toward the closed drapes.

When she was ready, she didn't say anything, she just came around and stood in front of him. As they walked out of the room, she seemed a little unsteady, so he had her hold his arm.

As they went downstairs and out of the hotel, she continued to hold his arm. They found a promenade, which appeared to go around the island. There were no other people to be seen. At first, they walked in silence. They passed by a large cinema building, which was closed. They still couldn't see any people anywhere. It looked like they had plenty of open space to roam and talk privately.

Svetlana was the first to speak. "I don't understand what has happened. Right after I left you last night, I requested a wakeup call, set my own alarm, brushed my teeth, took off my clothes and went to bed. That's all I did. I would guess that I fell asleep in ten minutes. The next thing I remember is waking up to your phone call. At four in the afternoon! This just isn't possible."

"Svetlana, when you went missing this morning, I got the hotel to let me in your room. I looked carefully everywhere. At nine thirty this morning, you weren't in there."

Bo figured that in her drowsy state she might need a little time to process the sinister implications of what he had just said.

It didn't take long. "What? No! Oh, my God." Bo felt his arm being squeezed. He could tell she was starting to breath heavily.

"Other than being drowsy, do you feel all right?"

"Yes, I think so. But...I'm frightened."

"Of course, by the unknown. Svetlana, I'm so sorry."

"Do I look any different?" she asked.

They stopped, she turned towards him, and he looked her over, mostly focusing on her face.

"You look the same. I don't see any physical changes or signs of trauma."

They resumed walking.

"I view everything here very differently now," he said. "Considering whatever it was they did to you, we can assume any less onerous tactic would be in play. It's a matter of authorization level.

"Which is why I think our rooms are probably bugged. I'll bet there are cameras in there too."

"Where do you think that stuff would be?" she asked.

"Oh, it could be in a lot of places: the lights, television, headboard, phone, drapes. Who knows? It could be anywhere. But let's not get upset about that. The only thing that matters right now is that we stay together for the rest of this visit, which has taken some oppressive and surreal turns.

"This morning, I was told not to worry, that the police would find you, and that I needed to focus on my meeting with Kim.

"When I met with him, he and I talked privately and also in a group setting, and I was introduced to a bunch of other people. It was something you'd expect to be conveniently done somewhere here in the capital. But, no, I was taken by helicopter and then by an off-road vehicle to somewhere out in the country, to some secret underground military installation.

"During the helicopter trip, I had to wear eye shades and earmuffs, so I wouldn't know where we were going. And when we got to this place, we went deep underground. I mean really deep.

"And down there in this army place, there was a little basketball arena, with a full court, nice hardwood floors and everything. When Kim arrived, he greeted me in English. 'Bo,' he said, 'welcome to the basketball underground!' Then he wanted to go out and stand at center court to shake hands.

"We were only on the court for a few minutes. Then we went into a canteen. He and I sat separately for a while to discuss my proposal. But first, he went on about what he saw as all the symbolism of the moment. Like, center court is for the beginning, underground is for confidential and toasting with delicate tea cups is for careful handling. The more I think about all the things that happened this morning, the crazier it seems.

"And Kim and I are sitting there talking with each other in English, with all these other people nearby. I thought speaking anything other than Korean was forbidden.

"Anyway, he accepted my proposal, without any reservation."

"Oh, Bo, that's good, congratulations."

"Yeah, I suppose. But considering how this has started, you have to wonder what we're really getting into.

"Then we joined the others in his entourage: some Army brass, his favorite coaches and trainers, staff and bodyguards.

"He talked to them about me. He said that he gave them some highlights of my career, and told them that I was going to help him promote the value of basketball for health and recreation.

"When he was done, they gave me a big round of applause. And then, as he had asked, I went around and shook everybody's hand. Then he left, and I was escorted out.

"Svetlana, are you sure you're okay?"

"I think so. I feel okay. Even the drowsiness is going away."

"Good, because if you wanted to see a doctor, I think it should wait until we get back home on Monday."

"That's what I think. I've got a doctor who will see me right away. I'll have her check me out when we get back."

For a while, as they continued to walk along the island promenade, neither of them talked. Then they stopped and silently looked at each other, as if what may have happened to Svetlana was unspeakable. Then slowly, they hugged each other. The hug lasted a very long time.

Later, in their final written report, the Guard Bureau surveillance team would conclude: *It appears that their relationship is, or is becoming, more than just business.*

After they moved on, Bo broke the silence.

"We may never know what happened to you.

"Maybe they didn't want you to go out to that secret place, so they just kept you sedated in another room, even though that would have been an unnecessary, extreme measure. Or maybe something more invasive was done. At a business seminar on industrial espionage, I learned that, in some countries, security officials delight in the use of so-called truth serums, like sodium thiopental, even though they're widely discredited."

"Maybe it was the Escort Bureau," Svetlana said. "Official name: Supreme Guard Command. Maybe the same, nice, courteous people who were so kind to help me with my expedited visa processing decided I should be abducted and probed with very dangerous drugs.

"Whoever it was, and whatever they did, why did they do it to me? I'm never political. I try very hard to appear neutral and objective. I'm Russian. And I've never acted in any unfriendly way toward the DPRK or its leader."

"Svetlana, remember, we're going to end up being very close to Kim in a lot of unguarded situations. Maybe their security people thought you needed to be cleared more thoroughly. Maybe they weren't worried about me, because since my school days, my life has been an open book. But most of your life would be unknown to them.

"My girlfriend did not want me to come here. She said that, just because you're Russian, doesn't mean you'll be safe. I disregarded what she said, but now I think she's right.

"Anyway, the important thing right now is for you to feel safe. Please, let's move you into my room. You should be with me at all times for the remainder of this visit."

"Yes, definitely, thank you." He felt her squeeze his arm again.

"Also, are you ready for this?" he said. "We've been invited to Kim's *spectacular* Sunday buffet. We're being picked up at ten."

"I would have expected nothing less," she said.

They looked at each other with somewhat dispirited smiles.

"You know, we should probably decide now, how we're going to deal with this incident for the remainder of our visit," he said.

"I think we ought to act like nothing has happened," he continued. "Completely downplay it. What do you think?"

"I agree. To do otherwise would just be a waste of time, and make everyone uncomfortable."

"When we get back home, that's another thing," he said. "Do we keep this to ourselves? Do we disclose this to certain other people? We can figure that out later."

"Yes, enough for now," she said.

Suddenly, they heard vehicles rapidly approaching, and watched with amusement as four taxis, in tandem, sped by. Moments later, the quiet and solitude returned.

"I think everything's going to be all right," she said.

"I think so too," he said. "Let's head back to the hotel."

First, they went to her room. Bo stayed while she got ready. She had said that she was going to examine her body for anything odd, like a needle mark, take a quick shower, and change clothes. He didn't want to anymore, but of course, again, he looked away.

When she was ready, they moved her things to his room and went to dinner.

After dinner, they took another long walk on the promenade around much of the island. They both returned waves to tired-looking men on a small fishing trawler, which closely passed by on the river. Otherwise, they didn't see any people beyond the hotel frontage.

She seemed to be back to her normal self. She said that she couldn't find any needle mark.

If she continued to appear unharmed, they made a tentative decision that they were going to keep what had happened as a secret between themselves.

They assumed that there were eyes and ears hidden in Bo's room. But they reached a kind of accommodation in which they didn't much care. They would simply adapt.

When they crawled into the king-size bed, they were both wearing underpants and socks. Svetlana also had on a t-shirt.

Despite all the extra room, they slept next to each other. Neither wanted any space between them. Where their bodies touched, they could both feel a soft, sweet, sexual electricity. The thought crossed both their minds that they could easily, suddenly, be engulfed in passion.

But this was going to be a night of stillness and comfort.

Chapter 17

When she woke up the next morning, Svetlana found herself cuddled up with Bo on the inside spooning position, with his left arm over her. She felt comfortable and didn't want to move, or disturb Bo. But she decided to find out what time it was and maybe start using the bathroom. As she tried to gently slip out from under his arm, he said, "How are you doing? How was your night?" He was wide awake.

As their conversation began, they were both mindful of the fact that there were almost certainly hidden eyes and ears in the room.

She continued crawling out of bed, sat up on the edge of it and turned to look back at him. What she saw in her mind's eye was a revealing, tender smile. *He's really very fond of me,* she thought. "Good morning," she said. "I feel fine. I slept all night, which is amazing considering my colossal sleep-in yesterday."

His smile broadened. "Good. Please, you use the bathroom first. While you're doing that, I can lay here and contemplate all of the ways I can help this magnificent country truly enjoy the health and recreational benefits of basketball.”

“Bo, you’re so on target. I’m proud of you. But right now, I’m not quite so ambitious. I only have one objective. I just want to actually show up in the main lobby at ten o’clock.”

She stepped into the bathroom and shut the door.

When she came back out, Bo was laying on his back, with his hands folded behind his head on a pillow. Her attention was immediately drawn to an alluring rise in the covers down in the middle of the bed. She imagined a pleasure tent, held up in the center by a thick, perfectly smooth, man pillar.

She removed the bath towel that had been wrapped around her, flung it over a chair, and breathlessly entered the tent.

A few minutes later, she managed to push away the blanket and bed spread, leaving only a sheet above them, which they pulled up for complete coverage.

Two members of the surveillance team, who had dutifully strained to observe as closely as possible, noted in their report, *We couldn’t see anything under that sheet, or make out what may have been said, but obviously a lot was going on. And we definitely heard her scream two different times; there was no mistaking that.*

An hour and a half later, Bo and Svetlana were out of bed.

“How about calling room service?” he said. “It’s only eight thirty. We probably won’t eat until almost lunchtime. How about a little snack to hold us over? Like orange juice and buttered toast.”

“That sounds good,” she replied.

"Please, ask them to bring it as quickly as possible," he said. "Even if it's only a little snack, we want as much time separation as possible from the Great Leader's buffet."

She made the call. Twenty minutes later, a large tray with their order was sitting on the table, tea and jam included.

"We should respect local customs and do this properly," she said. "I'll pour your tea, and if you're game, you should pour mine."

"Svetlana, I'll be happy to pour your cup of tea anytime."

*

At ten o'clock, Bo and his assistant were waiting in the main lobby when Tiger arrived. After greetings were exchanged, they followed her outside, where Lucky was standing by the car. The smiley face button was still in the backseat cup holder.

As Tiger looked in her mirrors and pulled away from the curb in front of the entrance, she said, "You're very fortunate to have this invitation from Marshal Kim. His Sunday buffets are known to be spectacular, and it's considered a great honor to be there."

"Where exactly is it?" Svetlana asked.

"At the Ryongsong Residence, the presidential palace north of the city, where we took you Friday night."

"Oh yes, about eight miles from here. The place that's ringed with exuberant guards. The locals call it the central luxury mansion."

"Exactly, you remember well."

About five minutes later, Tiger slowed down and pointed towards very tall, connected twin towers. "That's the hotel I was telling you about on Friday night, but you couldn't see it in the dark. The Koryo. It's forty-five stories, and as you can see, there's a bridge near the top. A lot of foreign visitors stay there. It's an interesting, entertaining place. We're making the offer again, if you have time before you leave and want to check it out, let us know, we'll take you over there."

"Thank you, Tiger, that's kind of you."

When they arrived at the palace compound, once again they went through multiple, rigorous and repetitious inspections. The friction between the military palace guards and the elite security detail was again palpable.

When they drove up to the entrance, Tiger stopped the car and she and Lucky got out and opened the doors for Bo and Svetlana. "We won't walk in with you this morning," Tiger said. "The palace staff will take good care of you. Please, have a wonderful time."

"Thank you," Svetlana said.

Even though there was a sizeable crowd waiting in the entry hall, as soon as Bo and Svetlana walked in, they were singled out by the reception staff and right away led through a maze of hallways and into the Sun Room.

The setting didn't disappoint. It was a long, narrow, high-ceilinged space that extended along the back of the palace and looked out over vast, lush gardens with several large fountains.

The room was populated with many huge flower arrangements on ornate pedestals. In the middle of the room was one long table with about thirty chairs on each side and elegant place settings. The food and beverages were being abundantly and colorfully presented with crystal and silver along the inside wall.

Bo and Svetlana were taken to their seats, but like many of the guests who were standing about, they did not sit down. They took notice of the place setting name cards. Bo would be sitting to Kim's immediate right, then Svetlana and Pak Hak Su. On the other side of Kim would be his wife, General Gu, General Ryang, and his sister Kim Yo Jong.

Many of the guests were drinking sparkling beverages out of crystal trumpet flutes. Bo and Svetlana were offered champagne or sparkling cider. They both chose the latter.

It was a scene of opulence and exclusivity. "These people must be some of the most privileged in the country," Svetlana said.

A string quartet was performing what Bo and Svetlana immediately recognized as the music of Dmitri Shostakovich. "Of course, this musical selection was not random," Svetlana said. "It's a thoughtful, classy way to make us feel welcome, and a demonstration of proper etiquette."

"And I appreciate it," Bo said.

"So do I."

Like many Russians, they were proud of their country's wealth of artistic achievement, and hearing this great composer's timeless music in a foreign land made them feel good.

About five minutes later, a man in a business suit, a palace staff supervisor, approached them. "Excuse me, honored guests, I'm part of the palace staff. I'll be here in this area. If you would like to go to the men's or ladies' room, please let me know. I'll be happy to show you the way."

"Thank you, sir," said Svetlana.

She translated for Bo.

"Tell him I'd like to do that right now," he said.

After Bo walked off with the staff supervisor, Svetlana took her trumpet flute and walked around the table to one of the French doors to get a better look out at the palace gardens.

After she returned to their seats and waited for ten or fifteen more minutes, she started to wonder why it was taking Bo so long.

Finally, he returned. As she went to pick up his sparkling cider to hand it to him, to her far left, she happened to catch a glimpse of the strikingly beautiful violin player, walking into the room through a hallway door near the end of the table.

Remembering how long Bo had stared at her image on that cinema poster, she wondered if the timing of her entry into the room was just a coincidence, or had they been discreetly brought together. She didn't see any other band members. Bo didn't offer an explanation as to why he was gone so long.

A short while later, a collective murmur of expectation, followed by a cascade of applause, sounded the entry of the Supreme Leader and his lovely wife Ri Sol Ju.

There was no announcement, but as soon as they entered the room, the guests cleared their path to the center of the table. Following right behind were the two generals, Kim's sister, and Pak. When they reached the center of the table, using Svetlana as an interpreter, Kim introduced Bo and Svetlana to his wife and the others in his entourage.

Bo and Svetlana were met by very friendly greetings by everyone in Kim's party, but it was his wife who extended the warmest and most gracious welcome, individually, to both Bo and Svetlana. In North Korea, this kind of attention from Ri Sol Ju was considered a rare and special honor.

Then a palace guard in ceremonial dress announced, "Attention please! May we have complete silence, please, as the Supreme Leader wishes to speak."

There was instant, total cooperation, and all eyes were on Kim.

"Please, my dear people, be seated," Kim said. Then he waited for everyone to get settled in their chairs.

"My wife and I welcome all of you here today." He paused. "I also want to introduce our special visitors from the Russian Federation: Bo Tenbinakov and Svetlana Vasiliev Baranovichi. As many of you know, in the world of basketball, Bo is a living legend. And back in her homeland, Svetlana is a distinguished scholar. We are so very happy to have them as guests in our country."

Kim then asked Bo and Svetlana to stand up, as he started to clap. As they stood together for the applause, Bo and Svetlana first looked at each other and smiled. Then Bo turned and looked at Kim and saluted. Then Svetlana stepped back, so she could see Kim directly. As a sign of gratitude, she put her hands together and bowed slightly. Then before sitting down, they looked both left and right and waved.

"Now, everyone, please, enjoy this wonderful feast," Kim said.

Then he and his wife lead the procession through the buffet. As ushered by staff supervisors, they were followed by Bo and Svetlana, the two generals, Kim's sister and Pak.

While they were eating, Svetlana said to Bo, "Pak wants to know if he could meet with us at three this afternoon in a conference room at our hotel. Would that be okay?"

"Yes, definitely."

After brunch was finished, Kim and his wife took Bo and Svetlana to see the palace indoor basketball half-court, and then outside for a stroll in the gardens. Svetlana continued to act as the interpreter. While they were in the gardens, Kim told Svetlana that he has given her the nickname of "Skysong" in recognition of the affection his country has for her. And he laughed and said that, besides, her formal name was too long. She told him that she was honored and very touched by this sentiment.

Kim brought up the subject of skiing. He told them that some of his fondest memories are from his days skiing in the Alps when he was in school in Switzerland. Especially, when he learned that both Bo and Skysong liked the thrills of downhill skiing, he insisted that they be his guests sometime this winter at his Masikryong Ski Resort. They accepted his invitation and said they very much looked forward to what would surely be a wonderful adventure.

When it was time to leave, Kim and his wife escorted Bo and Skysong all the way to the entry hall, where very warm farewells were exchanged between them.

Standing off to the side, Tiger and Lucky were a little stunned to witness this. They had underestimated the magnitude of importance for both of their charges.

*

At three o'clock, Bo and Svetlana met Pak in a conference room at their hotel. As the translator for both, Svetlana sat at the end of the table, with Bo and Pak next to her on opposite sides. The meeting lasted for two hours.

Of all the many details that were discussed between Bo and Pak, the one thing that Svetlana found surprising and intriguing was about hotel accommodations.

For their next, lengthier visit, while working under the contract, Pak offered to provide the best executive suite, but to have it described and billed as two separate rooms, one deluxe and one regular. Without skipping a beat, Bo accepted, thanked him and moved on to the next item.

For Svetlana, it was easy to appreciate the obvious dual purpose of comfortably facilitating her protection from fear and allowing their dalliance to be kept hidden from the folks back home. What she found interesting was that it appeared to be a scheme hatched by Pak.

*

That night after dinner, Bo and Svetlana again went for a walk around the island. There was one area in particular that they had come to enjoy: a stretch of wide path running between a wharf along the river and a retaining wall supporting a thicket of trees at an elevation about five feet higher.

It was where they had exchanged friendly waves with some tired fisherman the evening before, as the men passed by in their trawler about fifty feet away. That was a moment that stood out as a rare instance of nighttime detectable human activity and human contact, in the otherwise eerie stillness and silence of such a large city.

As they walked, Bo and Svetlana reflected on the whole weekend experience.

"It just seems like I was given some sort of test and passed with flying colors. In just three days, I've gone from being your assistant, to a drugged abductee, to a specially honored guest."

"Yeah, it's amazing. Seemingly overnight, you've reached some sort of exalted status."

"I'm trying to figure out why," she said. "My guess is it's two things. The assumption that I'm close to the basketball legend who may be able to do magical things for Kim. And their desire to be seen in a favorable light by someone who is becoming an authoritative scholar in Korean studies."

"By the way, Skysong, I like your new nickname."

"I do too. And when you consider my career ambitions, it's pretty cool that the leader of North Korea has a nickname for me. Now to round out my professional image, I just need to have a South Korean president do the same."

"You know, I can't stop thinking about your abduction. I just keep thinking about it. Another reason I'm quite sure our rooms are under surveillance is because the abductors had to know that I wouldn't stumble onto their maneuvers."

"And I was thinking, I'll bet that initially, to get me out of my room, I was given anesthesia gas to render me unconscious. But if during those fifteen hours, I was subjected to interrogation, why wouldn't I remember something?"

Bo took her hand and they stopped. Then he slid all of his fingers up the back of her neck into her hair like a comb, and gently pulled until their lips met...

She pushed away. "Bo, I think tonight, here in the land of hidden cameras and microphones, we should be chaste and forbearing."

"Think there were any cameras under that sheet?" he asked.

"I do," she replied. "And one of the guys spying on us probably sold the recording on the black market, and now we're all the rage on the Internet. There's probably millions watching it."

"Svetlana, can we go on a date, tomorrow night back in Vlad?"

"Only if you promise to be fun," she replied.

"I promise," he said.

*

On Monday morning, when they went to the front desk to check out, they were told that everything was taken care of and the entire staff at the hotel considered it a great honor to have them as guests and very much hoped to see them again soon.

Standing over by the entrance, were all three of the official escorts. Bo introduced Moon to Svetlana. Moon said that he stopped by in the hope of meeting Svetlana, and to bid them farewell. When they got to the car, as Tiger and Lucky put the luggage in the trunk, Moon opened the door for Svetlana and told her that he was very happy to have had the pleasure of meeting her. After he closed the door, he stepped back and walked over to the front of the car, and waved as they drove off. Bo noticed that the smiley face button was gone.

At the airport, Tiger and Lucky took the luggage straight to baggage check-in, and then walked Bo and Svetlana through all the security checkpoints to the boarding area, flashing their badges at every stop.

Svetlana thanked both escorts. Then, out of character, Lucky looked at Svetlana and said that it had been an extraordinary honor and pleasure. He had one more line to deliver, one that he'd been practicing. He looked at Bo and said the same thing, in somewhat broken Russian.

This was the first time Svetlana had heard Lucky speak. Now everyone was smiling. They all shook hands, and then the escorts left. Bo and Svetlana watched them as they walked away. Just before going out of view, they saw Tiger pat Lucky on the back.

*

When they got to the Vladivostok airport they were met by Nick, the Pacific operations manager, and Max, Bo's personal assistant. As he had been asked, Max brought his boss' regular smartphone.

Nick was very excited to hear how the trip had gone. But he didn't get any more than a "good" and "a success." The returning travelers were too busy regaining the use of their phones and going online. They felt like they had lost contact with their world for three days, and they were both anxious to catch up.

Back at the office, Bo called a meeting for late afternoon with Nick, branch manager Valeria, Svetlana, and Youri via a video hookup seven hours behind them in Sochi. At the meeting, Bo reviewed the scope and stages of work for Kim. Nick, with Svetlana's support, would interface with Pak Hak Su. Youri would deal with the Video All Stars. And Youri, Nick and Valeria were informed of Svetlana's official North Korean nickname.

Bo would be very busy with other things the rest of the week. On Tuesday, he'd spend most of the day preparing

159

for a New Zealand trip, which would last from Wednesday to Saturday. On Tuesday, he would also meet with Lucy.

*

On Monday, at the end of the day, Bo and Svetlana left the office separately, and then met for dinner at a restaurant in another part of town. Bo knew he could count on her to be discreet in the workplace. He also knew it was time to agree on some additional ground rules.

While they were eating, he broached the subject. "You know, as I mentioned in Pyongyang, I have a girlfriend. We love each other, and I'm sure we always will. Eventually, we'll get married. Someday, we hope to have several children. I'm bringing this up because I want you to know, if we're going to be seeing each other, I'm going to have to be very careful to keep it a secret. I have to be mindful of sneaky tabloid reporters and their cameras. Which means that we can't meet at my place, and wherever we do meet, I have to take circuitous routes to get there, and use necessary precautions. If the sensational news chasers are on my tail, I have to shake them off.

"This can get quite involved. If these guys decide that I'm going to be a catch, and commit to putting a crew on me, they'll use every tool available, which means they'll get into our phones. If I spot them waiting near your place, I won't stop. As soon as I can safely pull over, I'll call you on my burner phone."

He paused while he took a little, unmarked, brown box out of a bag that he had sitting on the seat next to him. He sat the box in front of her.

160

"What's this, a ring?" she asked coyly. "I thought you were already almost betrothed."

He laughed. He enjoyed her sense of humor. As she started to open the box, he said, "It's your burner phone, which must only be used for my incoming. If I don't show up when I'm supposed to, I'll be calling you on this phone."

"It's a new flip phone!" she exclaimed. "Or rather, I should say it's a new *old* flip phone. It's not a foldable smartphone, it's like those phones we used years ago for calls and messages." She laughed as she finished taking everything out of the box. "And a charger," she said. "How quaint. Are these things still being made?"

"Yeah, there's still a market for them. They're popular with spies and drug dealers and all sorts of nefarious characters. They're also useful for an upstanding gentleman like myself, who doesn't want his girlfriend to be blindsided, embarrassed and hurt by someone showing her some headline like 'Caught in His Love Nest!' with incriminating photographs and some lurid made-up story to match.

"Now seriously, Svetlana, I have to ask you, do you understand where I'm coming from? Is this okay with you?"

"Yes, Bo, I understand, and it's fine. I'll be more comfortable at my place anyway.

"Wow," she continued, "I never would have imagined that our illicit affair would include a new flip phone. I sure have hooked up with the right guy. I'll bet you've got a whole bunch of these."

And so, that night and the next, in Svetlana's invitingly pleasant, well-appointed abode, they wildly indulged themselves in the privacy they coveted.

When Bo met with Lucy at the predetermined place and time, it was their first rendezvous in which he did what she'd been doing all along. He executed lengthy, convoluted evasive actions to ensure he wasn't under any surveillance when he arrived at the destination.

It was also the first use of a safe house, which in this case was a garden apartment. It had an ideal feature. Its front door wasn't visible from the street or any neighbor windows, and there was ingress and egress in three different directions.

Lucy started by saying that it would certainly be much appreciated if he didn't make any wisecracks about her disguise at the Bell Burger. He laughed and said that, until he heard her voice, he actually fell for it.

While they ate chicken salad sandwiches that Lucy had brought, they identified signal sites, so that either of them could call for a meeting or leave certain other messages. They settled on code for meeting locations. They adopted a time converter. And then Bo told her about the trip.

He told her that, in small private groups, Kim was not as averse to speaking English as previously reported.

He told her that the reports about Kim having a secret basketball facility in the city of Anju may be erroneous.

He told her about the underground military base. How he was unable to see or hear during the helicopter trip. That at whatever speed it was going, or route that it took, the chopper was in the air for sixty minutes.

He described his perspective in the open field and what looked like a smokestack past some rolling hills.

He estimated the distance traversed in the off-road utility vehicle at six miles. And described the deceptive maneuvers under canopies of large thick trees.

He described the destination at the foot of a mountain, and gave an inventory of the military vehicles he was able to see.

He described how entry was gained down into the installation to a depth he estimated at eighty feet and the layout of the facilities he saw, but cautioned that he had no idea what may exist beyond or below.

He told her which generals were in the central luxury mansion, on two different occasions, and which ones were deep underground out in the country.

Bo told Lucy many things, in precise detail. But he did not tell her about the abduction of his assistant.

Chapter 18

It was four years ago when Emma Darling first met Bo. She was in her seat next to a window on the express service from Heathrow to Paddington Station. She could see a young man quickly approaching. She watched him move across a broad stretch of the terminal floor, then go around a glass wall and then come onto the platform. She imagined that he might be a ballet dancer, or a figure skater. No, he was more like some prehistoric man, a hunter-gatherer moving in on his prey. She thought he was gorgeous.

She was sitting close to the doors with an empty seat next to her. She looked around and saw that the only other empty seats were in the back. Maybe, just maybe, she could corral him. She hoped he'd make it inside before the doors closed. He did.

And as he lifted up his large bag and slid it into a rack, she got a glimpse of his luggage tag and saw that he was Russian. She also noticed that he handled the large bag like it was filled with feathers.

Bo was on his second trip to Britain scouting for resources. So far, everything had gone smoothly. His flight had arrived on time, he cleared security and customs without any delay, he impressed himself with how he had remembered where to catch this fast-direct train without even looking at signs, and how he had managed to get in just before it left.

As it started to move, he turned away from the luggage rack to look for a seat. He was immediately beckoned with a welcoming hand gesture for an empty seat only a few feet away. He delighted in plopping down next to an attractive young woman. It never ceased to amaze him how many there were in airports, always, without fail.

"Thank you," he said. Most of the time, in his quest for the next amorous adventure, he had to scan the terrain and use some clever approach tactic. Not this time. Not with this one. He just about landed in her lap without any effort at all.

"You're welcome."

After a few seconds, she said, "Now, I'm going to go way out on a limb here, and ask if you're Russian? That is, if you don't mind. I like calibrating the accuracy of my perceptions. I suppose it's kind of silly, but why not?"

He looked at her and smiled, but said nothing.

"It seems like you might speak English," she said. "Now that I'm out here on the limb, it'd be nice if you could say something."

"Yes, I am certainly Russian. And I thank you for recognizing that."

"You're welcome."

Her expression and nod said that she knew it.

His smile got bigger.

For a few minutes, they both just looked forward or down or away from each other. Then Bo broke the silence.

"May I ask where you're coming from and headed to?"

"For business reasons, I can't tell you where I'm coming from, except to say it's from a great distance. I've travelled a very long way. I live and work in London. Right now, though, I'm just going to make a brief stop here, and then continue on to North Yorkshire to visit my mum and dad."

"It sounds like maybe you can't tell me, but I'll ask anyway. What kind of work do you do?"

"Oh, I can tell you what I do. Just not necessarily whom I do it for. I'm a videographer."

"What an amazing coincidence," he said. "That's why I'm here. I'm looking for video production people."

"Well, you just found one. But, most likely, I won't be what you're looking for. My company only does a very specialized type of work."

"And what type would that be?"

"Before I answer that, I must compliment you on your English. It's quite good, quite good indeed."

"Thank you, again. You're most kind. What's your name?"

"Emma, and yours?"

"Bo Tenbinakov."

He wondered if his full name might ring a bell. It didn't.

"Well, Bo, I'm part of a company that's small in size, but big on talent. It's called VAS or the Video All Stars. We like to say that's what we make all our clients – stars. We operate behind the scenes and anonymously transform a client's image.

"We're expensive, and we tend to deal with extremely wealthy and powerful people. But don't misunderstand me, we're not snobbish. It's just that we've found a niche that allows us to make a lot of money. And we all seem to like making a lot of money.

"We're sort of a rare breed. Even though we'd probably be very good at it, we don't ever do things like popular entertainment or commercials or live events or public documentaries.

"Now, please, do tell me, what sort of videographers are you looking for? What type of business are you in?"

He had a strong feeling that this encounter would be going places. She wouldn't normally be eye-catching, not even strangely attractive. She was rather plain and simple. No makeup. Pale skin. Blonde hair pulled back in an untidy ponytail. Blonde eyebrows. Black sweatshirt, black cargo pants, hiking boots.

But he could already feel the chemistry. She was beautiful. Natural. Wholesome. Her blue eyes were filled with adventure. And her voice was enchanting.

Their arms had touched several times. Some of the chemicals had spilled into each other and were getting warm. He could sense an electrical charge and figured that eventually sparks would start to fly. He contemplated many possibilities.

"I own a company called Bo Brand Basketball. It's a global enterprise, which is based in Sochi. I sell anything and everything related to the sport that I love. I consult on arena construction, furnish dazzling scoreboards, recruit coaches and players, run marketing campaigns, supply bobbleheads and peanuts. You name it, I do it.

"For clients who want a whole package, I take their game to a higher level. An important part of what I do involves images -- to define, to promote, to excite. Which brings me to my current search for video talent. I'm looking in several countries, but I've especially admired the particular techniques and look of many British productions in recent years."

She wondered if she could trust this guy. She wondered for less than a minute. She found him irresistible. She was going to go for it.

"I see," she said. "That's interesting. So, maybe it is possible that my company could be a resource for some of your needs."

"That's what I'm thinking," he said. "You know, Emma, in this short span of time, I've already thanked you three times for your kindness, and now it's obvious we should explore the possibility of a business relationship. How about you let me treat you to lunch or dinner at a restaurant of your choosing sometime in the next couple of days?"

"The thing is," she replied, "I'm not staying here at all. I'm leaving right away. As I said, I'm going to visit my parents up in Yorkshire. Have you ever been to the North of England?"

"No, I haven't. I'll bet it's nice."

"Oh yes, a lot of it's lovely.

"If you can spare the time, it's only two hours by train up to York. I could pick you up and give you a taste of the North. And it would be good to talk seriously about business. Who knows, we could be a good match, your business and mine. But I wouldn't suggest making that trip unless you could spend the night.

"If you could do it, from York we'd head west to Harrogate. That's where I stay when I visit mum and dad. They live out in the country, near a village north of there.

"I'll bet you'd really enjoy Harrogate; it's a delightful town. I'll be up there for a week. You could pretty much come up any time."

"That's sounds nice. I'd love to see more of England. I've never been outside of the London area.

"Of course, I do have an itinerary, but I left some free time for new discoveries and the unexpected, for opportunities just like this. Let me look at my calendar."

He studied his phone for a couple of minutes.

"I could do it in three days, would that work?"

"Sure, while I'm up there it's mostly like I'm on a vacation. And I can visit with my parents just about any time. So, I'm flexible."

When they parted ways at Paddington, they had agreed to finalize the details with text messages.

Within twenty-four hours, Bo was booked in first-class for the train trip to York, and had reserved a spot on his calendar for a tentative meeting later in the week at the VAS offices back in London.

*

As she waited inside the York railway station, Emma couldn't help but wonder if she may have made a mistake. When she met him, she was exhausted from the work she had been doing in Johannesburg and the long journey home with hardly any sleep. Maybe her first impression would turn out to be somewhat illusional.

She spotted him as soon as he got off the train. He was about two hundred feet away when he started walking towards her. By the time he was half that distance, her doubts had vanished. Once again, as she studied the fluid, graceful movements of his body, she was certain she wanted him. They waived at each other.

"Emma, how nice to see you again."

"Likewise, and thank you for making the trip up here."

"Oh, I enjoyed it thoroughly. This is a beautiful country you have. And that was a wonderful way to see some of it up close."

"Good.

"Well, follow me, and we'll go to my car and head to Harrogate."

He was surprised to find her driving an old Land Rover.

"I didn't know you were a professional basketball star," she said as they fastened their seat belts.

"How'd you find that out?"

"One of the guys in our company, Charlie, recognized your name.

"So, you were in a good position to go into a basketball business," she added.

"Yeah, in the basketball world, I've got a lot of name recognition and a treasure trove of goodwill, and I'm taking full advantage of it."

"Good for you."

"This vehicle is a classic," he said.

"Yeah, it's my dad's. He insists that I use it when I'm up here. He seldom drives anymore. But he still pampers this thing. And he says that it's bad to let it sit idle for too long."

"What year is it?"

"Nineteen seventy-seven.

"He'd want you to know the paint's authentic British racing green."

Bo stretched forward to get a better look at the hood.

"Yeah, this is a beauty," he said.

"Honestly, I'd rather be driving something else, but I know this makes dad happy. He also has a late-model Aston Martin, which also sits idle, but he doesn't seem to care as much about that.

"Don't get me wrong, I love him, and my mum. They're both good people who always, in their own way, try to do the right thing. But to put it mildly, they're both quite eccentric, especially my dad. I can only be around them for so long, and then they start to drive me nuts."

About thirty-five minutes later, they arrived at the place where Emma was staying. She had a suite on the top floor of a three-level Georgian building with a view overlooking a large park.

They spent most of the day and early evening talking about their respective businesses, as they dined in popular tea rooms, strolled through lush gardens and walked along wooded trails.

They both became convinced that VAS might very well become Bo's go-to guys for many of his important projects.

That night they sat close together on a love seat looking out at the large park, called the Stray, that began across the street. Then they slept together.

He loved her music collection and the soft soothing playlist she put on after they kissed. The last thing he remembered about that night in her bed was falling asleep to the gently-flickering golden candlelight and Mozart's Ave Verum Corpus.

*

The next day, Bo's appointment to visit the VAS offices was no longer considered tentative. It was now a must.

Emma would not be there. She explained that VAS consisted of six partners. That they were all equal, but Roger Arnett was the first among equals. He was their leader. He would be there. So would Charlie. The other three -- Helen, Toby and Jack -- like her, were off elsewhere during this little break between projects.

When they arrived at York Station for Bo to catch his train back to London, Emma didn't park. She pulled up into a passenger unloading zone. Before he got out of the vehicle, they thanked each other for a great time. After he shut the door, they smiled and waved at each other. As she drove away, she was sure that he would keep their little dalliance a secret.

Chapter 19

Two days later, as Bo walked up the steps at the address in Fitzrovia, having not seen any signage from the street, he was relieved to spot the small brass engraving, about six inches wide and three inches high, near the door and an intercom. It said VAS.

"Yes, may I help you?"

"Hi, I'm Bo Tenbinakov. I have a three o'clock appointment with the Video All Stars."

"Welcome sir. Please step inside. I'll be right there to take you to your meeting."

Inside, Bo was led by an older man, who introduced himself as Edward, through a maze of corridors into what appeared to be a lounge and kitchen, where three people were standing by a counter engaged in a conversation in which they seemed to be talking over each other and almost shouting.

One of them immediately broke away and hurriedly walked over to Bo.

"Mr. Tenbinakov, this is fantastic that you would come to see us! We have so much looked forward to meeting you."

The other two now also gathered around Bo.

"This is one of my partners, the incomparable Charlie Stafford; this is our very tolerant, forgiving, and most capable business manager Carol Hudson; I'm Roger Arnett." As hands were shaking, Edward was already making a large pot of tea.

"We could have met in a formal office or conference room, we do have them here," Roger continued, "but I thought we might benefit from a more relaxed casual setting."

"Yes, this is good. We won't be so stiff," Bo said, with a chuckle.

"Let's sit at the dining table," Charlie said. "It'll be good for the tea and biscuits."

As they sat down at the long dining hall table, Carol and Charlie sat on one side facing Bo and Roger on the other.

"This building was constructed in the early nineteen-thirties for the garment industry," Charlie said. "It was mainly used as a warehouse. We bought it six years ago and spent two years renovating it. We love the brick and beam structure and how well we were able to suitably adapt it for our studios and offices. We've got everything here, from large-format rooms with twenty-seven-foot ceilings and isolated recording booths to private showers and rooms for hair and makeup and wardrobe. We've got it all."

"When we finish our tea, we'll give you a tour," Roger said, "and then we can come back here and talk about our possible mutual business interests."

When they started the tour, Carol excused herself. Before she left, Bo told her about Youri, her counterpart in his organization.

As Roger and Charlie showed Bo around, they referred to their place as Palmer House, its original name. As they moved through the facilities highlighting a lot of their state-of-the-art equipment and their in-house-developed software, several times they gave demonstrations of their capabilities, which were astonishing. Bo had seen quite a few demos before, at top-notch companies, but never anything like this. He was very impressed.

When they returned to the lounge, Roger and Charlie talked briefly about how Carol handled contract terms, bookings, rates, billables and the like. And they acknowledged that their fees were considered to be very high. Then they talked at length about the backgrounds of all six partners, mostly about their technical skills and artistry. Finally, they talked about how all six partners make significant contributions to worthwhile causes, which at the present time include addiction, abuse, hunger, homelessness, cancer, and the blind.

Bo talked about several of his projects in which videography was a key part. And about how much more and how much better he needed to use video.

When the meeting ended three hours later, they all enthusiastically agreed that it seemed like a Bo-VAS era was probably about to begin.

Charlie left first. He said that he had a dinner engagement with the Lord Mayor of London. As Roger and Bo watched him leave the room, Roger said, "He's joking, mate." Then as the two of them chatted about Palmer House and Fitzrovia, Roger invited Bo to join him at an art opening, which was at a nearby gallery called the

Next Quarter. He said that its openings were usually packed with a lot of interesting good-looking women and a lot of fun. It was only five blocks away.

Bo said that he was game. As the two of them walked to the gallery, Roger explained how it came about that he always tried to attend the openings at the Next Quarter. He was first made aware of them from such an unlikely source -- a member of the diplomatic corps at the Embassy of Croatia, who is a friend of his. As it turns out, his friend apparently has some romantic link with the gallery owner.

He said that the Next Quarter openings have become a unique Fitzrovia phenomenon. "It's hard to describe," he said. "It's so many different things all at once. It's almost like a little carnival or a little circus. There's usually a theme. For this one it's *time*.

"Of course, there's the art exhibit; that's its raison d'être. But it has evolved into also being something else. It has become a creature that seeks to entertain and amuse in many different ways. There is always this menagerie of performers, staged and roaming, which may include musicians, comedians, actors, dancers, magicians, mimes, and various other surprises.

"Often, some of this stuff will drown out other stuff or make it incomprehensible. But that kind of dysfunctional chaos has become an acceptable part of this. It's kind of anything goes. Art in anarchy. There is only one rule. No politics. The owner says she doesn't want political discord to ruin her party.

"There it is, overflowing as usual," he concluded, as they turned down a narrow dead-end street. Bo could see a crowd of people about half a block away that had spilled out onto the pavement with their glasses and bottles. In the middle of the street, a placard said Private Party.

They hurried through about two dozen people to get past the outside smoking and vaping. Then, fortunately, one of the doormen recognized and greeted Roger, and in they went.

Inside, almost immediately, three women in colorful nineteen-forties' dress and hairdos, in one synchronized motion, swooped in. Like it was choreographed, in rapid succession, cascading from left to right, each blurted out a one-liner.

"Roger, this guy's *so* handsome, where'd you get him?"

"Roger, you're still keeping secrets from us!"

"Roger, you heart throb, don't pay attention to them."

Then, without pause, the one-liners rolled out again from left to right.

"Well, Roger, are you going to introduce us?"

"Will he tell us what he does? *You never have.*"

"Wait a minute, I've seen this guy before."

And then again, from left to right, again without any pause.

"Yeah, in your dreams, and mine too."

"I'm so glad I came to this party."

"I'm telling you, I know who this is."

Always from left to right without pause, the rotation continued.

"What? Are you sure?"

"Like as in wishful thinking."

"No, I know who this is. He's a basketball player. He's a big-time basketball player. I saw him play several times on the telly when I was in college. He played for some Russian team. We used to all be amazed at how good he was. His name's Bo. I definitely remember his first name.

I just don't remember his last name, but now, hopefully, Roger will tell us."

The rotation continued.

"I'm not going to let my jaw drop here. I'll maintain composure."

"Behold, man of mystery and sports hero. Wow, it's a double shot!"

"Yeah, but don't flip your wig. Maybe they're rationed." Roger and Bo were both chuckling by now. And Roger hesitated to interrupt this delightful comedy act with a proper introduction.

"Okay, which one of us gets to introduce these two main attractions to the artist?"

"Oh, I think we all should, don't you?"

"But they should see the art first, otherwise it might be sort of awkward."

Roger put up both his hands, which caused a pause in the act. Then he put his hands down.

"Ladies, this is Bo Tenbinakov.

"Bo, this is Connie, Babs and Daisy."

"It's a pleasure to meet all of you," Bo said.

"And thanks, Daisy, for being so nice to recognize my playing days."

As the evening progressed, Roger and Bo eventually checked out the artwork, which they both found to be perplexing. They didn't meet the artist, who was from Western Australia. They did read a description of him at the entrance to his exhibit.

Leon Hauser

a silent night rambler plying to find his rhythm an off the wall romeo boxed in a cheap blue suit a wild man hiding in the bush off the beaten path spilling the beans in the café of last resort hanging out in the middle of nowhere down a dusty road past an old broken tower clock a desolate outpost a place with no identity or purpose an abandoned camp in an art desert wasteland sometimes under the southern cross he drifts along in the stillness by a field of sweet lavender and dreams

footlights flash hearts throb hips sway souls shake the band stages as he imagines something like that may never happen again or maybe the most magical of all is just around the corner in a cool fresh autumn breeze gently flowing down the pink neon glowing avenue in the town of time the rendezvous ballroom a saxophone air force dancing piano keys a thundering rumbling guitars riff wholly rolling driving drums the salvation show

They talked with Roger's Croatian embassy friend and the gallery owner. They flirted with a whole raft of beauties. They tried to listen to an eighteenth-century costumed town crier's doubletalk proclamation. And they enjoyed the soulful vocal harmonies of a sixties-style R&B group called the Detroit Whistle.

It was ten thirty when they left for Roger's favorite, local, late-night, Italian café. As the night had worn on, something had clicked between Bo and Roger. They felt comfortable and open around each other. They were on the same wavelength. It was an auspicious beginning to their nascent business relationship.

By the time Bo decided to enlist VAS for the job in North Korean, he had worked with them on a total of eleven projects across three continents. Along the way, they had all become good friends.

Chapter 20

There was one person who wouldn't be calling Svetlana by her new nickname. Mrs. Natasha Alexandrov would always call her Mom.

As she had planned during her senior year in high school back in Novosibirsk, Svetlana's daughter graduated from the Far Eastern Federal University in Vladivostok. But then, instead of beginning work in oceanography, as she had earlier intended, she accepted a lucrative offer from Mazda. She has been employed by the automotive giant as a human resources recruitment specialist for the last two years.

Now twenty-four years old, she's married to Stefan Alexandrov, a young ophthalmologist. Her husband calls her Natasha. Svetlana, and just about everyone else, calls her Tasha.

Mother and daughter usually get together at least once a week to keep up with what's happening in each other's lives. Their relationship is no longer anything like that of a parent and child. There's only a fifteen-year age difference between them. They act like two very close sisters or two very close friends. They famously enjoy each other's company.

Before the North Korea trip, Tasha told her mother that they had to get together soon after her return. That it would be fascinating to hear about being inside such an exotic place. On Tuesday, they exchanged messages. Svetlana would go over to Tasha's for dinner on Wednesday, the first night Bo would be gone. Stefan would be joining them. He also wanted to hear about the trip.

After she accepted the dinner invitation, Svetlana starting thinking about what she would be telling her daughter and son-in-law. It wouldn't be much. She would be forced to leave out all of the really important parts of the story.

For the many professional and business reasons she and Bo had discussed, she would keep her pledge not to talk with anyone about the abduction. Without that key piece of the puzzle, how could she talk about the radically different ways she was treated and the suspicions she harbored?

And there was Bo's "absolute confidentially" agreement with Kim. That removed a big part of the storytelling material. She wouldn't even be able to talk about the true purpose of the trip.

She was dying to tell Tasha about her new affair, but she wouldn't be comfortable doing that in front of Stefan. Svetlana liked Stefan. But sex with Bo was not something she wanted to talk about in front of her very proper son-in-law. And she didn't like being guarded and unforthcoming in conversations with Tasha.

She felt overwhelmed by so many constraints on disclosure.

At the dinner table on Wednesday, it would be a difficult task to navigate through only the superficial, permitted parts of the story, and answer questions. And such a gutted version would be nothing like a realistic account. She wanted Bo to participate in such a coverup.

Off and on, over the next twenty-four hours, she debated with herself. Should she show up alone and self-muzzled? Or should she cancel? Early Wednesday afternoon, she sent Tasha a message that she was going to have to work late, and wouldn't be able to make it. As an alternative, she asked about the possibility of bringing Bo for dinner on Sunday.

Within seconds, Tasha was calling her. "Mom, what's going on? Sure, Sunday's fine, but you've got to tell me what's going on. You're bringing him to your daughter's house for dinner? Wow. Can we meet at the Baker's Hut at nine on Saturday morning?"

"Sure," Svetlana said, "but I can't talk now, see you on Saturday."

"I can't wait," said Tasha. The call ended.

Svetlana really wanted to talk about her unexpected and exciting affair. But first, she had to get her story straight. She would have to figure out how to safely get to the titillating details.

*

Bo had made it very clear to his staff that he needed to concentrate on the New Zealand trip. He had told them he was confident they could put Kim's whole package together and get it to Pak Hak Su without delay.

Everyone now understood that the official written contract was a necessary mechanism for setting forth the performance timeframe, the price and the payments schedule. A description of the true nature of the work was omitted. Instead, it contained generic verbiage about consulting to promote the health and recreational benefits of basketball.

Nick received a message from Pak that they wanted Skysong included under Key Personnel. They considered it vital for her to be personally engaged throughout the performance of the contract.

Nick checked with Svetlana, quickly exchanged documentation with the International Academy for Language and Culture, and then inserted her name under that provision. He was determined to kept things moving along.

On Wednesday, while he was in Manila to change planes, Bo read a message from Svetlana. She asked him to please join her for dinner on Sunday at her daughter's. He replied that he'd be happy to, and wanted to know if they could get together early that afternoon. He said it would be nice to spend some time alone first. She replied that she'd be ready any time after twelve noon.

*

It was crowded on Saturday morning when Svetlana and Tasha met inside the Baker's Hut and started looking for a place to sit. As they often did, this almost matching pair of tall beautiful blondes caused some heads to turn.

Luckily, a few minutes later, they found two seats, as a couple got up to leave.

"The usual Mom?"

"Yes, please."

While Tasha went to get coffee and pastries, Svetlana sat down, so they wouldn't lose their little table.

When Tasha returned with their items on a tray, she set them out on the table, quickly took the tray back to the counter and quickly returned to her seat. "Okay Mom, I'm all ears."

"I'm not going to talk about the whole trip," Svetlana said. "That should wait until tomorrow. Otherwise, Stefan would feel cheated, and Bo's commentary wouldn't be mixed in. So, this morning, I'll just tell you the stuff I can't talk about at dinner."

"Right Mom, just give me the juicy part about Bo. I know you went to bed with him."

"I admit it, I did."

"Oh Mom, my life's so tame and appropriate, please, you've got to satisfy my prurient curiosity."

"Well, it all started innocent enough," Svetlana began. "I don't think either one of us expected it to happen. It was all so professional and business-like at first. But we went together, alone, on that trip. Of course, we stayed close to each other; that's why I went. He doesn't understand or speak the language, and hardly knows anything about North Korean customs.

"On the second night, we were working in his room to prepare for the next day, and it just happened. We had been sitting side by side at a table going over some material, and it just happened. It came out of the blue, and we both dove in."

Svetlana's head went back, she took a deep breath, and then let out a slow exhale. Tasha's eyes got bigger and her chin dropped slightly, but otherwise she was motionless, and silent, as she stared at her mom. She knew what her mom's body language meant.

Svetlana looked around to see who was sitting close by and realized she had to be careful with what she was going to say.

"Tasha, this guy's got the nicest one I've ever seen."

"Mom! You're bad." Tasha pointed a finger. "Now tell me more."

"Well, there's an important caveat here," Svetlana said. "When we got back to Vlad, we spent Monday and Tuesday nights together. On Wednesday, he left for a business trip to New Zealand. He probably gets back tonight. We're planning to get together early tomorrow afternoon and then go to your place for dinner.

"When we were having dinner on Monday, he gave me the caveat. Although he had previously alluded to some girlfriend, I had no idea how involved they might be. On Monday, he elaborated. He said that he was in love with her, and knew he always would be. He said that eventually they'd get married and wanted to have several children.

"He said that he had no intention of getting involved with me, but as I well knew, it happened -- unexpectedly, suddenly, naturally."

"Where does this girlfriend live?"

"I have no idea. I asked him, and he wouldn't tell me. He said that she will not know anything about me, so it wouldn't seem fair to have me know any more about her. That he respects both of us, and doesn't want to be unfair to either of us. He also said that, although we can't change what's happened, if I wanted to stop seeing him outside of work, he'd understand. But that it would have to be me to end it, because he wouldn't."

"Oh, wow," said Tasha, "what are you going to do?"

Svetlana took a little sip of her hot coffee, and then smiled.

"I'm going to continue my relentless pursuit of a stellar career, and, for who knows how long, have a legendary basketball player as a part-time boyfriend.

"In fact, the more I think about it, the more appealing it sounds. Maybe it will change, but right now I'm in lust, but I'm not in love. And this sort of arrangement might suit me perfectly fine.

"Not only is he an amazing erotic dream in the flesh, but he's also a thoughtful, considerate gentleman. What more could I ask for?"

"Mom, I can't believe this. Twenty-five years ago, it was a famous football star. Now, it's a famous basketball star. You're a magnet for celebrity athletes." They both raised their cups as a toast.

"I'm sure he's a bigtime womanizer," Svetlana said. "I don't have any doubt about that. He's probably got a girl in every port. He probably likes a lot of diversity. He probably can't ever get enough of it. I may just be the flavor of the month. We'll see. What I'm curious about is this woman he's planning to marry. Is she real, or is that some story he's made up to control the expectations of his lady friends?"

*

It was ten thirty on Saturday night, when Bo returned home from his New Zealand trip. His first order of business was to call Zella. It had been a long time since they last talked. It would be three thirty in the afternoon in Cluj. He hoped this would be a good time to catch her.

She answered. "My mom died this past Monday. The funeral was this morning."

"Oh Zella, I'm so sorry." He paused for a moment. "Why didn't you tell me?"

"You were so far away," she said. "And I didn't want you to feel obligated to interrupt important business. It wouldn't have mattered anyway. What really mattered was your visit with her before she died. I know that gave her a lot of comfort. Anyway, right now I just need some time to mourn."

"Zella, I'm going to arrange to see you as soon as possible. I should be there in two days, three at the most."

"I...miss you," she said. It sounded like she was starting to cry, and then she hung up.

*

On Sunday afternoon, Bo and Svetlana had hardly begun getting their story straight for the dinner engagement, when they started fooling around with each other and ended up on the bed. Two hours later they were spent, and fell asleep.

By the time Svetlana awoke and startled a still-sleeping Bo, there wasn't enough time left to go over everything. "Bo, wake up! Oh no. We're supposed to be there in thirty minutes. We're not going to be prepared."

"I'm sure we can wing it," Bo said. "Let's just error on the side of caution, and rely heavily on the confidentiality agreement."

*

When they rang her daughter's doorbell, they were greeted by Tasha and her husband, who both appeared excited to welcome them into their home for the evening.

Tasha was every bit as beautiful as her mother, but with a more lighthearted airy appeal. Her husband was tall, nice-looking, and courtly. After introductions, they passed through the living room, library, and dining room, with a casual table setting, and ended up in the kitchen, which had a sliding-glass door opening out into a large garden.

As Tasha finished cooking and preparing the dishes, Stefan served cocktails. Bo was amused as he recalled exactly how Svetlana had described the eye doctor. *He's an affable and quite cerebral fellow. And pretty cute.*

After a round of drinks and some hors d'oeuvres, Stefan insisted that his mother-in-law follow him out to the garden, which was lit up with floodlights. He wanted to show her how beautiful the plants she had given them were turning out.

They were gone less than ten minutes. That's all it took. When she returned, and for the rest of the evening, Svetlana could see that Bo and Tasha were very much in tune with each other, as if they were communicating through some invisible aura. Stefan noticed it too, and wondered if there was a danger looming in their midst.

Chapter 21

Svetlana was asleep and dreaming.

The evening air is chilly, as my friend Nasiba Danilova and I glide on bikes down a sidewalk in an old, lonely, commercial part of town. Now, racing on a bike to catch up with us, we're joined by our friend Angelina Volkov. There isn't hardly any noise, or traffic or pedestrians.

It looks and feels like it did when we were little kids. Block after block of one- and two-story, dirty red brick buildings, with wired-glass windows, and alleyways of grimy potholed asphalt and graffitied dumpsters.

I see my dad standing by the back of his pickup truck holding a sledgehammer. He puts it next to some paint cans, rags and brushes, and ties a long piece of bright red cloth to the end of an extension ladder that is hanging out the back.

In a deep inside pocket of my denim jacket, I'm carrying a police-grade pepper spray canister. I know Nasiba has one too. And probably Angelina, since it was her brother who sold them to us, after we promised not to tell. We think he stole them.

Anyway, no one better mess with us.

I stop for a moment to study a clever, seductive poster, on a large boarded-up building entrance. It's right next to a Post No Bills sign. It has the image of that Korean girl, that violin player. Her face is so pure and irresistible.

I need to pee.

I start going into a diner, but then I see a sign with a big bold exclamation mark that says the toilets are for customers only.

Around the next corner, there is an antique store, or maybe it's a pawn shop, with the front door open. I look inside. There's a bird cage with two parrots on top of the counter. An old man comes up from the back and says that he is sorry that his toilet is out of order.

Angelina says I should just do it in the side alley and she and Nasiba will stand guard by the street entrance.

I decide to do it. Get relief. Be liberating. Pee in the alley for fuck sake. I find a dark spot behind a pile of wood pallets next to a forklift. I look for the slope and position myself so the stream will run away from me. Then I pull down my panties, lift up my skirt and start to squat down...I hear three distinctive clicking sounds. Then blinding floodlights come on!

Svetlana woke up and realized she really needed to pee and was also very thirsty. After a moment, she swung around and sat up on the side of the bed. What happened in the dream was rapidly fading. By the time she sat down on the toilet, it was almost all gone, with only a vague, fleeting recollection of Nasiba, Angelina and her dad.

It was three in the morning on Tuesday. She took two long swigs from a water bottle, crawled back into bed, closed her eyes, and tried to go back to sleep.

But that didn't happen. She laid there wide awake for a long time with all kinds of thoughts swirling around in her head.

She couldn't stop worrying about her abduction. What if they had done something awful, and it just wasn't apparent yet? Could they have put some sort of implant in her?

Tomorrow she had to make an appointment with her physician. She couldn't believe she hadn't done that yet.

She had been taken by surprise with Bo's abrupt departure before the office opened on Monday. And she was more than a little ticked off he didn't even so much as say goodbye with a simple text message.

She shouldn't have drunk so much vodka. She probably shouldn't have drunk any vodka. It wasn't at all like her to do that, to drink so much alone. It had disturbed her sleep, and she'd probably have a terrible headache in the morning. It was stupid.

She pondered what Max had said about Bo's itinerary. That he was going to Cluj-Napoca and then Baku, with private jets for two legs of his journey: Vlad to Beijing and Istanbul to Cluj.

Who was Bo going to see? She was sure his trip wasn't all business. Maybe none of it was.

She wondered if Bo's fiancée lived in one of those destinations. She could have asked Max, but didn't. If Bo found out she'd asked, there could be very negative consequences. He'd said that he didn't want her to know; that it wouldn't be fair.

What if Bo was a smooth act, but really a coldhearted prodigious womanizer? He sure left town in a hurry. Back late Saturday night, and already gone again early Monday morning. Here just long enough to fuck her brains out and flirt with her daughter.

Why would she care if Bo had an out-of-control seduction habit? Didn't she believe what she told Tasha, that part-time would be okay? She had to admit to herself, if it was going to be hardly any time, and she was going to be disregarded like this, then, that wouldn't work.

What if Max tried to make a move on her? That could create an uncomfortable situation. And worse, her source of information about Bo could dry up.

She didn't think Max was unattractive, but he wasn't her type. And she definitely wasn't getting involved with someone else in the office.

Doesn't Max know his boss is sleeping with her? Surely, he won't make a move if he does. Maybe he's just biding his time. Maybe he figures this won't last long and thinks she'll be available soon enough.

She tried over and over to put these worries and fears out of her mind, so she could go back to sleep. But many of them kept racing back into her thoughts.

Would she be crazy to go back to North Korea?

Would she really be a fool to continue a relationship with Bo?

Around four o'clock, the anticipated headache started to kick in. She felt like she was beginning to sink into a morass of distrust and contradiction, and soon wouldn't be able to find her way out of it with a throbbing head.

She'd take ibuprofen with breakfast and lunch. That would safely get her through the work day. Right now, she needed something else.

Like it was a life raft, she latched onto a mantra. *I'll stay focused on my career goal. I'll stay on track with Bo and Kim. The rewards will be fantastic.*

Chapter 22

It had not been easy for Bo to leave so quickly. After learning of Maria's death, as soon as he got off the phone with Zella, he called Max, even though it was late on a Saturday night.

"Max, I need you to help me tomorrow morning with some travel arrangements. Sorry I have to interrupt your weekend, but this is a matter of urgency. Can we meet at nine o'clock?"

"Sure, I'll be there at nine."

"Thanks."

"No problem. I'll bring some good coffee. See you then."

Max was use to this sort of thing. He actually liked it. He liked the feeling that came with unexpected matters of urgency, the rushes, the tactics, helping a famous important boss. This, he thought, was what bigtime personal assistants did.

In the office the next morning, Bo laid out the basic parameters: getting to Cluj as quickly as possible without any consideration of cost, followed by routine travel to

Baku, at least seventy-two hours later, for one day of business.

It wasn't easy to sort out, and it became very expensive, but by twelve noon, everything was booked, and Bo was able to make his early afternoon date with Svetlana.

At four o'clock the next morning, Max would pick up Bo and drive him to the airport.

*

A man in a white captain's uniform came out of the cockpit, motioned to someone on the ground through the open cabin door, then shut and secured it. As he approached with an extended hand, Bo couldn't help but appreciate the completeness in this guy's professional image. He had it all: a black cap with gold trim, gold on black four-bar epaulets, a black tie, and a *Top Aero* insignia.

Bo was shaking hands with a slender middle-aged Armenian man. "Mr. Tenbinakov, I'm your pilot, Captain Areg Topalian. If you please, sir, everyone calls me Top. I wanted to tell you that this is a special honor for me. You are a legend in the sports world, and now here you are, gracing one of my planes with your presence."

"That's most kind of you. Please call me Bo. And Top, it's my pleasure to be flying with you."

"Thank you very much." Top broke from his serious demeanor to nod with a proud smile, obviously grateful for the compliment. "Bo, I also wanted to tell you that the weather looks good and we can expect to have a pleasant flight into the Chinese capital."

After Top went back to the cockpit, Bo suddenly found himself being gripped with fear about losing Zella. He has been oblivious to her side of their relationship. He knew that was a dangerous thing. *I've taken her for granted*, he thought, and it scared him.

She was a physical attraction and sexual experience like none other. And she was his only true soulmate. He wanted to marry her and have children with her.

He could not bear to lose her. But at this moment, that struck him as a real possibility. The more he thought about it, the more he imagined that she could just say goodbye, and really mean it.

How could I be so foolish?

He wanted her to believe that he was devoted to her. But now he feared he might have convinced her that he was more devoted to his business. These long absences may have become intolerable. And what if she knew he was involved with someone else?

*

Bo was both amused and impressed to observe the unconventional measures Top was permitted to employ to rapidly access a spot near Bo's regularly-scheduled flight from Beijing to Istanbul.

After he was in his first-class seat on the big bird, his thoughts turned to the next stop. *Sarah Shannon Doyle.* It pained Bo that he wouldn't be able to visit her in Istanbul. But he had to get to Zella without any delay, and it would be risky to meet a British journalist before he was done with Kim.

Sarah was a top-notch Middle East correspondent for *The Sunday Times.* At the age of only twenty-six, she had already earned a reputation as a fearless dogged pursuer and reporter of critical events, as they unfold. Bo was fascinated by what she did, and how she did it.

Her eyes were sleepy, droopy, and irresistible. Their brown color exactly the same as her eyelashes, eyebrows and hair. All of it soft and fine, and connected, as her long bangs brushed across her face and her hair gracefully dropped down around both sides of her neck. Perhaps a rose-colored blouse would match the shade of her lips.

Bo was captivated by Sarah. He thought everything about her was perfect, and perfectly mysterious. She had a look of pure, delicate, girlish innocence. Considering what she did for a living, it was an incongruity he was unable to reconcile.

He had many fond memories. How they met at a coffee stand. How they delighted in squeezing together along teeming sidewalks. How they first kissed in bumper-to-bumper traffic. In historical places, quiet enclaves, chaotic bazaars and Turkish baths, in this surge of humanity at the dramatic divide between East and West, she was his dream guide. She made him melt.

Oh Sarah! he thought, as he closed his eyes. He wouldn't let her know he was passing through without a visit. Anyway, maybe she wouldn't even be there. Maybe she'd be somewhere like Syria or Iraq.

He promised himself that he would do whatever was necessary to hook up with her when he was done with his mission for the SVR.

*

When Bo finally reached Zella, he was greatly relieved to find her still devoted to him. They enjoyed three happy days together, and agreed to a Paris wedding in June.

For right now, she would continue working at the school in Cluj. At some point in the future, they'd start having children and then she would take a long break from her teaching career. In the meantime, since she would now be able to travel, they'd see each other much more often.

Bo said he would continue to spend a lot of time in the Far East for only about eighteen more months, at the most. Eventually, they'd make their home in Sochi. Zella would certainly miss Cluj, but she liked Sochi, and she thought it would be exciting to move there.

When they parted, they said that they would see each other soon. They would spend Christmas and New Year's together.

*

When Bo returned to Vladivostok, he told Svetlana that he has been with his girlfriend for over four years and that they have decided to get married in June. He told her again that he didn't want their relationship to end, but it would definitely have to be discreet and deferential to his future wife.

He said that he hoped they could continue working together, in the office and as travel companions. That the circumstances that had inadvertently thrown them together had created something beautiful. Again, he told her that he would not be the one to end it.

He hoped that she would not end it either. But if she did, he would understand and respect that, and if she still wanted to work for him, she certainly could.

She told him not to worry, that she wanted to continue working and playing together, and he could trust her to be discreet and deferential.

She also told him that she had the most comprehensive physical examination she's ever had, including a lot of unnecessary imaging. That it was very expensive, but well worth the peace of mind that all the normal results have now brought her.

He insisted that his company reimburse her for what was obviously a business-related expense. She smiled and gladly accepted the anticipated offer.

Because of the timing of the wedding news, Svetlana figured Bo's girlfriend was probably in Romania. She had been able to determine that there were two existing contracts in Baku, but nothing she saw indicated any business activity in Cluj.

*

A few days later, they were back in North Korea, in the same hotel, on a higher floor, sharing what was described by Pak Hak Su as, "the finest, deluxe, executive suite." Svetlana was surprised to find that her role in an illicit part-time affair was once again appealing to her. She told Bo that she loved his body.

There was another thing that surprised her. She was not only becoming knowledgeable about basketball, she was actually starting to really enjoy it. This bode well for her ambitions.

She was determined to broaden her skill set in Bo's business. She wanted to be indispensable. And when the Kim project was finished, she was sure the attention would shift to South Korea. That would be very fertile ground for his business and her professional development.

In advance of this visit, she had translated a frank conversation Bo had with Pak about having a suite without hidden microphones or cameras. Otherwise, Bo had said, he would cancel the project. Pak promised to make sure they had privacy. She and Bo both thought that the threat might work, but realized that they'd never know.

They quickly got settled into their new digs. Bo said that they had only seventeen days to get the whole job done. And when it was successfully completed, it would be considered a most remarkable achievement.

The circumstances on this trip allowed Bo, each night, to plan for the following days. The work was always done first. Then he had fun with Skysong. But they always quit early enough to get a good night's sleep.

On this visit, they were equipped to work much more efficiently. As called for in the contract, Pak had made special arrangements for them to have unlimited internet and international phone services.

Bo was glad he could still go after her sexy lips and feel up her irresistible thighs. In their sojourn, high over Pyongyang, they spent many hours taking care of business and taking care of each other.

*

The first task was working on Kim, who always acted delighted to see them both. During long one-on-one sessions on the half court in the central luxury mansion,

Bo was now often called "Coach" and frequently interrupted by Kim's celebratory dances and high fives.

These sessions consisted of demonstrations, instructions and drills for ball handling in a variety of situations, point guard mannerisms, various sorts of fakes, passing, three-point shooting, and understated signs of teamwork and conquest. During these sessions, Skysong was occasionally asked to participate, but she was mostly an observer.

*

The second task didn't involve Kim in person, only his images. In advance of the trip, Bo had obtained copies of the videos Kim had of himself playing in several games. These images were treated as highly sensitive and had to be handled in accordance with strict, demanding custodial procedures.

Bo also got what he needed to identify each player on both teams. He made a roster of photos, names, jersey numbers, and comments. He did the same thing for the referees. Everyone was notified to keep the same jersey or uniform number. Bo was working on reorganizing the teams and changing the nature and atmosphere of the competition.

Bo and Skysong were flown by military helicopter to a basketball facility in the city of Anju. There were no restrictions on what they could see or hear. It took about twenty minutes to get there.

Inside the facility, they met a contingent of reserve military who constituted the players and referees in the games with Kim. They were part of the original pool of talent that had been carefully selected as suitable for the assignment. They were the survivors of several purges for loose lips, lack of proper enthusiasm, or inadequate performance.

The Coach worked with this cast of characters to establish the most convincing and impactful lineups and plays. Skysong was totally involved in these sessions, constantly translating between Russian and Korean. She was frequently shouting out directions like she knew exactly what she was doing.

These players and referees understood they were "the Cast" who would help facilitate the Supreme Leader "shining like a star" and they were bursting with pride and excitement to make it a great success. The Coach, Skysong and the Cast had some heartwarming moments together, sharing laughs and groans and cheers.

*

On the last two days in Anju, Kim joined them for a Bo-created, dramatized, whole new take on a game. Kim was placed in his point guard position on the underdog team, the People's Army Choir, to play against the highly-touted, semi-professional Korea Dragons.

When the Anju sessions were finished, Bo told Kim that they were making wonderful progress. Kim was apologetic that these seventeen days would be all work. He said they needed to make definite plans for the Masikryong ski trip. Since the weather forecasts all continued to point to an early-season heavy snowfall, they decided to do it on the second weekend in January.

*

After the last Anju session, after a room service dinner back at the hotel in Pyongyang, Bo asked Svetlana to join him up in the bar on the forty-seventh floor. He expected the Video All Stars to be arriving soon, and that was the designated meeting spot.

As they headed up to the forty-seventh, he told her, "These guys have unbreakable commitments for all of January. Initially, they weren't available in December either. But good ol' Youri somehow was able to negotiate his way into getting them booked for eleven days during the second and third weeks of December. Since they're coming from London, a lot of travel time will cut into the working days.

"To make that loss as little as possible, we got special permission to allow a private jet to bring them in here. As soon as they landed in Beijing, they were escorted to an awaiting plane operated by a pilot named Top, who I recently met. I'm telling you, that's a guy with some amazing aviation connections."

Bo and Svetlana were waiting in the rooftop bar when they heard a commotion coming from the elevator bay, and then Bo heard familiar voices and accents.

He swung around to face their approach, threw his arms out wide and shouted, "Well, if it isn't my favorite Brits!"

The one leading the approaching pack shouted, "Bo! Damn, you're lookin' good!"

"Roger, it's so great to see you," Bo said, while they hugged. As they separated, Bo motioned towards Svetlana. "Roger, this is my special assistant, Svetlana, known around these parts as Skysong. By the way, she's off limits."

"Everything's off limits, mate!" Roger said. "Youri gave us a sizzling lecture. We didn't just read the contract, we memorized it. We promised to be well behaved, around the clock. That's what it says. We have to show the utmost respect for all our hosts. Don't laugh at anything, except ourselves. Believe you me, we know the score, mate.

"When we leave here," Roger continued, "the only thing we'll be taking with us is a shitload of money.

"After we've disappeared, they'll look at our video and they'll say, 'This is a fuckin' masterpiece!'

"It's all good, mate. I told Youri, if we can work with Bo, that would be fantastic! Let's make it happen. And we did.

"Well, I should say, Youri made it happen. We didn't have any time in December, but we let him deal with everybody, and somehow, he made them all happy. He's a fuckin' genius."

"I should do some introductions," Bo said. He raised his voice. "Everyone, please come closer. It's wonderful to see you all!

"Svetlana, this is Charlie...Helen...Emma...Toby...and Jack. As you'll soon realize, this is the most amazing video crew in the world.

"And you guys, please meet Svetlana, my assistant and expert on Korean language and culture. Marshall Kim has nicknamed her Skysong. She's happy to be called either. And conveniently, we all speak English.

"Tomorrow morning we'll meet downstairs for breakfast, promptly at seven o'clock. There'll be signs directing you to the right room.

"Now, the first round is on me, and the second one's on Roger!"

"Okay, I'm having a Taedonggang," Roger said. "Are you familiar with it, Bo? It's a light lager, which is made here at the state-owned Taedonggang Brewing Company. It's the most popular beer in the country, and it's exported."

"You're up on the local brewing scene, are you Roger?" Bo replied.

"You won't believe this," Roger said. "In two thousand, Kim's father bought a brewery that had been operating in England since eighteen twenty-four. Lock, stock and barrel. Over one and a half million pounds, in cash, through a German broker. That was back in two thousand, mind you. They moved all the brewery equipment to here, and reconstructed everything just like it was in Wiltshire."

"That's the brewery Tiger wanted to show us," Svetlana said to Bo.

"No wonder you want to try it," Bo said to Roger.

Roger lowered his voice. "Say, listen mate, I have to ask, do you know why we had to do double room occupancy?"

The VAS crew was paired up into three suites. It was Bo who insisted on two to a room. He told Pak that it would help keep everybody out of trouble.

The real reason was the same one that caused Svetlana to move into his room on the first trip. He told Svetlana about it. He told her that he didn't think anything would happen. That he was being overly cautious. But with VAS, he said, it was better to be safe than sorry.

"Roger, you know how we've learned to just trust each other on some things? Well, this is one of those. It's no mistake. It would be best to go with it. Please, just trust me on this one."

"Okay Bo, if you say so."

"Do you think all your guys will be okay with it?" Bo asked.

"They'll be fine. They trust you, just like I do."

"Thanks, Roger."

*

Four vans were used to transport crew and equipment, two for each. The drivers and other escorts included the familiar faces of Tiger and Lucky, who were in the lead passenger van.

All the equipment was constantly in the custody of the authorities. The security detail totaled eleven. There were thorough searches of everyone every morning. No one was allowed to bring any personal recording devices.

Moon was also there. He was keeping a close eye on everything.

The schedule was tight. They would be working at a furious pace. In the final product, the game will appear to have been played in the capital's indoor sports arena, which is the largest in the country.

A special concert in this venue by the People's Army Choir had been hastily organized. The arena had a capacity of twelve thousand three hundred. There were sufficient incentives to guarantee that every seat would be filled.

Large-scale projected images and cheerleaders would be used to stir the crowd into an emotional, patriotic frenzy. The results would include thunderous roars. This would give the Video All Stars what they needed for crowd images and noise.

Additional cast members had been selected based on their ability to announce a game with an infectious enthusiasm, flair, and a penchant for drama.

The contract with VAS included their videography services under Bo's direction, and an unusual provision for the transfer of all of their equipment -- after their proprietary software was uninstalled -- to the DPRK at the end of the job. All of it had arrived safely on a cargo plane.

Pak made sure that all the additional equipment and tools they needed, like high-rise hydraulic platforms and aerial camera support cables, were at the ready.

VAS worked tirelessly for eight long days. They were always in good spirits, several times breaking into spontaneous, comical, improvised renditions of the Irving Berlin classic, *There's No Business Like Show Business*.

By the time VAS started doing special effects and editing, they had amassed a huge collection of images of Kim and the other participants in actual games and in staged game scenes. The Choir concert was a tremendous success and a rich source of sights and sounds.

So as not to in any way compromise the appearance of authenticity, there were a limited number of crowd close-ups, and in those, all the identifiable faces were doctored. It would be most unfortunate to have people recognize themselves, knowing they weren't at such a game.

The reverse was true of the players and referees, and superstar Kim. The facial close-up was fundamental to the VAS style, and it would be a major factor in giving this production its dramatic power.

In the pre-game warmups, the Korea Dragons team exhibited all of the poise and confidence one would expect from highly-favored semi-professionals. There had only been rumors that Kim might be able to play for the People's Army Choir.

During interviews before the game, in response to questions about such rumors, several commentators had said that they hoped this would happen. They said that Marshall Kim's father had a special place in his heart for the Choir, so it would pay honor to the Eternal Leader. They also noted that the amateurish Choir team would certainly be a sad underdog. It would be good, they said, if the playing field could be more level and the game a little fairer.

At the tip off to start the contest, Kim was nowhere to be seen. Against great odds, the Choir team fought valiantly to keep the game within reach. When the first half ended, they were behind by only nine points. Their fans, which seemed to be everybody in the arena, were further pumped-up during halftime by the projection of video highlights from a rousing, patriotic Choir concert.

It was in the middle of the third quarter, with the Choir down by thirteen points, that a roar spread from seats near a tunnel onto the floor. It was the Great Leader. He had suited up for the underdogs.

To tumultuous applause and screams, he went to his team's bench, a timeout was called, and he entered the game as a point guard.

Kim's presence almost immediately inspired his teammates to unbelievable feats, on both ends of the court. The tide had turned. And because of his brilliant play calling, and amazing fakes and fast passes for assists, the comeback continued deep into the final quarter.

Then, the Great Leader took over the game. Everyone in the arena rose to their feet and did not sit down again.

In describing Kim's performance during those final minutes, the announcer was screaming hysterically. "Yes! He did it! He scored from way downtown!" Followed a couple of minutes later with, "Another three-pointer!" And finally, with only a few seconds remaining, "This is truly unbelievable. It's absolutely stunning. He actually did it yet again, nothing but net, from way downtown!"

In the end, the Choir won by a single point.

Just as Bo had envisioned, Kim's performance was a breathtaking, glorious, unforgettable moment of leadership and triumph. And just as Kim had wished, it was an emphatic, resounding demonstration of his supremacy and power.

*

When their job was done, everyone was in a hurry to head home for Christmas. When they parted, Bo, Svetlana and the Video All Stars all hugged each other affectionately. Together, they had pulled it off. Based on a fantasy, they had created a believable reality, and it was a masterpiece.

Kim was ecstatic. He was beside himself. He wanted everyone to see it. But he knew Bo was right. The smart thing to do would be to keep it under wraps for quite a while, to help ensure its authenticity.

At a later time, it would quietly be released into the nation's files, where it would eventually be discovered by millions of his people.

Chapter 23

After he was back at the Vladivostok office, Bo went into the empty lunchroom. He got an apple juice out of the fridge, opened it, took a drink, and stood in front of a desktop computer, which was on the counter for everyone's convenience. He logged on to a neighborhood business networking website, and posted a comment.

Business: Bo Brand Basketball
Contact: Valeria
It was reported that at 16:15 yesterday an electric scooter carelessly left in street was moved to sidewalk against pole

This was a coded message. It told Lucy that they needed to meet at the safehouse tomorrow afternoon at one fifteen.

On this website, only registered businesses within the district could post comments. But anyone could read them. Very few people wanted to. When Bo might be in town, Lucy looked at it frequently.

The next day, Bo was the first to arrive at the Burdenko Lane garden apartment. He was completely confident in the lengthy surveillance-evasion measures he had executed. Lucy arrived about ten minutes later.

In her latest disguise, Lucy had a hair net over a bouffant-style wig and a white apron. She looked like an assembly line food preparer. Sloping down from the top of her forehead, covering her eyes, was a pink sun visor.

As they greeted each other, Bo smiled, but he didn't laugh. Lucy immediately started taking pasta salads out of her bag, and asked him to begin his report.

Bo described how Kim's "basketball hero" video turned out and the various stages they went through to get there. "Lucy, I don't think it would be an exaggeration to say that, in Kim's eyes, I have been elevated to some sort of deity."

He told her that the reports about Anju weren't erroneous after all. That he and Svetlana had been there. And there were no restrictions on what they could see and hear during the trip. He went over details, which neither of them considered significant.

He again described how elated and grateful Kim was about the video, and how Kim apologized profusely about seventeen days of nothing but work. And he told her about the ski trip plans.

"Okay, let me talk for a bit now," she said, "so you can eat your lunch. The pasta salad is really good; I hope you enjoy it.

"First, I want to say that I'm amazed at how fast you have moved towards our goal. You have done in weeks, what we thought would take many months, if not well over a year.

"It's now easy to see how we figured this so wrong. For Kim, your attraction was incredibly compelling, and so you've been able to basically determine the schedule. And you have always moved at blistering speed. In hindsight, we should have expected this.

"We had hoped that you would be able to eventually become his buddy. Well, you've already done that, in spades. I'm not going to underestimate you again. And now what looms ahead is an ideal setting to begin attaining our goal.

"I have a hunch that during those nights at Masikryong he might privately share with you the kind of thoughts we want to hear about. He's never going to reveal military secrets. We don't expect that. What we hope to discover is his strategic thinking. And I think there's a chance he might loosen up and begin confiding in you about that.

"We have ways to find out a lot about their military operations and military research and development. Our reconnaissance and spies give us many facts, which we are able to analyze. What we want you to do is tell us what Kim is thinking, what he is assuming and believing. We want you to get in his head.

"Before I go any further, I need to ask you a question. Before you answer, please pause and realize that it's critical that you give me a deliberate, thoughtful answer.

"Do you think you might be an alcoholic?"

As she had requested, he didn't answer immediately. Then after a moment, he looked at her and simply said, "No."

"We didn't see anything in your background to suggest that. In fact, you don't seem to be much of a drinker at all, but I had to ask.

"Now here's the thing. We need you to temporarily become a heavy drinker. We need you to build up a tolerance for alcohol. And you should start working on that tonight.

"Kim's a heavy drinker. You're going to have to be able to keep up with him during those nights at the ski resort, and at the same time, rely on your memory for what he said. As I mentioned before, we sure as hell can't put a wire on you. If they found that, deity or not, you'd die quickly in a tragic accident.

"We're quite sure that if you don't drink or drink very little, out of respect for you, he'll respond by doing the same. And then the chances of him loosing up and telling us what we want to hear will be drastically reduced; then it probably won't happen.

"So, we want you to go with him down that path leading to a state of inebriated, unrestrained disclosure.

"But first, you've got to build up your tolerance so that you'll be capable of accurately retaining a lot of information. I know you have an extraordinary memory, but if you don't go through this tolerance training, up at the ski resort, your memory will be greatly diminished.

"Also, to further strengthen your capability, you should do listening and memory exercises with the heavy drinking. This involves making a concentrated effort to listen carefully, keeping what you've heard in clear focus, repeating it to yourself and then, at the first opportunity, doing an undistracted, total recall.

"This tolerance training may cause you problems. Drinking too much can cause anybody problems. But it's a risk we need to take."

She paused, and just looked at him for a moment.

"What do you think, Bo?"

"I get it. I'll do it. By the way, I like this pasta salad."

"Good. All right then, next subject. Let me now go over the arrangements for the debriefing after Masikryong."

She took an envelope out of her bag and pulled out a map and photos of some streets, businesses, a parking lot and a white cargo van and spread them out on the table.

"You drive to the corner of Kashira Avenue and Mira Street. There are three businesses sharing a building at that location, fronting along Kashira: a hardware store, a furniture store and a crafts and art supply store. There's a large parking lot across the back and on one side, which can be entered from Kashira or Mira.

"The lot is seldom more than half full. The customers tend to park near the two ends to be closer to a store entrance. In the back, behind the building, nearer to the middle of the lot, look for an unmarked, white, Ford cargo van. It will be backed into a space, with enough room left to open the rear doors.

"Use the Mira entrance into the lot. There will be two guys sitting in the front of the van. If either one has his arm outside of the window, drive on through, exit on Kashira, and do fifteen more minutes of evasive driving. Then come back and try the same thing again.

"If you're waived off, it's because someone may be able to see you when you switch vehicles. Even though in all probability it would just be some inconsequential customer or employee, after three misses, we'll have to cancel this location, and revert to initial contact.

"If you don't see an arm outside the window, pull into a space next to the van. Get out, lock your car, don't look around, go to the back of the van, open a door, get in and have a seat. One of the guys will come around to the back and shut and lock the door.

"You'll be riding in the van for quite a while, including some stops. Eventually, it will go inside the Navy base. It will back up into the receiving dock of a building, and then you'll be discreetly escorted to the room where I'll be waiting.

"If necessary, we can change this, but let's set the time now. I think we can assume that you'll return on Monday morning. Plan to stay out of your office on Tuesday until late afternoon. Meet the guys in the van at eight in the morning. That parking lot should be quiet then. How does that sound, eight o'clock on Tuesday?"

"That sounds good," he replied.

"Bo, I can't emphasize enough that the critical part of this is how thoroughly you do your anti-surveillance driving maneuvers."

He nodded, and then studied the map and photos again.

"Okay Lucy, I'm good to go."

"Okay Bo, I'll see you after your ski trip."

As they prepared to leave, Lucy asked, "How's it going with Zella?"

"Good. I recently spent three days with her in Cluj, we're spending two weeks together for the holidays in Sochi, and in June we're getting married in Paris."

"Wow! Congratulations."

"Thanks."

As they approached the door, Lucy paused.

"Bo, I hope the heavy drinking doesn't mess things up with Zella."

"Don't worry. Yeah, it may get a little messy, but I'll manage."

*

After the meeting with Lucy, Bo spent a few more hours in the office, then he got together with Svetlana for dinner. He told her that he'd be in Vlad for one more day, and then he'd be joining his fiancée for two weeks.

The previous night was the first time they hadn't slept together in eighteen days. Tonight would be their last night together for at least two weeks.

On the way to her place, he stopped and bought a quart of vodka and a six-pack of beer. During the evening, he drank a lot.

When he woke up the next morning, Svetlana was in the bathroom. The door was open and he could see her looking in the mirror.

"Good morning, Skysong."

"You gave me a hickey on my neck!" she said. "It looks awful!"

His eyes got big and he stared at her, trying to see it, as she started moving rapidly around the bedroom picking up things.

"Svetlana, I'm so sorry about that."

"You know, Bo. Maybe it would be a good idea if you took off sooner rather than later. Because I'm really mad, and I don't want to say something I might regret later."

Neither one of them said another word as Bo gathered up his things and left.

She had overplayed the hickey thing. They both knew that her anger was more about his two weeks with Zella during Christmastime and New Year's.

After he was gone, she started working on convincing herself that it was actually going to be nice to be home alone for a change.

She was ready for some rest and relaxation, a good book and music. She was going to check on a couple friends. She would do a little Christmas shopping. She was going to watch some televised basketball games. She would have Christmas Eve dinner with her daughter and son-in-law. Stefan would probably be relieved to know that Bo wouldn't be with her.

In a few weeks, I'll be the one skiing with him.

Chapter 24

She had begun to think that maybe he was taking the place of the father she never had. Whether it was that, or he had just become a very good friend, Zella cherished her relationship with Oleg.

And he seemed to fill a void left by the loss of her mother and the departure of Sabrina. Zella had other friends, but no one she felt like talking with about Bo, which was the biggest thing on her mind.

Oleg was so easy to converse with. He was so caring and seemed so wise. And he was always pleasant. When she was in his presence, she always felt relaxed and comfortable. And she knew she could confide in him. She knew she could trust him to keep her secrets.

As a student of hers, the first thing that caused him to be special was how much he knew about Bo. He was a basketball fan, Bo was his favorite player, and he was always excited to talk about him.

Oleg said that because of his lessons with Zella, he was finally mastering the Romanian language. And they were both very happy about that.

On the way between where Zella taught and her home, there was a bookstore, which had a small simple café upstairs. When they first ran into each other in that bookstore and enjoyed tea together in its café, they exchanged phone numbers and began inviting each other to meet there.

At the highest levels of the Russian government, Bo was viewed as a national treasure. It had been made very clear that serious harm to his personal life -- most particularly his relationship with Zella -- should be avoided. The SVR officer who assumed the identity of a Pavel Olegovich Pankova whenever he prepared to cross the border into Romania had been tasked with monitoring the situation.

Oleg, as he preferred to be called, was seventy-five. Zella had been led to believe that he was retired, after a long career with the Russian space agency. He told her that he had fallen in love with Transylvania, and now treated it like a second home.

She felt so lucky that their paths had crossed.

Up in the bookstore café, it even seemed like they had their own special table. It was in a back corner. It was always empty, like it was meant just for them.

"When we first got together at Christmas, I thought it was going to be wonderful," Zella told Oleg. "At night, Sochi was so bright and colorful. The first thing we did was go out and buy a small tree, some decorations, and a bunch of indulgent things, like cognac, eggnog and little cakes. The whole time we were shopping, we could barely stop holding hands, laughing and sneaking kisses.

"But within a few hours, he was drunk. If we hadn't decorated the tree as soon as we got home, he wouldn't have been able to even do that with me. He didn't say so, but I could tell that he had a terrible headache the next morning.

"On the second day, we went to what we call the 'sacred ground.' We stood in front of the Archangel Column. That's the spot where we met. I have two selfies we took, one smiling at the camera, and one kissing. At that point, I still thought we would have a great time together. By four o'clock that afternoon, he was smashed again.

"Oleg, this went on for three straight days. A flask in his pocket, clumsiness, sloppiness, impoliteness, nodding off. He's never been like this before. It was more than disappointing; it was very troubling. When I asked him about it on the third day, you won't believe what he told me.

"It was for Kim Jong Un. And he was going to keep drinking a lot. It was a type of training. He needed to build up tolerance for alcohol. He was going to visit Kim at his ski resort. It was going to be social and business. Kim was a heavy drinker. He wanted to be able to keep up with him, and still be able to make smart business decisions.

"He implored me to understand and to realize this was a one-time, temporary thing. He told me that maybe enormous financial gain would be hanging in the balance.

"I think what really got to me was when he drunkenly told me that I shouldn't be so intolerant, because what he was doing was definitely for a worthwhile objective.

"So, my Christmas was ruined, he was determined to keep getting drunk every day, and now I was accused of being intolerant. It was too much. I was gone on the next flight out."

"Oh Zella, I'm sorry this happened to you. I'm sure he didn't mean what he said about you being intolerant. You know, people can say ridiculous things when they're drunk.

"It must be strange for him in North Korea," Oleg continued, "and it could be frightening dealing with a dictator inside a totalitarian state. Rightly or wrongly, Bo must believe this will help him deal with it. Regardless, it sure will be good when he's done with this."

"He shouldn't have gone there to begin with," she said. "I tried to talk him out of it. But he said he'd make a ton of money. But you know, he's very wealthy. He didn't need to do that."

For a moment, although she was talking to Oleg, she appeared to be lost in thought and staring into the distance. "Christmas in Sochi. What a disaster." She paused, and then continued. "He's been trying to reach me since I took off. I'm ignoring him, except I sent a message with six words: That tyrant is wrecking your life."

Then she appeared to snap out of her brooding. "How about you, Oleg, any plans for Orthodox Christmas?"

"Yes, I'll be going back to Russia for a week. The second to the ninth to be exact. My dear wife passed away a couple of years ago, but I have family I want to visit."

Oleg's wife would have to be dead, otherwise his extended stay in Romania by himself would probably raise undesirable questions.

"Zella, I'll be in church on that holy day, and while I'm there, I'll pray that your Bo, who I'm sure has good intentions, quickly finishes up his business with Kim and gets back to his normal self."

*

As Lucy had suggested, Bo had started doing listening and memory exercises with his heavy drinking. It may not have seemed like it to others, but he was sharpening these skills.

Against the onset of distraction, confusion and the other conditions of alcohol-induced impairment, he was making a tremendous effort with close attention, clear focus, repetition and total recall.

There were two things he didn't want to keep repeating, but he couldn't stop hearing them over and over. One was, "Telling me that constant drunkenness is a business necessity is bullshit!" The other was, "I want to go home, now!"

His travel agent got her a shared charter flight that very night, and she was gone. He felt awful. Again, she was suffering collateral harm from his secret work. He drank himself into a stupor and passed out on the sofa.

The next morning, he got rid of the little Christmas tree. Looking at it just made him feel worse. He threw out all of the other Christmas goodies too. All of it made him feel worse.

He went into the office that afternoon. Not surprisingly, there wasn't anyone there. And he could do very little. This wasn't the time of year to be contacting people about business.

He decided that he needed to take his disreputable act on the road, to the Far East. If he was going to soil anything, it would be better if he didn't do it in Sochi, where his home office was, and his future life with Zella was going to be, hopefully.

Before he left town, he did manage to do something good. He took Youri to lunch at one of Sochi's nicest restaurants -- to thank him for doing a great job.

The trip to Vladivostok took much longer than usual. He drank in every airport and on every plane. After he was back in Vlad, he upped his consumption.

He did not contact Svetlana, and avoided places where he might run into her. Even though it was met with scorn and ridicule, he was at least able to give Zella a "business necessity" story. There was no credible explanation that he could give Svetlana.

Twice, he picked up women in bars. One of them drank as much as he did. He doubted she could hold it. He was right. When they went outside, she lost her balance, fell straight down onto parking lot gravel and was bleeding from a cut on her forehead.

He left her with a wet towel and a well-paid taxi driver. He used his smartphone video to capture her profuse apologies and thank yous, and the cabbie's identification.

The other pickup wanted to show him her "artsy" apartment. He bought more booze on the way. In her extremely cluttered apartment, with all sorts of weird objects hanging from the ceilings, she smoked half a joint, and then got very paranoid.

After recording some of her bizarre behavior, he took the first opportunity to quietly duck out. He wasn't sure if she would realize he was gone or even if he had actually ever been there.

On a third occasion in a Vlad bar, he got into an altercation with a longshoreman, who was going to teach Bo a lesson. Although the woman didn't think so, this guy thought "bigshot" Bo was butting in.

It was fortunate that several other patrons broke it up quickly. He could have ended up being arrested and subjected to embarrassing publicity. A lot of his business was based on a clean-cut image.

As a bouncer was seeing the tough guy to the door, Bo took a video of the dockworker looking back at him, shaking his clenched fist and shouting, "I would've kicked your ass!"

Bo didn't consider these three nights to be a total a waste of time. He used the verbal sources in each one to do his listening and memory exercises. And he watched each video the next morning after breakfast. They were all perfect. He was definitely maintaining better. His training was going well.

Of course, to be cautious, he kept all three videos, just in case any of these people got the bright idea they could easily do a shakedown on a wealthy celebrity.

After almost a week back in Vlad, he finally came to the realization that he needed to stay home at night while finishing his training. It was too risky out in public.

So, on each of the remaining evenings, he got hammered at home and picked some verbal source of information on television or the internet and faithfully did his memory exercises.

*

When she got into bed, Svetlana had hoped for an uninterrupted good night's sleep.

Down the alley, with mud, debris and broken-up asphalt, the back of the old red brick buildings with their wired-glass windows. So forlorn, so haunting.

The line to get into the hip nightclub is long, and people are making fun of each other. Maybe I'll take a poster. I see them tacked up near the entrance, but not too close to the bouncer. Then I'd have that Korean girl's face, that violin player's face. But I might get caught. They might have ways to pounce on me that I don't know about. And Nasiba Danilova is with me, and I don't want to get her in trouble.

I'll ride my bike and get flowers. When I come back, surely, things will be different. Those people in line with all their smoke and overdone makeup will get tired of saying mean things.

Nasiba doesn't think so. She thinks they'll only get worse, and it's disgusting. She's leaving.

I can't remember where I left my bike. I have no idea where it is. I can't believe it. I feel so stupid. Polina Alekseeva is going to help me find it. She is such a good friend. Sometimes, secretly, scandalously, we take turns pretending that one of us is a beautiful, scheming, Imperial Russian princess and the other is her lady-in-waiting. When we play those characters, we talk about things we would never talk about otherwise.

Polina and I walk through a maze of alleys and around lots of corners, past many large garbage bags, which are stacked next to dumpsters with big padlocks. We go up some ramps and then we see two sets of stairs. I go up one, and Polina goes up the other.

At every level, I look for my bike or something familiar that might jog my memory. I find nothing. How could I have no idea where it is? I go back down. I'm very frustrated, and feeling more embarrassed by the minute.

I go up the other stairs and start yelling for Polina. As I reach the top level, suddenly, from somewhere, there is a lot of honking. It has been quiet all along, and now a loud cacophony of car and scooter horns? I look over the side.

I can see something odd down by the bottom of the stairs, but it's hard to tell what it is because it's very dark down there. Oh God! Is that Polina? Did she fall?

Svetlana woke up. It was the middle of the night. She looked over to see Bo. There was no Bo. *Of course, he's not here. He's with his real girlfriend. They're spending Christmas and New Year's together.*

Then she tried to remember the dream. For an instant, she saw that old rundown Novosibirsk neighborhood and Polina and Nasiba. But after a few seconds, it all evaporated.

Chapter 25

At noontime on the Friday of the second weekend after New Year's, Bo and Svetlana were buckled into their cushy seats in a chartered flight to Kalma Airport in Wonsan on North Korea's east coast. Like everything else on this trip, it was compliments of their official host, the ministry of physical culture and sports.

Bo looked distracted. He was worried about Zella. Svetlana was smiling. She was looking forward to a good time and being treated like royalty.

In Wonsan, they were greeted by two business-suited gentlemen. After their bags were gathered, they were led to an awaiting helicopter for the trip to Masikryong. It was a spectacular way to approach the ski resort at the summit of Taehwa Peak. All the mountains were covered with snow.

Two Masikryong Hotel employees in uniforms whisked them away from the chopper. They were led into the hotel, shown their suite and given their key cards. Then they were taken to the ski rental store. After they picked out all of their gear, the hotel staff carried it back to the hotel front desk luggage room.

Then they were shown around the hotel and informed of its amenities. Finally, the staff wished them a pleasant stay and excused themselves. At this particular moment, all Bo cared about was getting Svetlana back to the suite for sober sex. She knew what was coming, and she couldn't wait.

It was about four hours later, while they were having dinner, that Svetlana was handed a phone. An aide of Kim's told her that the Supreme Leader would be joining them at eight thirty in the morning for a day of skiing. For Bo, this meant another night of heavy drinking. After dinner, they went to a bar. Svetlana was with Bo on his first night of training, and now his last. There'd be no hickey on this bookend.

*

The next morning, as they began waiting in the hotel front lobby with their skis, poles, boots and other gear, they noticed a sudden presence of what appeared to be plainclothes security personnel, coming and going in all directions. And then two of them in ski outfits came over and escorted Bo and Svetlana on the short walk to the lift.

Minutes later, they were on their way to the summit. It had snowed overnight and there was lots of fresh powder. It was a tantalizing sight. At the top, they were greeted by Kim and his wife Ri Sol Ju, who said they were very happy to welcome their guests to one of their favorite spots. Kim said that it should be a wonderful day on the slopes, and asked them to please excuse the presence of so many bodyguards.

First, they took in the breathtaking panoramic views. Then they began that unique pleasure of long exhilarating runs. Not surprisingly, there were no lift lines. Every time they got to the bottom, they couldn't wait to get back to the top. There didn't appear to be any skiers on the mountain other than Kim's security people. Except for lunch in the summit restaurant, they were on the slopes all day.

After their last run, they agreed to reconvene in an hour and a half. At that time, an escort would come and take Bo and Skysong to the chairman's suite. Ri said that her favorite chef was preparing a dinner.

*

As Bo and Svetlana entered Kim's suite, they were not at all surprised to find it very large and very luxurious. They were mostly taken by the broad view of the snow-covered mountain, which looked majestic bathed in bright moonlight.

The food was phenomenal. The chef was asked to the table twice to receive everyone's praise. He bowed to their accolades.

Ri was enchanting. She was reserved, but she was also expressive and spoke with a polished eloquence. A lady of sophistication and good taste, she was quite at ease engaging equally with both guests.

As dinner seemed to flow to an end, Ri gracefully directed an invitation to Svetlana. "Skysong, please, would you join me in the library? At the moment, nothing could seem more appealing than the pleasure of having a fireside chat with the visiting Russian scholar of our Korean peninsula."

"Oh yes, thank you, that sounds delightful," Svetlana replied.

Kim took notice of this, smiled, and looked over at Bo. "Coach, since we haven't been invited to join the ladies in their fireside chat, we should have our own." His smile broadened. "Please, follow me to the gentlemen's bar, or in popular parlance, the man cave."

The first thing Bo noticed inside the cave was a familiar image, a framed still from the video production showing Kim dribbling with one hand and pointing with the other.

Kim poured two glasses of Courvoisier and brought out Bo's gift of Cuban cigars. They lit up two of the torpedoes and then sat down in front of the fire, which servants had prepared.

"The aromas from the cognac and cigar are magnificent," Kim said.

The conversation soon turned to Kim's many questions about professional basketball. He was fascinated to hear about Bo's playing days, about memorable games and plays, and insights into other players and coaches. He even expressed a curiosity about certain officials and the fairness of their calls.

Kim was intrigued by any of the behind-the-scenes, unauthorized, rumored, locker room, and scandalous sorts of things that typically weren't reported in the media. Bo did much more than satisfy his curiosity. He purposely embellished and dramatized his inside scoop. He cleverly intended to set the tone for an evening of speaking freely, openly and candidly.

As Kim listened to one account after another, he veered back and forth from serious rapt attention to knee-slapping laughter. He was so entertained, he probably didn't notice that after his fourth cognac, Bo was still on his first.

At dinner, Kim had three double whiskeys; Bo had a single vodka. Amidst all the distractions from the ladies, the servers, dishing food, the chef, and the lively group conversations, Kim didn't seem to notice the discrepancy then either.

Finally, Kim stopped asking basketball questions. He refilled both of their glasses and toasted to a great day of skiing. Bo followed with a toast to their friendship.

And then as he started his eighth drink, Kim drifted into what seemed like the beginning of a determined, unreserved narrative. And while he was talking, sometimes it seemed like he was talking to himself, or for the approval of others not present.

Bo didn't let his mind wonder. He didn't miss a thing. He kept his focus. And he stored it well. Every word.

"Bo, as my good friend, I'm going to tell you about a global illusion, and different way to view my country. Out there in the world, among so-called advanced societies, there has been a certain smugness that has looked down on my country and considered it primitive and deprived. They have laughed at us.

"But you know what? The last laugh could be on them.

"Anyone who has been down in our subway system has marveled at its beauty – the marble floors, chandeliers, sculpted columns and colorful murals. Few tourists appreciate its national survival aspect. It is the deepest system in the world.

"And what passengers see is just part of an underground network. There are offshoots that go even deeper and become large areas that are equipped to protect and sustain many people in the event of an enemy attack.

"By contrast, the so-called advanced societies are so incredibly fragile! They have become so overly complicated and so completely dependent on electricity that their very existence is at risk.

"For example, let's consider the Americans. We have the capability with our intercontinental ballistic missiles and nuclear warheads to detonate a blast three hundred miles above Kansas.

"If we did that, the immediate effect of the nuclear explosion at that altitude would be a coast-to-coast electromagnetic pulse that would fry electronics all across the forty-eight states.

"If you aren't familiar with this stuff, an electromagnetic pulse is a short burst of electromagnetic energy, specifically gamma rays, that all nuclear explosions produce in varying degrees.

"The Americans worry about the wrong thing. Even though it should be obvious, most of them don't understand that they've become totally vulnerable. And the few that do, are in denial.

"If we went to war, our missiles wouldn't be aimed at their cities. There wouldn't be mushroom clouds with millions of people being vaporized. No, even though we have lots of missiles, all we need to do is get just one of them about three hundred miles above Kansas.

"Such an attack would destroy their civilian infrastructure. Their electric grid would be gone. Power lines and transformers would be fried. Many power plants would be on fire.

"Pitifully, if they were hit with such an attack, their electric grid would be sitting there waiting to act like an immense antenna for us. And the missile doesn't have to be accurate. It just has to be high enough. With our intercontinental ballistic missiles, that would be easily accomplished.

"The warhead doesn't even have to be that large. It's gamma ray output that matters. And we've learned how to maximize that.

"And it's the interaction with the geomagnetic field that matters. It's a strong field over the forty-eight states. That's what would produce the most devastating consequences, and the effects would be fairly uniform from coast to coast.

"At the beginning of the *so-called blackout,* people wouldn't realize what's happened and what they're facing because there wouldn't be any communication. People in California and New York would be saying, 'Oh well, we'll go outside and we'll build a campfire and we'll have a nice evening at home; we'll break out the candles, it'll be fine.'

"A couple of days like that would be okay. A week like that might be okay. But when you start looking at two or three months and beyond, you're looking at an unthinkable scenario in a society that is totally dependent on electric supply.

"In the blink of an eye, there would no longer be any electricity, and they would lose access to communication, transportation, food, prescriptions, medical attention, fuel, heat, air conditioning, banking and financial institutions, security, and emergency services. No more internet or phone service. No more television or radio.

"Computers in cars and trucks, railways, air traffic control and airplanes themselves -- it would all be useless. Food would rot in refrigerators, and in farm fields, with no means of transporting agricultural products to population centers.

"Their apocalypse would have arrived. Our invisible gamma rays would be the beginning of the end of their way of life. Simultaneously, our cyberspace warriors would inflict severe damage in areas not directly hit, as conflicting and confusing commands would show up in Alaska, Hawaii, Guam and elsewhere.

"Of course, they have great offensive weapons, which would cause mass destruction, and we would suffer very heavy losses. But so much of what we do can go deep underground, far more than they realize, and we would survive.

"Like a lot of other countries, they have laughed at the images from outer space that have shown how dark our country can look at night. The last laugh would be on them.

"In such a conflict, the America empire would rapidly disintegrate. The world would be amazed at how quickly it would cease to exist."

Kim paused to finish his ninth drink before continuing.

"And my good friend, there is something else that is not what it appears to be.

"The 'supreme' in 'Supreme Leader' isn't as 'supreme' as people have been led to believe.

"It's a great image, which captivates hearts and minds, and it has the support of all sectors in our power structure. But I must constantly stay on a path that is viewed as self-sustaining for that power structure. They all want the Kim dynasty to continue; it has served them well. But if they ever conclude that I was becoming an existential threat, there could be a regime change.

"Which, my good friend, brings me, regrettably, to the last thing I need to tell you.

"What you have done for me is something I will always be so very grateful for, and I have so much enjoyed our time together.

"But I have learned that, in some very influential quarters, there is a rather widespread concern about foreign influence and the amount of time and resources I have devoted to my interest in basketball.

"So, I'm sure you can see where I'm going with this. We need to bid each other adieu.

"As sad as that will be, there is a silver lining. Consistent with what you wisely advised me, the authenticity and impact of what we have made is best served by our relationship sliding into obscurity."

And then, right on cue, as Kim appeared to be done, there was a knock at the door and the butler stepped inside to announce that Ri was entering the room. A moment later, she walked inside, but only a few feet past the doorway, to ask Kim if he could let Bo go, so that he could take Skysong back to their suite. "It's been a long day," she said.

"Yes, of course, my dear, and how fortuitous your timing. We were just finishing up."

Excellent timing, or did he push some button? Bo wondered.

"We should all ski together tomorrow morning," Kim said. "At noon, unfortunately, I must go back to the capital. So, how about we meet again at the summit at eight thirty. How does that sound Bo?"

"It sounds perfect."

*

Within twenty minutes, Bo was sitting on a toilet lid in his suite, so he could be alone and undistracted, to do a total recall.

He had to resist intruding thoughts: Tomorrow, would Kim regret some of the things he had said? Was Kim too inebriated to realize what he had said? Would Kim worry that he may have said even more than he actually had? And, alarmingly, that an adored basketball idol has now been banished from the king's court.

*

The skiing on Sunday started off much like the previous day. The foursome, surrounded by bodyguards, enjoyed great conditions and the incomparable fun of long runs.

At about eleven thirty, after everyone had all just gotten off the lift at the top, Kim announced that this would have to be the last time down for him and his wife.

When they all gathered at the bottom, Kim and Ri handed off their skis and poles to aides, but Kim insisted that Bo and Skysong keep their skis on. He said that a special lunch was being prepared for them at the summit restaurant, so they should get back on the lift right away.

Even though it was awkward with Bo and Svetlana still on skis and holding poles, Kim and Ri came over and gave them what seemed like obligatory hugs. Everyone said their thankyous and best wishes. And then Kim and Ri turned towards the hotel and walked away.

Bo and Svetlana didn't move. They stood and watched, expecting Kim and Ri to turn around and wave. But they never did. When they went out of view, Bo and Svetlana looked at each other, said nothing, and headed to the lift.

About two hours after lunch, the weather seemed to suddenly change. A storm moved in and it became darker and there was moderate snowfall. Bo and Svetlana both knew how thrilling such conditions could be.

In their skiing experience, this was when it seemed like everyone else sought shelter, and it became just you and the mountain, just you and the elements, just you and mother nature. Conditions that can scare you into praying for the ability to just get down safely, but then you regain visibility and your speed, and as you approach the bottom, you can't get back to the top fast enough.

Thankfully, the lifts were still operating, apparently just for them. They found it unbelievably amazing that they probably had the whole mountain to themselves. They were in a skiing paradise.

Bo and Svetlana both thought that these remaining hours alone on the slopes with the inclement weather would be something they'd never forget.

It happened in late afternoon. A total whiteout. They were about three hundred feet below the summit. At first, they were separated, but fortunately within yelling distance, so they were able to get back together. Then they started very slowly to find their way down, not knowing at all how close they might be to a tree, a rock, or a steep perilous drop.

About ten minutes later, as they were continuing to very slowly and cautiously go down, they were suddenly startled to hear approaching noises. What exactly, wasn't clear. Then for a brief instant, it was. The sounds of skiers *flying* past them, just out of view, on the other side of the white curtain. They stood motionless. Only their eyes moved. It was very scary.

"What the hell was that?" Bo finally uttered.

"Whoever they were, they sure know the terrain," Svetlana replied.

"For some reason, that gives me the creeps," he said.

"Can you imagine, if we had been standing in their path?" she said.

"I counted four, how about you?" he asked.

"Same," she said.

After about ten more minutes, as they slowly, carefully continued their descent, visibility returned, and they resumed full speed. At the bottom, spooked by the dangerous and mysterious skiers, they called it a day.

When they returned to their suite, they found two wrapped gifts laying on the bed, one for each of them. They were identical framed pictures of Kim and Ri, in elegant winter coats, with a snow-covered hillside in the background. There were inscriptions in the bottom right corners. To someone else, the way Kim and Ri were smiling and waving could be interpreted as a greeting or a farewell. Bo knew it was goodbye.

To Bo
A Sports Legend
A Great Coach
Our Dear Friend
Best Wishes Always
Kim Jong Un & Ri Sol Ju

To Svetlana
A Gifted Scholar
Brilliant Skysong
Our Dear Friend
Best Wishes Always
Kim Jong Un & Ri Sol Ju

On Monday morning, Bo and Svetlana were taken by a helicopter to Wonsan, and then flown on a charter flight to Vladivostok. This was Kim's final extravagant treat, courtesy of the ministry of physical culture and sports.

Neither one of them would ever return to that country.

Chapter 26

As Bo turned into the mostly empty parking lot behind
the stores on Kashira Avenue, he saw the white van, two
guys inside and no arm outside a window. He pulled in
next to it. Got out of his car, locked it, went to the back of
the van, opened a door, got in and sat down.

"Good morning, sir, please use your seat belt," a young
man said, before he shut the door and locked it. There
were three front-facing seats on each side. Bo sat on the
middle one on the right. A partition separated the cargo
compartment from the front cabin. It had a sliding door,
which was shut.

About an hour later, they were at the front gate of the
Naval base. The two in front showed their identifications,
told the attendant that the back doors were not to be
opened, and asked him to contact the base commander
for confirmation. A few minutes later, they were waived
on through.

After they backed into a loading dock at an office
building, the driver and his partner escorted Bo down two
flights of stairs to a door marked Auxiliary 9-7. From the

moment he stepped out of the van, other than his escorts, Bo didn't see anyone. He doubted that was just happenstance.

"That's it, sir," the driver said, pointing to the door. "It's unlocked. There's no point in knocking. Just go on in." Then the two escorts started walking back up the stairs.

The first thing Bo noticed was how heavy the door was, and how thick the door and wall were. Otherwise, inside, it appeared to be a typical conference room. Lucy was sitting in the middle of the table, facing the door side of the room. She had electronic equipment in front of her. She was the only one there.

She stood up. "Nice to see you, Bo."

"Thanks, nice to see you too."

"Please, have a seat right across from me, in front of the recorders."

She continued talking as she walked around the table to the door, locked it, and came back to her seat.

"I call this 'the tomb.' Nobody will be eavesdropping on us here.

"Now, I'm not going to do any preliminaries, and we should save our friendly chat for another time. Let's get right to it.

"I'm turning on two machines, as a redundant backup precaution, and then I'm just going to sit back and listen." She did it, observed the recording indicator lights, and gave him a thumbs-up.

Lucy appeared to be calm. In fact, she was having a hard time containing herself because she was so excited. The gaining of any new insights into Kim would be a remarkable accomplishment, and the Center would be impressed and grateful. She was anxious to ask all sorts of questions. But she kept quiet, and tried to look relaxed.

Along with the decision not to have anyone else present, for the same reason, she was determined to have a demeanor that would be most conducive to complete and accurate recollections.

Bo's thoughts and emotions were quite different. With pride, he was going to put his extraordinary memory on full display. He wanted the bigshots at the Center to be astonished at how well he delivered the goods.

In a way, he also wanted to say that the alcohol tolerance training was regrettable. That it was totally unnecessary, and caused harm in his personal life. But he decided not to do that. He wouldn't whine. Besides, it would be pointless, and such complaining would only take some of the luster off of his showboating.

Bo looked at Lucy, smiled, and began his very long verbal report, which chronicled the entire weekend. It varied greatly in the level of detail. It varied somewhat in tone and emphasis, most prominently at a point when he emphatically imparted his own sort of imprimatur.

"So, Saturday night after dinner, it was just Kim and me in what he called the gentlemen's bar. That's when he said some very surprising things. Now, I want to preface with the alcohol report. I kept tabs.

"The need for me to keep up with him turned out to be incorrect. Kim had three double whiskeys and five cognacs. Whereas, along with eating a big meal and spread out over almost four hours, I had only one single vodka and one and a half cognacs.

"And my insignificant imbibing immediately followed several weeks of alcohol tolerance training.

"In other words, I was stone-cold sober.

"My listening, memory and recall for that evening was not, and is not now, impaired in any way or degree whatsoever.

"I'm now going to tell you what Kim said about the execution and effects of an electromagnetic pulse attack, their underground survival, his regime, and my dismissal. What I say will be true and exact to his meaning in all parts, and mostly, it will actually be verbatim."

*

When Bo finished his report that afternoon, he and Lucy did not discuss it. As Lucy wished, they agreed to meet again in eight days at the safe house, which would give the Center time to respond to Bo's report and the abrupt end of the mission.

*

Bo had considered it his official duty to report his banishment from North Korea to Lucy before he told Zella that he would never be going back there. As soon as he got to his office, he sent her a message.

> Zella
> Kim job finished
> Will not return to NK
> I'm very sorry about
> alcohol tolerance
> training
> Please forgive me
> You are the love of
> my life

*

Back at his desk, Bo began to put together some ideas he had for new business development and a tantalizing sexual pursuit. Among other things, he would send Nick and Svetlana into South Korea. This move would be a logical progression into Nick's role and responsibilities as the Pacific operations manager. And it would give her some of the additional Korean experience she so much desired.

Chapter 27

Center deputy director Ivan Stogov could not believe that this would be his last meeting about the scheme involving Bo Tenbinakov. Regina Baranova and Anton Malenkov, its top two project managers, were just about to be brought into his office. *Fuck!* he shouted to himself as his arms and fists shook in anger.

As the three of them convened around Stogov's conference table, he didn't offer tea. And after they were all seated, no one talked for a moment, which was strange.

"How could this happen?" Stogov asked. "How could so much planning, so much effort, so much money, and so much risk, end up like this? The door was slammed in our face. Just like that -- one, two, three, bam! Terminated! It's unbelievable."

"Well, he did everything he was supposed to do," Malenkov said. "In fact, it appears that *everything* was done perfectly. The problem was, sir -- and I guess this was so from beginning to end -- we never fully appreciated the incredible speed at which this guy moves. It turns out, he was too good."

"And honestly, sir, there was no way to anticipate what Kim did," Baranova added.

"Really?" Stogov mocked. "No way to anticipate?"

Again, for a few moments, no one said anything.

"We overestimated Kim's adoration of basketball stars in relation to his basic survival instincts," Baranova said. "And, I must admit, we underestimated how compelling it would be for him to protect the authenticity of what he'd been given. In hindsight, once he got that thing he wanted, a prolonged relationship with Bo was probably never in the cards."

"Two words I never like to hear are *in hindsight*. They're usually synonymous with failure," Stogov said.

"Mr. Malenkov and I agree that there's no point in working up a full-blown, official, lessons-learned report for this one," Baranova said. "It was a unique plan that can't ever be repeated. We don't see any point in devoting more resources to..."

"Nonsense," Stogov said, interrupting her. "Almost all our cases are unique. And especially when they end with the use of those two failure words, a final analysis must be properly done. Just make sure that it's securely locked away in the vault. Now how are you going to wrap it up with the case officer and Bo?"

"Of course, case officer Lucy Wong shares our dismay and disappointment," Baranova said, "but she's not going to let it show when she meets with him to say goodbye."

Chapter 28

When Bo arrived at the safe house eight days after his final report in what Lucy had called "the tomb," he found her setting the table for a fancy meal. She had spent the night. This time, she was doing some fancy cooking.

She couldn't believe that the case with the code name NATURAL was already coming to an end.

"Bo, you are about to be served my signature dish, sautéed scallops. Everything is just about ready."

"Lucy, you didn't have to, but that sounds really good."

"So, please tell me, has your relationship with Zella survived this strange adventure?"

"Yeah, it has; we're still looking forward to that June wedding.

"I wish I could invite you," he added.

"Well, thank you for that sentiment," she said. "Now I'm going to dish up the plates. You can get the bottle of sparkling water out of the fridge and open it."

Once they were seated, Lucy poured the chilled beverage into the crystal stemware, which she pointed out, was made in Romania.

"I was asked by the Center to do this: They wanted me to tell you that they're certainly here in spirit. They're very proud of you. They're joining in this toast."

She raised her glass, and he followed.

"To you, Bo, congratulations on doing a fantastic job."

"Thanks, Lucy." He smiled, but only a little and only for a second.

"I feel bad," he said. "I'm sure everyone is upset that we got shut out so soon.

"I know I was sure stunned when it happened," he said. "I didn't see it coming before he dropped it on me in his man cave."

"I know, none of us saw that coming," she said.

"We can't control the vicissitudes of Kim Jong Un," she said, "but today, at this moment, we can acknowledge something admirable. You, Bo Tenbinakov, carried out your assignment perfectly; you were stellar."

"Kim's an enigma," she added, "and so, we shouldn't be surprised about anything he does; we shouldn't be too surprised how this ended."

*

Near the end of the meal -- she dreaded to do it -- she brought up the financial matters. She said that since Service funding of staff salaries, rent, equipment and utilities for the Vladivostok office terminates sixty days after his engagement with Kim ends, that would now be in fifty-one days, and the final payment would be prorated.

Bo said that he understood, and would be ready to assume all of the expenses for his branch office, which was going to continue operating.

"I have one special favor to ask of the Service," he said. "I believe we owe a debt of gratitude to Svetlana. Throughout this mission, she always maintained her poise and command of the situation. Her knowledge of Korean culture, her competence with its language and her often nuanced guidance to me was invaluable. I couldn't have done it without her.

"As a scholar in Far East studies, particularly the Korean peninsula, she is a talented rising star. She should have the opportunity to, not only reach her full potential, but also to make a significant and lasting contribution to Russian academia.

"I believe it would be in our country's best interest if she were offered an appointment to the prestigious faculty of my alma mater, Saint Petersburg State University.

"The favor I am asking is to be put in contact with someone in the Government who might be able to help me with that wish."

Lucy took a drink of her sparkling water, and appeared to be pondering the request.

"Bo, I completely understand, and I promise you, I'll champion that."

They both nodded.

"Now, let's clear off the table, and I'll serve my signature dessert. Incredibly, it's from a recipe I acquired many years ago when I was visiting the Center. It's from a Headquarters dining room pastry chef."

Bo thought Lucy's apple croustade was one of the best desserts he ever had. When he finished, he closed his eyes for a moment to reflect on it, and savor it.

"Lucy, that may have been the best dessert I've ever had in my life."

"Thanks." She smiled and nodded.

"Now, is there anything else in particular you wanted to ask me about or discuss?" she asked.

"No, I don't think so. I think that's it for me."

"Okay then, may I ask a favor of you?"

"Of course," he replied.

"This is, in all probability, the last time we'll ever see each other," she said. "It's been quite an honor for me to work with you. Now it's time to part. Here's the favor: Please, just get up and leave, without any hesitation. Sometimes, it's hard for me to say goodbye, and this is one of those times."

Bo did not skip a beat.

He looked at her and said, "You're one of my heroes. I'll never forget you."

Then in one, continuous, smooth movement, he got up from the table, pushed his chair back in, walked across the apartment, opened the front door, walked out and shut it behind him.

They would never see each other again.

Chapter 29

Two days after his final meeting with Lucy, Bo received a text message from his friend Sarah, the British journalist. Seeing her name caused *So Fucking Cute* to light up and pulse in glowing pink letters on a marquee in his mind. Then he read the content.

> You've been visiting
> the hermit kingdom
> How interesting!
> Learn any secrets?

He froze. *What the... How does she know? VAS? No, they wouldn't do that. How much does she know?*

Even though he was really taken aback, he responded right away.

> How'd you find out?
> I thought your beat
> was ottoman empire

About five minutes later, she replied.

> Word gets around
> Want to stop by and
> tell me about it?
> There could be a
> kebab in this for ya

He decided not to pry any further about her source. That might only raise suspicion. He'd react in a low-key fashion.

He'd have to give her answers, but he'd downplay the whole thing. He'd be nonchalant about it.

A few minutes later, he sent her two messages.

> That changes things
> I'm sure you know where
> the best kebobs are
> Let me get back with you

> Don't get excited re NK
> Not much to tell

The more he thought about it, he figured her news organization probably had some sort of online topical information sharing among its correspondents. That's probably how she got wind of it. Because she knew him, she was probably given the okay from whoever's turf it was on to take it. Which would seem to indicate that, as a possible story, it hadn't generated much enthusiasm.

He felt bad that his first reaction was to suspect VAS of violating their trust. *They're good loyal friends; they deserve better.*

*

On Friday of the following week, Bo took off for two destinations. First, he would visit Zella in Cluj, and then on his way back to Vlad, he would stayover in Istanbul to see Sarah.

*

When he left Zella's after visiting her for three days, he felt very good about their relationship, and apparently, so did she. They both reaffirmed that they would always love each other. They began making detailed arrangements for their June wedding in Paris, and were starting to imagine how romantic it would be.

For Bo, there was only one disconcerting note in his visit with Zella. It was when she told him about a Russian visitor in Cluj named Oleg. It was the way she portrayed this old, supposedly dignified gentleman. How they had become fast friends. That he was such a caring person, always such a good listener and always so understanding. That he was so intelligent and seemed to be so wise. How he had been such a comforting friend and helped her through her fears and worries.

When she got to the timing of his departure, Bo knew it for sure. A week ago, this Oleg went home to Russia. He told Zella that he was going to his favorite grandniece's wedding, and that it was time to go back home anyway.

He was SVR, Bo said to himself.

*

Bo took two taxis from the Istanbul Airport to Sarah's apartment on the European side of the Bosporus. As they approached the center of the city, he told the driver of the first cab to pull over next to an open-air marketplace that he was familiar with. He knew it had multiple exit points onto other streets and would be crowded.

After he got out of the cab, he quickly maneuvered through the mass of people, picked his egress and came out to a curb on another street, about two hundred and fifty yards away.

He hailed the only taxi he saw, which immediately pulled up in front of him. After he put his bag in the vehicle, before he jumped in, he took another look around. *Perfect!* he thought. At the moment, there were no other taxis in the area. As his cab sped away, he was confident, if he was being followed, he would now be losing them.

Sarah greeted him with a cup of tea. Then, after he freshened up, she took him for that kebab at one of her favorite cafés.

While they were sitting at a table waiting for their food, she got to the original question. "So, what motivated you to go to North Korea, of all places?"

"Oh Sarah, a lot has happened since I last saw you. I opened a branch office in the Far East, in Vladivostok. My business is now spreading into the western Pacific, all the way down to New Zealand.

"It didn't make sense to me to simply ignore North Korea. To me, customers are customers. And to those people who don't think one should do business with that regime, I say that the sport of basketball is a universal way to build bridges and spread goodwill.

"But I must admit, I did have mixed feelings about North Korea. The thing is, Kim Jong Un is crazy about basketball. I had a hunch that it could be a very lucrative business opportunity. But I hesitated, because I knew that some people close to me and some of my other customers wouldn't approve."

Bo knew, if someday, Sarah was to became aware of that video depicting Kim in an astonishing performance of basketball heroism, she would know right away that it was his work, she would know that's what he really did in North Korea. And he certainly didn't want to ever alienate her, so he didn't want to lie. But he had no choice.

"I'm a businessman. In the end, the big money possibility won out, and I decided to go for it."

"What were you going to sell them?"

"I presented a comprehensive plan for gradually developing a vast national infrastructure for basketball, which highlighted the health and recreational benefits of the sport, and team building and community spirit values. It was going to go all the way from young school children to the professional level."

"So, what happened?"

"In hindsight, I don't think that Kim ever seriously considered buying anything. I think he just used my proposal visits as an opportunity to hang out with a basketball star and show off a celebrity to his in-crowd.

"So, I ended up with the worst of both worlds. No income, only proposal expenses. And some painful consequences for going there. My girlfriend had been adamantly opposed to it. It caused a lot of discord between us. Fortunately, after I told her that I'm not going back there anymore, she's gotten over it.

"By the way, we're getting married, in June, in Paris!"

"Congratulations!"

They were sitting opposite each other at a little table. She leaned back in her chair and seemed to be studying him as her head moved slightly from side to side.

"Well, I say that," she continued, "but you're going to leave a lot of broken hearts, including mine."

"Sarah, nothing has to change between us."

"Oh good, you really had me worried there for a minute." She looked at him with a mischievous smile, and then leaned forward again and took another bite out of her kebob, which she seemed to particularly savor, with her eyes closed.

*

By the time Bo left Sarah two days later, he was confident that the information her news organization had about his trips to North Korea would have been of a routine and superficial nature, probably gleaned off of a passenger manifest or picked up from some marginal tipster.

*

Bo returned to Vladivostok the same day Nick and Svetlana left for South Korea. He arrived nine hours after their departure.

Bo was optimistic about Nick and Svetlana's trip. The research, planning and advance work had been meticulously and artfully done. He expected it to pay off. They had six destinations and would be gone for almost three weeks.

Bo would now turn his business attention to a different type of project. As he told Zella, it was time to share some of his good fortune by helping others. He told her that he had been approached by different community leaders in Vladivostok about contributing to youth sports. He had decided that he would create a foundation for youth basketball in Vlad. He would develop an organization with broad support and partnerships among a wide variety of businesses and community groups and involve its professional basketball team.

He would be instrumental in establishing an ongoing leadership and administrative structure. He would work out location agreements with various entities. He would provide specifications and sources for construction, equipment, maintenance and supplies.

He would provide seed money, recruit promotional talent, and create the framework for ongoing fundraising.

Once it was all on a solid footing and moving forward on its own, he would step down as the executive director, and only remain as a historic reference, as the founder. And then, of course, going into the indefinite future, he would be listed as a financial supporter.

Zella was never pleased about anything that would cause him to be away for long periods, but especially after North Korea, she was able to adapt to this latest project much more easily. She had no trouble imagining how beneficial it would be to the young people, especially the more disadvantaged. She had to respect his decision. Someday, their children would become aware of this legacy, and be proud of their father.

*

About a month after his final Lucy meeting, Bo received a letter from an Elena Abramovich, an official in the Russian ministry of education. It read in part,

Please contact me at your convenience so that we may discuss details about how I should assist in the pursuit of gaining the valuable addition of Svetlana to the faculty of that institution, which plays such a vital role in the affairs of our country.

Chapter 30

Bo was startled to see an incoming FaceTime call from Youri. His eyes got big and he stared at it for a moment with riveting apprehension.

Youri never did this. His initial contact was almost always by text or email. Occasionally, his initial contact would be by voice call, but only when the circumstances warranted it. Never with FaceTime.

When Bo answered, he could see Youri sitting at his desk with a somber look.

"Hey Youri, what's up?"

"I'm afraid I've got some very upsetting news. The Video All Stars have gone missing, off the coast of Myanmar. They were being ferried somewhere along the coast, the boat didn't show up at the destination, and there hasn't been any sign of them for over two days."

"Oh no." Bo closed his eyes and felt chills.

"I'm in touch with their office in London, which is in touch with the British authorities, who are now beginning to look into this."

Bo opened his eyes and looked at Youri.

"Any indication of bad weather?"

"They didn't say anything about weather conditions, and without a more precise location, there wouldn't be any point in me trying to figure out what it's been like. Myanmar has a very long coastline. It's about twelve hundred miles long.

"Let's try not to imagine the worst right now," Youri continued. "I'll work on finding out more. There are probably a lot of possible explanations. Maybe it's just something like faulty communications."

"Okay Youri, I'll wait to hear from you."

Then Youri and Bo silently continued to look at each other for a moment.

"Bo, I know, this is scary."

It appeared to Youri that Bo was in shock, as he didn't move at all, and seemed transfixed, with a blank vacuous look on his face.

"Bo, I'll talk with you soon."

Youri ended the call.

Bo sat back in his desk chair. It had been three months since they all said good-bye to each other in Pyongyang.

He closed his eyes again. He tried not to think of the worst. But it was irrepressible. He couldn't stop his mind from imaging the kind of thing that he feared probably happened.

They were approached by another boat, which appeared friendly and in need of some assistance – an old man, an old woman and a young man. Once alongside and within reach, the elimination action began. From below deck, up rushed a group of commandos, who quickly propelled themselves onto the other boat and before the victims could even realize what was happening, they were being riddled with bullets. Then everything that might float was secured in iron mesh containers. An explosive device was used to make a large hole in the bottom of the hull. Finally, a camera drone was used to find any floating debris, which was then all scooped up with nets.

Bo opened his eyes. *My God, what have I done?*

It was early to do it, but he decided to go home, as quickly and as quietly as he could. He was afraid that he might throw up.

*

It was just about midnight when he answered another FaceTime call from Youri.

"Bo, I'm sorry to have to tell you that it's not looking good. They were traveling in a small boat with two crew members off the far southern coast of Myanmar, in the Andaman Sea. They had left a town called Myeik and were headed northward to Dawei, a city where they were scheduled to catch a local flight to Yangon where they were to catch another flight to Dubai, and then home.

"The two crew members are guys who have been running a private ferry service up and down the coast for at least ten years, probably a lot longer. They have a good reputation for being careful and safe and having all the right equipment. There hasn't been any contact since they left Myeik. No distress signals. Nothing.

"You had asked about the weather. It certainly had nothing to do with this. The weather conditions were excellent."

Youri paused, folded his hands on the desk in front of him, looked down at them for a moment of silence, and then looked up again and continued. "They've been missing longer than we previously thought. Somehow, in the first information I was given, almost two days were left out. It breaks my heart to say that it's now been four days. Officially, this is now being described as lost at sea, cause unknown."

After another short pause, he continued, "They were working on a project for a very wealthy developer and the state tourism board to promote the construction of a massive tourist resort in an area near Myeik.

"It's a project that has become very controversial. In some ways, it sounds like a typical sort of controversy for this type of development. Some of the locals want what's being proposed for the jobs and economic development. Some see it as a threat to natural beauty and a bucolic way of life.

"There have been several incidents of violence. There's a lot of anger on both sides. The developer has been accused of corruption, including fraud, bribery and strong-arm tactics.

"Also, the area inland from Myeik is a notorious smuggling route into Thailand. It's hard to tell how those interests might play into this battle over the proposed development."

Youri paused again. He thought Bo might want to say something. But Bo just continued to stare at him with a sad look and said nothing. So, Youri continued.

"I know how much these guys mean to you. I'm fond of them too, and value them very much. And I don't mean to sound insensitive, but I think sometimes they may have chosen to work for some pretty shadowy characters.

"They're so good at what they do, that they've been able to command enormous fees. Sometimes the lure of the big bucks can be too tempting. Sometimes the risk can be too big. Again, I don't want to sound cold here, but we may be looking at the consequences of an occupational hazard."

"Okay Youri, anything else?"

"No, that's all I've got at the moment."

"Okay, thanks, good night." Bo immediately ended the call, cutting off Youri before he could say his own parting 'good night.'

Bo knew that Youri would not say anything that might suggest that his decision to work for Kim might have been a horrible mistake. *What does he really think?* Bo asked himself. *He's alluded to other possible suspects, but doesn't he know what I know? Isn't he, being the always loyal right-hand man, just helping me find a way to cope with a horrible mistake that can't be corrected? Wouldn't he see me as having foolishly put my friends in peril for big bucks?*

*

On the twelfth day of its disappearance, the search for the *Sea Prince*, as it was called in Burmese, and the eight people presumed to be on board, was officially discontinued. The investigation was left open. Practically speaking, it would become inactive. It had a one-word tag: inconclusive. There was not a single clue of where, when, how or why it happened.

In the days, weeks, months and years that would follow, whenever Bo would think of them as the Video All Stars, as a group, it was bad enough.

When he would dearly remember them individually as Roger, Charlie, Helen, Emma, Toby and Jack, he felt the presence of horror deep in his soul.

He agonized over it like nothing before in his life, and a feeling of unspeakable guilt became a permanent fixture nailed to the center of his being, where it would hang secretly forever.

They were his good friends. They trusted him. He would never be able to stop asking himself why he hadn't seen how this would end? Why didn't he realize that by making something so believable and so enormously valuable to Kim, their lives would be sacrificed?

From the moment he first heard the news that their boat was missing, it became intuitively obvious that Kim would not risk letting any of these Brits ever have the chance to undermine the authenticity of his legend as a basketball hero.

Those six beautiful good-natured people. His friends, who trusted him. Slaughtered.

If he had known how that spy mission would turn out – the profound loss that it would cause -- he never would have done it.

Sixteen Years Later

Chapter 31

When Bo visited his alma mater, Saint Petersburg State University, for his thirtieth reunion, he was joined by his wife Zella and all three of their children, two girls and a boy. Natalia was eleven, Mira nine and Leo seven. Bo was now fifty-one. Zella was forty-two.

Over the years, Bo's many global business ventures had grown enormously, particularly Down Under and in Africa. He now had bustling offices in Melbourne and Lagos.

After being a stay-at-home mom before all the children became school age, Zella was now active on the board of an international youth sports organization, which focused primarily on basketball, particularly in disadvantaged areas, and had been founded by her husband. It was an organization that, among other things, had evolved into an impressive machine of athletic talent scouting and recruiting. She was also active on the Sochi sister cities committee, which had ties to fourteen cities around the globe; she was the chair of its sports subcommittee.

The alumni reunion events organizing committee had recruited Bo to be a co-chair. They had told him that they were sure having his name on the save-the-date notices and invitations would be a big draw. That he would be instrumental in making this reunion a wonderful event and a tremendous success.

Bo was happy to oblige. He was proud of his degree from Russia's oldest university, which was one of its most distinguished institutions. As always, he valued positive publicity. And it was an opportunity to see an old friend.

After moving to the opposite Russian coast to gratefully accept an enviable appointment to the SPSU faculty, Svetlana had blossomed in academia. She was now a distinguished professor in the university's Korean studies institute. And her prominence extended far beyond the ivory tower into government and industry. She was now widely considered to be one of the most respected Russian authorities on the Far East.

Bo had told Zella that he needed to work with the events organizing committee the day before the reunion started, and for that day he had arranged for her and their children to be given a special private tour of the Hermitage, the world's largest and oldest museum.

Their Hermitage tour would be conducted by Veronika Lesnoy, who was a very entertaining assistant curator. She was the museum's media star for television shows, documentaries, and internet videos. Even those people who were not fascinated by treasured objects and works of art from antiquity, even those people would almost always become enthralled with Veronika Lesnoy.

For that day, Bo had also reserved a room in a small boutique hotel near the university campus. Online, the accommodations did not look like something he would normally choose, nothing at all like something that would suit his taste. But it was the only thing available, and he definitely needed a discreet place to meet Svetlana.

*

In the morning on the day before the reunion started, Bo did meet with the events organizing committee for a short time, but then he apologized and told them that he had to excuse himself to deal with a critical, unexpected business matter. By late morning, wearing a cap and sunglasses, he was on his way to the rendezvous destination.

He had booked the room for two nights, so he would not be hampered by the standard check in and check out time requirements. He had used an alias and had paid in advance with a credit card from one of his subsidiaries, a generically-named equipment leasing business.

As he entered the Hotel Lebedev, he found the front desk clerk occupied with an elderly couple. As he stood and waited, he heard enough of their conversation to realize that the couple's room had some sort of plumbing problem.

The young clerk, who looked to be no more than sixteen or seventeen, was telling them that, under the circumstances, for the remainder of their stay, they were being moved into a suite, which was much larger and much nicer, and, of course, at no additional cost to them.

These guests were obviously very pleased. After expressing their appreciation, the gentleman told the clerk that he reminded him of their grandson. And the lady concurred. She said that the resemblance was remarkable. Then the couple and the clerk proceeded to delve into questions about where each of them was from, where the couple wanted to go on their trip, what the clerk wanted to do with his life, how much the couple wished him success. Bo began to wonder if this would ever end.

Then, mercifully, someone from housekeeping got off the elevator and told the clerk that their suite was ready. These two very happy guests were obviously quite excited to see it and went on their way.

"Yes, sir, and how may I help you?" the young clerk said to Bo.

"Good morning. I'm Aleksey Kotov. If you please, I'd like to check into my room, which is booked for two days, which actually started yesterday. You see, we didn't know when I'd be able to get here."

"Oh yes, I remember seeing that. Just a second please," as he looked over at his computer screen. "Ah, yes, there it is. I see everything's already been filled out. If there aren't any changes..." Before the clerk got a chance to ask for it, Bo put his phony identification on the counter. "Thank you, sir," the clerk said, "and if you'll just sign the register here."

When Bo walked into the room, he looked around in disbelief. For his purposes, the décor was dysfunctional and off-putting. He sat down for a few minutes and pondered the absurdity of the setting.

He couldn't imagine that many travelers would want to stay in a room like this. It was so extremely overdone with glittering gold and frilly things. Everywhere he looked, there were antique figurines and other knickknacks on top of crocheted doilies. This peculiar ornamental obsession had so overpopulated the room with porcelain that there was no place left to set anything down, not even a purse and a couple of water glasses.

And the bed didn't look like something anyone would sleep in, or have sex on, or even lay still on. It didn't appear to welcome any sort of intrusion or disturbance. It was presented like a well-preserved period piece one might see in a museum gallery, with many layered adornments of intricate motifs over a lace ruffle coverlet.

The whole room was so delicate, you got the sense that, if you weren't always extremely careful, something could easily be damaged. It almost made you afraid to move. As a hotel room to accommodate travelers, it was utterly ridiculous.

He got up and went back downstairs to the front desk. The same clerk was still there. Fortunately, he was alone.

"Young man, I can't begin to tell you how much I would appreciate it if you could change me to a different room. One that's... I'm not sure exactly how to put this... I can image that for certain people, it would be lovely. But I was just hoping you might have something without so many delicate things, you know, maybe a little bit more... Again, I'm not quite sure how to put this..."

When Bo stalled again, the clerk interrupted. "Oh, sir, I'm sorry you don't like the decor, but I'm not permitted to make room assignment changes."

"Listen, I'm more than willing to compensate the hotel in whatever amount you consider appropriate in order to waive that restriction. And I'll certainly want to reward you for your extra trouble. Just please, change me to a room more in line with my age, gender and disposition. Please!"

"I'm sorry, sir, I'm simply not able to do that."

Bo stood there and looked at this kid, who wouldn't have been born yet when his basketball playing days in the EuroLeague ended more than twenty-one years ago.

At the moment, Bo was anonymous, and he wanted to keep it that way. He entertained thoughts of asking for the manager or the owner -- anyone who might exercise discretion for financial gain.

But then he thought the better of it. He just let out a loud sigh and said, "Okay, thanks anyway." He was not going to bring more attention into his arrival and possibly draw someone into the picture who might recognize him.

"Oh, by the way," Bo said, "I'm expecting a visitor, a lady who will be here part of the day for a private business management consultation."

Better not break anything, the clerk thought. "Oh yes, of course, sir," the clerk said. "Thank you, sir, for letting me know."

While he waited for Svetlana back in the room, he had to admit that it certainly felt comfortable sitting in the plush rose-colored chair, which faced the bed.

About the time Svetlana was due to arrive, there was a loud knock on the door. It had been a very long time, but he thought that he would recognize her knock. This harsh demanding sound wasn't it.

No one else knew he was there. He wondered if it could be a maid, perhaps mistakenly thinking this was a room that needed cleaning. Or staff checking to see if everything was satisfactory; but surely, they would use the phone for that. In either case, no one would knock like that.

He was struck by a reoccurring fear of being executed. There were all sorts of scenarios. What if Kim found out it was a spy mission? What if some SVR braggart was careless and the RGB got wind of it? Or the most likely, that Kim would eventually decide to eliminate him before he got too old and maybe too chatty.

He had expected this fear to dissipate over the years. Instead, the reverse happened. The older he got, the more it seemed to settle in. Maybe that just came with having a family.

Many times, he reflected on what happened to Kim's half-brother in a busy Macao airport. Kim Jong Nam, who was suspected of being an informant for a foreign intel agency, died after fifteen minutes of terrible pain, when two women rushed up and rubbed two chemicals on his face that combined to form a deadly nerve agent.

The women, one was from Vietnam and the other from Indonesia, were arrested for murder. They claimed that they thought they were part of a television prank show and were later released. Many times, Bo thought about that execution and how elaborate and far-fetched it was.

And, of course, there was the haunting, unspeakable horror about what happened to his six British friends. Gone without trace.

He had no doubt, if they ever wanted to, they could easily get to him, and it could be almost anywhere, and it could be in the most unlikely of circumstances.

Apropos, even though he was definitely unhappy with the room, he did appreciate one feature; thankfully, it had a peephole. As he got up to look through it, he did so with some trepidation.

He was surprised to find that the unfamiliar knock was actually Svetlana. He opened the door, stepped aside, invitingly swung his arm inward and said, "Welcome to the ultimate man cave."

She passed through without smiling, stopped in front of the bed, and silently glared at it.

Bo was taken aback.

Obviously, the joke had fallen flat, and her body language left him disoriented. Why didn't she smile? Why didn't she say anything? He wouldn't blame her for being disappointed with the room, the bed in particular, but at the moment, she appeared to be mad about the bed, which was really strange.

"Yeah, I know. This room is ridiculous," he said.

As she turned around to face him, he spread both arms out wide and started to walk towards her for an embrace, but she backed away and said, "We need to sit down."

He was now finding her offishness to be shocking. He offered her the plush chair and sat on the bed so he could face her.

She was now fifty-five, and he was not surprised to find her looking young for her age. She still had her sex appeal, and to him, in a certain way, she had become even more erotic with age.

"Svetlana Vasiliev Baranovichi, Skysong, what's wrong?"

Her head was tilted back a little and her eyelids were down slightly, as she gave him a piercing look. "*I know*," she said.

"What?" he said, with a startled look.

"You heard me. *I know*."

Only Bo's lower jaw moved and ever so slightly. The rest of his body froze.

After a moment, he started breathing again and awkwardly took a gulp. He broke away from her stare by pensively looking down and then out the window. He realized he was not reacting well. This too, was a surprise.

The woman sitting across from him was a different person from the one he had known in the past.

She now seemed to possess an unrestrained fierceness, which he hadn't ever seen before. At the moment, she seemed like a bomb he might unintentionally detonate.

As he looked away, her piercing glare remained fixed. He knew he could not continue to avoid it. He resumed eye contact, and sensed that an indictment was about to begin. He had no choice, but to face the charges. "Please, tell me, what is it you know?"

For almost a minute, she just glared, and said nothing.

Then, finally, the words, like daggers: "She told me all about it. How you started an affair, not too long after you first met that night when we went over to their house for Sunday dinner. A torrid affair that lasted two years.

"Now I understand why you sent me into South Korea with Nick. At the time, I thought you were glad it would benefit my career goals. Now I understand why you pulled strings to get me the job of a lifetime, where my career dreams could all be fulfilled. You couldn't wait to get me as far away as possible -- over six thousand miles away.

"I have to hand it to you, Bo, you really know how to mastermind things, and you can sure put on an act. I really believed that you cared so much about me that you were willing to put my future above your own pleasures. I was such a fool."

She paused for a moment to glance around the room with a look of disgust, and then continued, "Tasha and I were always so close. Always transparent with each other. That is, until then.

"I knew she was keeping something important from me. I thought it was probably something about Stefan. I didn't want to press her about it. I knew she would tell me in due course.

"Then I left for St. Petersburg. After I moved, I attributed our growing estrangement to the great distance separating us. I guess I was so thrilled and awed by my new position that I was distracted from the obvious truth. My beautiful relationship with my daughter had withered, and for no apparent reason."

She broke eye contact with him only long enough to look down at the floor and take a deep breath before her closing remarks.

"Fortunately, for Tasha and me, our cherished relationship is on the mend. We're getting close again. When we reflect on those times, we can commiserate with each other, as we were both taken in by the same master of deception, the same guile, the same temptation."

She paused and glanced around the room again, now with a smirk on her face. After a forced laugh, she continued, "Later, I heard about your well-publicized efforts to build a youth basketball program in Vladivostok. As I look back, I realize that was just another one of your elaborate diversions, another one of your perfect plays. That one to fake out your wife, while you scored with my daughter."

She stopped talking, looked down, and shook her head.

Bo finally responded. "Life can be so complicated and sometimes we end up doing things that we did not intend to do or never imagined we could do. Look at us, we never intended to get involved like we did. It happened because we were thrown together by an incident over which we had no control and..."

He didn't finish what he was saying, as she hurriedly got up and started towards the door.

But then she stopped and swung around, appearing to be even more enraged.

"That incident at the Yanggakdo Hotel?" she said. "I'm not so sure you weren't behind that. I'm not so sure that wasn't another one of your brilliant plays.

"I certainly wouldn't put it past you. It quickly served to set up an intimate clinging and emotional dependency."

Then she stormed out, leaving the door open behind her in a final gesture of contempt.

Chapter 32

Svetlana woke up and looked at the time. She felt a victory of sorts, as she realized her alarm would disturb the peace in only two minutes. She reached over and canceled it, and as she put her head back on the pillow, she appreciated her biological clock for being so precise in averting that much less pleasant awakening.

Before she got out of bed to start the day, she laid there and thought about the dream she'd just had before she woke up. She only vaguely remembered something about climbing over a barricade. Naturally, almost all of it had already evaporated. But to her, perhaps, not the most significant thing. The people in it. She remembered that it was some childhood friends, who were central to whatever was going on.

Her adult life has included many dramatic chapters on both coasts. But she seldom dreams about any of the people involved in any of that. Her teenage years were a nonstop, screaming, rollercoaster ride of thrills and crises, but the people involved in her late teenage years are usually absent as well.

Instead, her dream world is most often occupied by childhood friends. It's a phenomenon that she never ceases to find surprising, curious and precious. Occasionally, there are others too, but three stand out with the most recurring presence: Nasiba Danilova, Polina Alekseeva, Angelina Volkov.

She reflected on the end of that age of mischief and make-believe. She knew she hadn't had contact with Polina since she was thirteen because it didn't continue past eighth grade. She guessed she probably lost track of Nasiba and Angelina at around fifteen.

She looked at the time again and changed thoughts. She needed to get moving. As she got out of bed and headed to the bathroom, she reviewed her expectations about the two highlights that awaited her in what should be an especially meaningful day ahead.

In the morning, she would be leading a class of graduate students into a fascinating period of Korean history, one which she particularly enjoyed. Those students would be eager in their quest for knowledge. For Svetlana, it would be a most satisfying academic experience.

At lunch, she had a much-anticipated date with her daughter Tasha. She was going to give her a report about the end of a period in their lives, about her meeting with Bo the previous day.

Eighteen months ago, Tasha and her husband Stefan relocated from Vladivostok to St. Petersburg. They now had children, two girls. Raisa was nine, Anastasia was six.

Stefan had joined a St. Petersburg ophthalmology group, which was well-established and very busy. It had four other doctors. Two of them were getting up there in years, and were beginning to wind down their practices.

Stefan landed in this plum spot, thanks, in part, to the connections and influence of someone who was intimate with his mother-in-law. Svetlana's very helpful close friend was the widely-respected medical director at a prestigious St. Petersburg hospital.

Tasha was now a devoted stay-at-home mom. It felt like her calling. After years working as a corporate recruiter, she was thankful that she had found the right job for herself. She relished every minute of it. Her daughters were very fortunate.

Stefan and Tasha were very grateful to now be living in St. Petersburg. They loved this gorgeous city, with its incredible wealth of culture. They were awestruck by how vast it was -- hundreds of museums, thousands of libraries, thousands of grand architectural treasures.

Professionally, besides what he knew was going to be a very rewarding practice, Stefan was grateful for the access he now had to so many comprehensive and advanced medical resources.

Tasha was back together again with her best friend, her mother. Sometimes, Stefan got a little jealous about that. But he always figured that it could be a lot worse. He had no idea that it actually had been.

*

Sergey's was a classy restaurant and quite a distance from the campus. It was Svetlana's regular go-to place when privacy was in order. Today, it also had the advantage of being in the direction of her daughter's home.

Tasha arrived first. As she waited inside the entrance, she admired the practical advantages and nostalgic charm of her mom's favorite hideaway.

It was off the main drag, tucked away on a quiet leafy side street. It was the last commercial business before the neighborhood became residential. It wasn't trendy. It was beautifully maintained, but it was dated.

Looking around at the furnishings, wall hangings and other decorations, she guessed that most of the patrons were probably quite old. It was a good bet for anonymity.

Ten minutes later, when Svetlana walked in, the host immediately led them to their table. After they sat down, read the menu and thanked the waiter for taking their order, Svetlana sighed. "What a relief. That final scene, so many years in coming, finally happening," she said.

"Excuse me, Tasha, I need some water first."

While Svetlana was taking a drink, her daughter just sat still and smiled.

As Svetlana put down her water glass, she started laughing. Then Tasha started laughing too.

Finally, Tasha said, "Okay Mom, *please*, tell me what happened."

"Well, it started when I got to his door. It was a really tacky hotel, by the way. He was embarrassed about it. I've heard there are a zillion conferences going on this week, so I'm sure he couldn't find anything else. If he had any choice, he never would have picked this place.

"Anyway, I knocked very loud, like someone who was really mad.

"I'm sure he looked through the peephole first, and was probably surprised to find that it was me who did the rude knocking. When he opened the door, he cracked some joke about a man cave, which I just ignored. I didn't smile or say anything. I just looked stern.

"Inside, he tried to hug me, but I backed away and told him that we needed to sit down. I said..."

Svetlana started laughing again, but then quickly suppressed it and continued, "So, I glared at him, and said, *I know.* At first, he tried to act puzzled. And I didn't say anything else for a long time. I just kept glaring at him.

"He lost his composure, which I've never seen happen before, and he seemed to be at a loss for how to respond. Finally, he says, 'Please, tell me what it is you know.'

"Tasha, I don't know how I was able to keep a straight face through all of this. It was quite a performance.

"Anyway, after glaring at him a while longer, I told him that you owned up to the whole thing. And then, I proceeded to go through the particulars, especially the terrible harm his treachery had inflicted on a beautiful mother-daughter relationship.

"That now I understood the motive for sending me into South Korea with Nick for three weeks. That, at the time, I thought he was unselfishly trying to help advance my career goals.

"That now I understood why he pulled strings to get me a job over six thousand miles away, an offer he knew I couldn't refuse. At the time, I thought he cared so much about me that he was unselfishly putting my future above his own desires.

"Of course, I didn't say anything about the fact that it was you who planted the St. Petersburg idea in his head.

"I told him I knew his Vladivostok youth basketball program was another clever play, a cunning diversion to fake out his wife while he scored with you.

"Then I stormed out and left the door open behind me. It was all a dramatic display of utter contempt. He made his bed, and I left him sitting on it."

"Wow," Tasha said.

"Yeah, it was something else," Svetlana said.

A young lady was now approaching with the soups they'd ordered. Svetlana had never seen her before, and assumed she was a new hire. She looked nervous.

As she started setting the soups down, Svetlana said, "Perfect timing!"

Mother and daughter both sat up a little straighter, placed Sergey's thick, dark green, linen napkins on their laps, smiled at each other, and started daintily sipping their soups.

The waiter returned, looked at the table and mumbled, "She didn't bring you the bread." He took a tensed-up, exasperated deep breath, blinked his eyes closed for a split second, and hurried away.

Svetlana put her soup spoon down on the plate under the bowl, and folded her hands on her lap.

"You know, Tasha, he's really a very smart and crafty guy, but I don't think he'll ever realize he was just a player in our game."

www.ingramcontent.com/pod-product-compliance
Lightning Source LLC
Chambersburg PA
CBHW021109110726
47900CB00007B/2104